SURVIV🔍R MAX

Trigger Warnings

by
Davi Barker

NORTON PRESS

Just because the mind is blank
Doesn't mean the words are empty

About the Author

A lifelong connoisseur of the undead, Davi believes that art should imitate life, and if it can't, art should at least eat life's brain. Frustrated by the big lurkers and shakers in the zombie genre, Davi aims to redefine the quintessential metaphor of the living dead. Zombies are unique among monsters in that they outnumber the living, enacting one of literature's most enduring themes: the triumph of the individual over the collective. And as the masses return from the dead to consume the living, it is the survivors who build the new world from the corpse of the old.

Survivor Max: Trigger Warnings
ISBN: 978-1978206403
Copyleft ⊚ 2018 by Norton Press

About Survivor Max

It started out as an alien story. An extraterrestrial on Earth in search of proof that humanity was ready to join the intergalactic community. There were thirteen kids from all over the world, but I kept getting stuck. What's a teenager's life like in China? Or Somalia? I was doing more research than actual writing.

Tarrin Lupo, author of The Pirates of Savannah, suggested that I had bitten off more than I could chew. That I shouldn't try to write an epic trilogy on my first try, and instead I should write about something I knew well enough to write without all the research. I reduced the cast to one kid and replaced the aliens with zombies.

The next day, by coincidence or providence, I found myself on a plane, seated next to a science teacher who was grading zombie stories written by students Max's age. Many of Max's best ideas came from them, and I dedicated Too Smart To Die to the 2015 graduating class of Thornton Central School.

When I started I folded and stapled by own chapbooks to hand out at festivals. My printing expenses were briefly sponsored by SurvivalGearBags.com, but ultimately Survivor Max was picked up by Prepper Press, a family-owned publishing house specializing in apocalyptic fiction and survival nonfiction. They wanted a book by that Christmas, but I was only a third done, so they offered me a three book deal, and published both Too Smart To Die and School Bites a year later.

The third book was delayed over a year, first by my divorce, and then by the death of my mother. It's difficult to write about grief when you're experiencing it yourself. Then the publisher decided not to publish the third book. This book. In the simplest terms, and the most convenient definitions, I imagine it was probably because the story was no longer the survival companion it began as (although that will always be part of the flavor). Max's story outgrew that box. Fans kept asking for it, and making suggestions, so in the age of self-publishing I decided that losing my publisher was no excuse not to continue.

Special Thanks to the Barrios Family,
Corinne, Dave, Tristan, Dylan and Temperance,
without whom this series may never have continued.

Preface: Wealth of the Inheritors

If you're still alive, congratulations. You've inherited the whole world. Who knows if you deserve it? You're probably some kind of psychologically predisposed lunatic. Crazy kept a lot of people alive in the beginning.

The first thing you've gotta understand is that my story is not that unusual. I spent the first weeks of Black Autumn alone. The virus spread fast . . . although it turned out it's not a virus.

The point is, people turned into ravenous undead cannibals so fast my entire apartment complex was swarming before I could bug-out.

I lost my dad the first night . . . and again twenty eight days later.

I was alone at Lochshire Estates, scrounging for food and water abandoned by my neighbors. But a lot of us thought they were the last man on earth before we found others. At least I avoided all the chaos in the big cities. The riots. The mass dead migrations.

Lochshire is where I met Ellie, and my cat, Stinky Romero. We managed to escape with our skin intact . . . mostly.

In those days lots of people huddled together for safety in shopping malls, and prisons, and schools. That's where we went. Thornton Middle School. It used to be ground zero for public indoctrination in Thornton, New Hampshire, but it got a lot more interesting after the infection. The Health Department turned the soccer field into a tent city for refugees. After they lost contact with the Capital, the school faculty and local police made it into their own private utopia called *Thornhaven*, but they never really agreed on a unified vision for the place.

By winter, a power struggle between Sheriff Napolitano of Thornhaven and Major Winters' group from the local S-Mart escalated into a full-blown armed conflict. I escaped with Ellie, Stinky, and our new friends, Scott and Niles.

The other thing you've gotta understand about our story is that we were all kids. I'd just turned twelve. Ellie was only a year older. Scott and Niles were both in my grade. Niles was a scrawny videography geek, and Scott was the jerk that bullied him. We'd also all lost family. Niles lost his brother Holland at Thornhaven, and Scott's dad . . . well, he was murdered.

Lots of people found themselves stuck in the middle of some blood feud between power mad tyrants in those days. Some mayor or priest. Some mad scientist or revolutionary. It's always some charismatic con artist tricking people into doing the work, while they sip chocolate milk at the end of the world.

***

It was Black Friday, literally. S-Mart attacked Thornhaven the day after Thanksgiving. We pretty much escaped Thornhaven with just our school uniforms. Ellie didn't even have shoes. Not exactly winter appropriate. I did manage to grab my bug-out bag.

We made it to a Denton's Sugar Shack, about a mile south of Thornhaven. It was a little breakfast place Dad used to bring me. Not ideal, but we needed somewhere to get warm and dry for the night, so we could make some distance in the morning. Niles had an old camera case, although the camera was long gone. Instead, he used it to carry a few personal items. Luckily, that included matches. We made a fire out of cash from the register and broken tables.

Once everyone stopped shivering, and the feeling came back to my fingers, I went for the med kit in my gear bag.

I had a tourniquet, tweezers, safety pins, ibuprofen, burn gel and single servings of sterile pads, bandages, adhesive tape, alcohol wipes, butterfly sutures, and a tube of antibiotic ointment I stole from the nurse's office at Thornhaven. *Looks like I'll need all the single servings.* Ellie was bitten on the arm and I needed to dress it as soon as possible. My pinky was also broken.

"We should go north," Ellie insisted, "back to that dead judge's house."

"Are you nuts?" I replied as I cleaned the bite with the alcohol wipes and pinched each tooth mark closed with butterfly sutures.

"Fine, what's your plan, Brainiac?" she asked. "Judge Burke's house has cupboards full of honey and rice. Not to mention a fireplace."

I dabbed the bite with the ointment, dressed it with a sterile pad, and wrapped it in a bandage. "If we go north we walk right past Thornhaven, and depending how things went down, they could be looking for us."

"If we go south we go right by S-Mart," she countered. "Besides, I got some payback to bring to the *Thornites.*"

"Not without shoes, you don't!" I found a knife in the kitchen and pressed it against my broken finger as a splint. Then I wrapped my hand in electrical tape I found in the restroom to keep it stable.

Ellie is what makes our story unique. She was bitten when the infection reached Boston, but she didn't change. Turns out Ellie's immune. She and her mom came looking for my dad, because he was researching the disease independently, but her mom died on the road. Lots of people died on the road.

With all our injuries dressed, we ate rat meat, crackers, and belt cheese. Once all our food was consumed, I turned my attention to inventory.

I still had Dad's handheld CB radio.

It had become sentimental to me. Dad trained me how to use it before he died, so we could stay in contact in a crisis. I could tell them apart because I had written "Property of Max Hartwell" on mine, and Dad had responded by writing "Property of Rich Hartwell" on his.

When Sheriff Nap took us into custody he confiscated both radios, but I managed to get Dad's back before we escaped. It was pretty useless without a second radio, but I just couldn't abandon it.

I was the only one with a backpack. I still had Dad's bug-out bag. It was full of all kinds of useful gear and some other things we'd picked up along the way. I had a water filter, fifty feet of paracord, a flashlight, a sewing kit, a signal mirror and my last MRE, which I was saving for an emergency. I also had a multi-tool, a photo of my family, and three packs of Mr. Romero's tomato seeds, for when we found a safe place to grow.

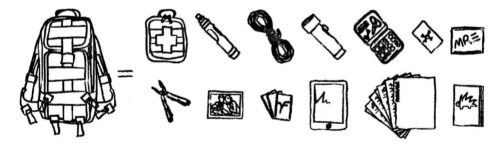

I also had Dad's zPad and hard copies of all his research. But I still needed to find a scientist who understood it. See, he knew something most researchers didn't: the active infection is bloodborne, but we're all carriers of a hidden airborne infection.

We all change when we die. No matter how we die.

Finally, I still had my copy of the *PorcScouts Survival Guide,* which was basically a field manual for worst-case scenarios.

The only weapon I had was a Sig Sauer Mosquito I pulled off a dead cop. I only had ten rounds.

Scott found a fire ax under the counter. Niles found a pantry full of maple syrup. Stinky sat by the window, looking out at the snow. He was our early warning system if anyone found us.

I scrounged through the restaurant's janitorial supplies and found a box of heavy duty garbage bags, which gave me an idea. Using duct tape to fashion straps and pockets, I created backpacks for everyone.

I took everything that was left and divided it into everyone's packs. Everyone had a water bottle, an emergency blanket, a roll of duct tape and three bottles of maple syrup. We'd be grateful for anything when the food ran out.

There was a map of other Denton's locations on a kid's menu. There were three in the area, which would all be good places to scavenge, but more importantly it was a crude road map of New Hampshire. So, I included a kid's menu with Dad's cabin marked on the map in everyone's bag, in case we got separated.

The most important thing about surviving freezing temperatures is staying dry. You can wear all the ugly sweaters in the world, but when your body heat melts the snow you're soaked to the bone and freezing to death before long. So I made everyone a suit out of garbage bags and duct tape to wear over their clothes. I padded them with insulation I tore out of the walls for warmth, and I made loops and pockets out of duct tape for essential items. I also lined the inside of my gear bag in plastic to protect it from water damage, and wrapped Dad's research in another bag just in case.

We'd spend the night at Denton's, and in the morning try to make it to the cabin. That was the best plan, but it was still about twenty five miles away by road. Not many people survive on the road.

One: Saturday Mourning

We were all asleep under emergency blankets on the floor of the dining area. The blankets were developed by the space program. Ultra thin. Lightweight. They looked like tin foil.

I was plenty warm, because Stinky was curled up with me, although sometimes his fur tickled my nose when he snuggled too close.

In the middle of the night I heard a tapping at the window and I sat up. Everyone else was asleep, and there was a chill in the room from the snow outside. Scott kept cuddling up against Niles for warmth, and Niles kept shoving him away. Ellie had nudged close to the fire, which was down to just a few glowing chair legs.

The tapping got louder as I walked to the window, and became more of a scratching. I pulled the curtain aside, but the windows had been boarded up. So, I peeked between the boards.

The wind howled outside, but the scratching sound was gone. All I could see was black night, and the bluster of snow.

I turned back to the fire, but the pounding sound started again, louder and harder, until it rattled the building. I peeked outside again. *Still nothing.* I squinted into the black and could just make out the swaying tree line through the snow.

Suddenly a huge branch swung out of the static, busting the boarded window to shards and splinters. A rush of air swirled through the restaurant, extinguishing the last bit of fire. Snow billowed in and quickly peppered everything.

My nose tickled.

Something about that smell.

I ran to Ellie, shaking her and screaming, "Come on! We gotta get out of here!" Snow piled up around her, but she didn't budge.

I ripped the blanket off Scott and Niles, "Wake up! Guys, I need your help!" In seconds they were practically covered in snow, but still didn't wake up. Scott was humming the tune of "Darling Clementine" in his sleep.

I pulled Niles up by the shoulders and jerked him violently, but he just went on snoring. Ellie and Scott were completely buried in snow.

"Max." A voice from nowhere.

I was trying to shake Niles awake when I realized the flakes on my hands weren't melting. They weren't even cold. They brushed off like little bits of shredded cardboard. I tasted the flakes on my fingers and they had a chalky flavor, more like sand. It wasn't snow at all.

"Max?" It was Ellie's voice, but she was still asleep.

Millions of little grey specks blew in from outside, piled up to my shoulders. *It was cat litter.*

"Max!" Her voice was right in my good ear.

The pile of cat litter rose over my head, until all I could see was endless grey.

"Wake up!" Her hand came fast and slapped me wide awake. "We got a situation here! Will you talk some sense into these lamebrains?" she asked.

I was laying on the ground, and Ellie was on top of me. Niles and Scott were by the window, peeking through the curtains. Stinky was hiding in a dead potted fern.

It was bright outside. None of it was real . . . except the tapping. "What's that noise?" I asked.

"There's a creeper outside and these softheads won't stop teasing it," Ellie answered.

I sat up. Scott was tapping spoons on the glass and Niles was making faces and giggling.

"Would you deal with your friends?" Ellie stood up. "They won't listen to me."

"What the heck are you guys doing!?" I demanded.

"What's the big deal?" Niles asked. "It's just one greyface, and it can't get in."

"Knock it off!" I insisted. "If it gets too excited it'll attract others."

"Not to mention that demented sheriff might be out looking for us," Ellie injected. "Where do you think he'll look first, with you two clowns drawing a crowd?"

"I'm pretty sure Sheriff Nap is dead." I said. "We left him tied up in the art supply closet for Major Winters to find. I don't think the Major would let him live."

"Great, then the demented army major is out looking for us. That's so much better!" she said sarcastically.

"Ok, fine. Let's let it in and take it out." Scott swung the fire ax like a baseball bat to warm up.

"I like this idea," Ellie added.

"What!? Why would you let it in?" I cried.

"Think about it," she explained. "If we leave it out there, it'll attract more. If we go out and deal with it, we might get spotted. We should let it in."

"No way!" I insisted. "This place has a back door. We should ignore it, and just keep moving."

"We could tie it up," Scott suggested. "Get a close look at it."

"Awesome!" Niles beamed with excitement.

"Um, no!" protested Ellie. "If you let that thing in here it's getting piked."

"I got a better idea!" Scott's eyes lit up as he thought of it. "You guys lure it over to the door. I'll climb into the rafters." The building was an old wooden construction, with support struts along the ceiling.

His plan was actually pretty good, so we agreed to try it. I would lure it to the main entrance and let it chase me into the dining area, where Niles and Ellie would be hiding behind two sideways tables. They'd trip it with a broom, and I'd slip a loop knot around it's ankles. Then Scott would jump down from the rafters, pull the creeper up by the feet, and *presto!* Neutralized.

But that isn't quite what happened.

I caught its eye in the window. It was a skinny woman in a sundress. Not really dressed for snow. I drew it over to the front door. "Everyone ready?" I hollered back.

"Ready!" they all confirmed.

I flung open the door and leapt back, ready for a chase.

The woman stepped in, its eyes locked on me.

I ran into the dining area, stepped over the broom, and turned back.

The woman took one heavy step into the waiting area and stopped again.

Ellie peeked her head out from behind the table. "What gives?"

The woman took a second solid step in, and its eyes drifted toward Ellie.

"What's it doing!?" yelled Scott from above. "I can't see!"

Niles came out from behind his table. "Maybe it's afraid." He tried to jump scare it.

Its eyes switched to Niles, and it turned toward him, almost losing its balance.

We all exchanged confused glances.

"I get it!" I grabbed an umbrella from behind the front desk and poked the woman with it. It swung at me so slow I was three paces back before it finished. "It's frozen."

"Since when do creepers freeze?" asked Ellie.

"Since forever," answered Scott. "Where have you been?"

"None of your business!" she barked.

"The cold slows them down," I explained. "But I've seen them freeze solid when it's cold enough."

The woman took another step inside, and I opened the umbrella to block her.

"Guys, get with the program!" Scott yelled. "What's going on down there? Where's the geek?"

"Can we please stop calling them *geeks*?" demanded Niles.

"Why?!" Scott protested. "What do you call them?"

It took another step toward me and swung, but I brushed it off.

"Greyfaces," said Niles.

"That's stupid!" replied Scott.

"You're stupid!" yelled Niles.

Scott wound back and socked Niles in the arm.

"Ow!" cried Niles, rubbing his shoulder. "Don't be such a jerk!"

"Guys!" I yelled as the grey-faced, geeky, creepy woman gurgled sludge on the umbrella. "Are we doing this or not? It's going to thaw out."

Niles nudged it and the woman stumbled and fell over, snapping her frozen fingers off when she hit the ground. He grabbed the paracord from me and started tying its ankles.

"Wait!" yelled Ellie. "Take her shoes. I need those."

"Seriously?" quipped Niles.

"Yeah! Excuse me if I don't feel like running through the snow with garbage bags on my feet," she answered.

The woman was wearing bright red cowboy boots. Niles pulled them off and handed them to Ellie before tying its ankles. The woman just rolled side to side on its back, trying to twist over. "Ready when you are, Scott!" He yelled.

Scott jumped down, and next thing we knew we had an authentic, sort of living, whatever you call them, hanging upside down from the ceiling, still reaching for us.

We all circled around to get a better look.

"So, what are we supposed to call these things?" asked Scott.

"Back at Thornhaven, Moses had a name for them," I explained. "It was some kind of monster from Caribbean folklore. Like a dead person brought back to life with magic."

They all gave me an incredulous look.

"I'm not saying they're magic. I'm just trying to remember the name," I protested.

"He called them *jumbies*," Ellie answered.

"What the heck is a *zumbie*?" asked Scott.

"She said *jumbie*," corrected Niles.

"That's what I said. *Zumbie*," repeated Scott.

"No. It's like a French J, like *jhee, jhee jhee,*" explained Niles.

"*Zuh, Zuh, Zuh, Zuh,*" Scott imitated.

"Repeat after me. *Jacque de Molay, thou art avenged!*" Niles spun his wrist and bowed like it was the end of a Shakespeare play.

"You are such a geek!" said Scott.

"That's the whole point, Scott," I injected. "You can't call Holland–"

"Niles," corrected Niles.

"Sorry. You can't call *Niles* a geek if you're going to call them geeks too," I insisted. "We have to call them something else. Something unique."

"We should call them *infected*," suggested Niles. "That's what they are?"

"We're all infected," Ellie replied.

"It's a parasite, and not a virus. Technically that makes them *inFESTed*?" I corrected.

"Fine, then we're all *inFESTed*," Ellie smirked.

"I got it!" Scott snapped his fingers. "They're vampires! They crave flesh, which is kinda like craving blood. You have to stake them in the head, which is kinda like staking them in the heart. They're brain-dead vampires!"

"Um . . . it's wearing a cross." Ellie pointed at the woman, whose dress had fallen over her head, exposing the crucifix tattoo on her butt. "Besides, they're not repulsed by sunlight."

"Actually they are," I corrected. "I saw it at Lochshire. Sunlight doesn't set them on fire or anything, but they spread out at night, and then herd together in shadows during the day to get out of the sun. So there'd always be a crowd on the shady side of a building."

Scott beamed, "See? Vampires! What about garlic?"

I thought a moment. "They track by smell, so it's possible garlic could throw them off. Plus garlic is effective against all kinds of microbes. Maybe it would aggravate them. It's worth testing."

"We don't have any garlic. I already searched the kitchen," Niles scoffed. "Besides, they're more like *ghouls* than vampires. But they aren't folklore. They're advanced science. What we're dealing with is probably extraterrestrial."

"What!?" we all exclaimed in unison.

"It's like the Psyborgs in Tsar Trek. Those parasites are probably like nano drones from outer space, sent here to hijack our brains with orbital mind control lasers. What we're dealing with is an alien invasion, and they're using our own dead against us."

There was a long silence before anyone responded.

"Look, I don't care if you call them *puppies and kittens*. If they're frozen out there, why are we still hanging around in here? Let's suit up and move out."

Suddenly, the fringe of the woman's sundress caught the licks of the flame and ignited. The woman began flailing her arms, and shrieking. I'd never seen them afraid of anything before. We watched as the flames engulfed her dress, and began to climb up into the rafters. *It's time to leave.*

"Look, *greyfaces, ghouls, geeks.* Let's just call them *G's* for short," I suggested.

Everyone nodded.

Two: Desperate Breakfast

We left Denton's in a pyre, and ran out into the cold. Everything outside was buried under knee-high snow, but we could still see the clearing in the tree line, which followed a buried two-lane highway. It was the only real path, except trudging straight through woods and over granite.

The northern sky was full of thick white smoke. Any PorcScout worth their quills knows that means they were already putting out the fires at Thornhaven. But now Denton's was billowing black smoke into the air, which would lead the Major right to us.

"Guys, we should keep moving. Even with the G's iced over, there are still people around." I looked over the map.

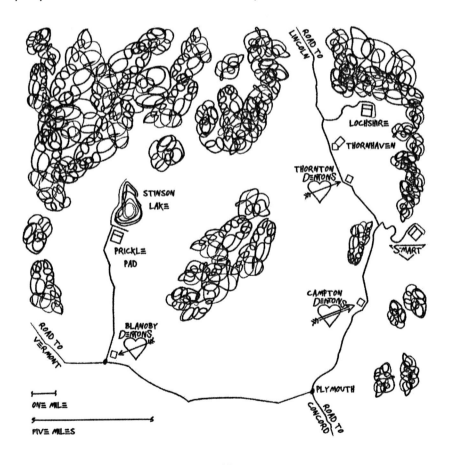

S-Mart was about two miles south in Campton. Thornhaven was a little over a mile north. I put them both on the map, along with Lochshire Estates.

To get to Dad's cabin we had to go south to Plymouth, west to Blanoby, and then north to Stinson Lake. It was only twenty-five miles, but no one was plowing the snow. We needed roads.

"We should stay out of sight, and head south. Keep an eye out for salvage along the way, especially warmer clothes. Maybe a vehicle."

I looked up from the map and Ellie was already trudging north. Niles followed after her and Scott shoved him playfully as he ran by.

"Wait!" I ran after them. "Where are you going?"

She turned around. "I told you, I'm going to that house we cleared out last month near Lochshire. It's got a fireplace, and we've got an ax." She pointed at Scott. "Plus it's got food. That's as good a place as any."

"When do we eat?" interrupted Scott.

"Ellie, everything within 3 miles of Thornhaven was picked clean weeks ago. That's why they stole the food from S-Mart in the first place. There won't be anything worth scavenging until we get further away. We should try to make it south to the Denton's in Campton before dark."

"And what makes you think S-Mart hasn't cleared the Denton's in Campton?" Ellie protested.

"They probably have, but it's still our best move. We need to get away from Thornhaven, and head toward the cabin. There are emergency supplies there."

"When do we eat?" asked Scott.

"Look, I've got a little rat meat leftover," I offered.

"Barf! No thank you!" exclaimed Niles. "Grab yourselves one of these." He stopped and opened the main compartment of his camera case.

"What do you got there?" inquired Ellie, as Niles opened the lid. It was filled with packed snow.

"I simmered some maple syrup over the fire last night while everyone was sleeping, and poured it into snow molds this morning. They should be ready. He pulled one out and it looked just like the amber scientists get dinosaur DNA from, with a spoon in it. "I call them *maple syrupsicles.*"

He'd made four, one for each of us. I don't know if the hype was real, but I swear it was as advertised. *The best maple syrup in New Hampshire.*

Everyone was silent for a minute as we ate frozen maple syrup and shivered in the snow. I thought about the fruit preserves stocked in Dad's pantry, and hoped they hadn't been looted.

"It's the closest sure thing," continued Ellie in a calmer tone. "Even if the food's gone, at least they'll have jackets. Besides, I don't like being out here unarmed. I'll bet the judge had golf clubs, or something."

"We can't get there without walking right back through that war zone." I pointed to the billows of smoke in the sky. "They'll be on high alert, not to mention all the fresh G's wandering around after the fight."

"Yeah, no way!" insisted Niles. "I'm not going back there."

"Me either," agreed Scott.

"Give me the gun and I'll put a bullet in the Major." Ellie held out her hand. "Maybe then you babies will stop wetting yourselves."

"I'll tell you what," I took out the pistol and checked the safety. "You can carry the pistol if you come south with us." I placed the handle in her hand, but held the barrel until she agreed. "You let Scott handle any G's with the ax, and you take the shot if you see anyone following us."

21

She nodded and tucked the pistol in her waistband.

We finished eating, Niles collected the spoons and we headed south.

We walked silently for a long time. I think everyone was a bit overwhelmed. Then Niles spoke first.

***

Have you ever missed someone so much you tried to keep them alive in your mind? Tried to imagine them alive in every situation, and pretended to be them?

I was in the AV Club room at school when the lockdown alarm went off. Back then we shared the computer lab with the school resource officer, Scott's dad. He kicked us off the computers and switched our screens to the outfacing cameras.

A caravan of armored vehicles pulled into the school parking lot, and riot police swarmed the campus.

The principal's voice came over the loudspeaker telling us a state of emergency had been declared, and to stay calm. "Teachers, please bring your students to the auditorium in an orderly fashion. Everything is under control."

On the internal cameras we saw the halls choked with panicked students, and Officer Pike left to herd traffic. The rest of the AV Club left too, but I stayed behind to watch the cameras.

In the front of the school, police were setting up roadblocks when an old man pushed passed and made it in the outer gate of the school parking lot. There was a struggle as an officer wrestled him to the ground, forced a pistol in his mouth and pulled the trigger.

I didn't know what was going on. I didn't know who the old man was.

The officer stood up, gripping his left hand, which was covered in blood. And when the other officers saw it, one of them raised a shotgun to his head and killed him too.

I freaked!

My first thought was Holland. He was the star keeper of the school lacrosse team, the Tigers. They were supposed to be outside in the field, but I didn't see him on the monitors. Coach Ramos was rushing everyone into the locker room, so that's where I went.

I ran straight to Holland's locker and wrapped my arms around him.

"Get your girly arms off me, Freak!"

We were twins, but we couldn't be more different. I'm socially awkward, he's popular. I build computers, he chases frogs. I'm good with systems, he's good at sports. I wanted to be a comedian, he wanted to compete . . . in anything. In everything.

Coach Ramos herded us into the auditorium to wait for our parents with the other kids, but when nobody came for us the faculty brought us cots and blankets and left us there overnight. We were all scared, but Holland and I had each other, you know?

For the first week, emergency broadcasts told everyone in town to come to the school. Police built barricades, and put up fences.

That weekend there was a soccer game scheduled against Gilman Middle School, but it was obviously cancelled. So, the school counselor, Miss Styx organized this big community barbeque to keep morale up. They played students vs. faculty.

We were so sure everything was safe.

All the commotion attracted more G's from town, so the police moved their patrols from the back of the school to double their numbers in front.

There were a couple of those things moving along the back fence. It was my first chance to get footage of them up close. We still had internet in the computer lab, and those #bitergram videos were getting popular, so I wanted to make one. I was going to call it, "Interview With The Infected" and have Holland film me asking questions I'd prepared. I was going to splice it together later, and do some bad lip reading for the G to make it work. But Holland didn't want to work the camera, so we switched. He put on my Channel 4 News jacket, and read my lines. I put on his orange Tigers hoodie to keep warm.

The interview was going well. It was really funny stuff. But something we did aggravated the G too much, and it managed to knock over a section of the fence. Suddenly it was on top of Holland, biting his face.

I should have helped. I know that once you're bitten it's too late, but I didn't know that then. Instead I ran back to the barbeque for help.

The G followed me, and attacked the crowd. It caused a panic. People died. And when they finally found Holland's body they just assumed he was me.

I decided right then that I enjoyed being dead. That it was better if he got to live. So, I let them think I was him.

When I first met Niles at Thornhaven he was still pretending to be Holland. I know Scott suspected that he was Niles all along, but I figured everyone's got a right to be addressed as they preferred, so I didn't question it much.

Three: Student Patrol

The road to Campton was serene, punctuated by only occasional sludgy bloodshed. The air was crisp, and the snow-covered forest was beautiful. Best of all, there was no sign of anyone following us, but that didn't mean we weren't entering hostile territory. We had to head right through S-Mart territory.

We passed many abandoned houses tucked away in the woods, but their front doors were all bashed open, so we assumed they'd already been looted.

We came across a few slow-moving G's shuffling along the road, but Scott disposed of them pretty easily with his ax. He seemed to enjoy it. It was shocking how much blood stained the snow.

Halfway between the two towns was a waste processing station.

Just outside Campton we came across a prison bus, rolled on its side across the highway. There were a few bodies inside, but they were putrid. They'd probably been there since the day of the outbreak. The front of the bus was blackened where the engine had caught fire.

Behind it the road was clogged with abandoned cars. So, we fanned out and brushed the snow off the windshields to look inside. Sometimes we found G's inside that were sluggish from the cold. So, Ellie and I teamed up to drag them out and pin them down, so Scott could bring the ax down on their heads.

It became routine, but once Niles admitted he was too afraid to help Scott joked that we should use Niles as bait. No one else found it funny.

We found keys in a half dozen vehicles or so, but someone had already siphoned all the gasoline. So we gave up trying to salvage a vehicle.

We found two coats along the way. An olive green field jacket that Ellie took, and a yellow Sugar Plum Golf Club blazer that Niles claimed.

At the end of the line was an empty station wagon with open doors that was obviously familiar to Scott.

"Scott, what is it?" asked Niles.

***

Man, I wasn't even supposed to be at school that day! They suspended me for having a can opener because of some stupid zero-tolerance policy. They said it was too close to a weapon. Nevermind that I actually had a can of peaches in my lunch. Nevermind that my dad, the security guard, packed it for me.

Whatever. I bet they're glad they have a can opener now.

I was with my mom running errands in Plymouth when this guy just walked into oncoming traffic. She slammed on her brakes, and swerved but still sideswiped him as we spun off the highway. She'd been drinking, but it wasn't her fault. He came out of nowhere!

Mom never handled crisis well, but when she saw he was in an orange prison jumpsuit she was relieved and said, "Well, at least no one will miss him."

I was so mad.

She freaked out when she saw he was still alive! She wanted to leave him there, but I insisted we had to get him to the hospital.

She made me help her lift him into the backseat. But he was broken and bloody.

"Mom, you have to call the police!" I insisted.

She dropped him. "I'll call your father. He'll know what to do."

Dad told us to abandon the man and the car and come to the school. Apparently, a prisoner on that bus was infected and attacked the guards. They crashed, and the dead prisoners escaped into the woods.

Police were trying to keep it contained, but it spread fast as the dead attacked the rubberneckers and emergency responders. When police found us on the side of the road they shuttled as many of us as they could to the school.

When we got there, mom still had blood on her blouse from the dead guy, so they put us in the quarantine tent in the yard, instead of with the general population.

It made sense. They didn't know how it spread yet. They were just being careful. But they put us in with the bite victims, so it wasn't long before the quarantine tent turned into a buffet.

I wasn't even sad when she died. More like relieved. My whole life, she was this fat, lazy drunk. She'd scream and yell when we were late with her feedings.

"I want more parmesan! Where's my mayonnaise sandwich? Get me another ice cream cone!"

Dad deserved better.

When they let me back in gen pop they put me on student patrol, so I could help Dad keep order. We kept the line moving in the cafeteria, and stopped people from running in the halls, or making too much noise.

That was before that bastard killed my Dad.

I wanted to kill the Major when I found out, but Sheriff Nap let him go! Some kind of professional courtesy.

After that, I spent a long time watching the G's in the yard. I gotta tell you, I don't think they're as braindead as people think. I mean most of them are, but I've seen some weird stuff. Like dead cops didn't just join the herd, like everyone else. They found each other, and picked partners.

Sports fans did it too, kinda. This one time, I saw a bird swoop down at a G in a Lancaster Rebels jersey. When it reached up to grab the bird, all the other Rebels fans in the crowd reached up, even though they were nowhere near the bird, like they were doing the wave.

I think it's like clans, or maybe bloodlines. They stick together instinctively because they were infected together.

Plus, I noticed some G's trying to get out. Either moving along the fences, testing the connections, or trying every door, over and over.

It's like they still have memory, so are they even really dead?

Four: The Fall of Boston

We followed the highway toward Campton until we started seeing civilization again. It was like a ghost town.

"We're getting close to S-Mart. We should keep off the street as much as possible," I suggested.

Everyone agreed, so we stayed behind hedges and parked cars as much as possible. We stopped scavenging and focused on getting through town as quickly as we could.

I lost my ear weeks ago when I was attacked by Scott's dead dad. I survived, but missing an ear made it hard to tell the direction of sounds. So, when I heard the rumble of an approaching engine I couldn't tell where it was coming from.

Everyone leapt for cover behind a garbage truck as some kind of armored personnel carrier roared into view from the south.

This thing was massive! It looked like a modified Humvee, with a steel wedge mounted to the front, and tank treads instead of rear wheels.

The engine revved as it smashed into an abandoned car, launching it out of the road.

Stinky was tense in the middle of the highway.

"Stinky! Get over here!" I yelled.

I ran into the street and grabbed the cat, but when I tried to reverse directions my legs slipped and flew out from under me.

The carrier honked a kind of truck horn, as if saying it saw me, but it wasn't going to stop.

The ground shook as the carrier approached. The sludge under me was so slippery I couldn't get to my feet. It was going too fast to slow down in time. I was dead for sure.

Then suddenly, it made a hard right turn toward downtown Campton.

Scott offered me his hand and pulled me to my feet. "What the heck was that? It looked like some kind of mutant tank!"

"It's called a half-track, a big one too. An M3 maybe . . . Or an M5," inserted Niles as he joined us in the middle of the street. "The US hasn't used them since World War Two, but the Israelis still use them."

"What's it doing here?" I wondered aloud.

"It's good for snow," answered Niles.

Ellie ran to the intersection to watch where it was going. "I'm going after it. I want to see who's in it," and she ran off.

We all scrambled to follow her. The tank treads left a distinct mark in the snow that made it easy to track once it was out of sight.

We spotted the half-track a few blocks away, stopped in the S-Mart parking lot, and we ducked behind a snowbank for cover.

A soldier got out of the driver's seat and was greeted by a woman in an S-Mart uniform that came from inside. But the weirdest thing was the G behind her. It was also dressed in a blue shirt and red apron, like an S-Mart employee. It's hands were strapped to a shopping cart full of bricks, but it wasn't attacking. *Why wasn't it attacking?*

The soldier signaled to the vehicle and a bald man in a grey lab coat got out, escorted by two more soldiers.

Something about him was familiar.

"Oh my gawd!" Ellie yelped and dropped behind the snowbank. "It's Dr. Blum!"

"The virologist from the CDC?" I asked. Before the internet went down I saw a panel discussion between Dr. Blum and a neurobiologist named Dr. Murphy on a show called *Info Planet* with Joel Saxen.

She nodded.

"That's perfect! That's the guy Dad was trying to send his research to before he died. He's working on a vaccine!" I stood up, ready to march down there and give him Dad's files.

Ellie grabbed me by the back of the collar and yanked me down to the ground. "So help me, if you hand me over to him I will feed you to the dead!" She looked genuinely terrified as she explained.

***

It was my thirteenth birthday. Mom and Dad originally planned this big pizza party with all my friends, but everyone in Boston was put on mandatory house arrest. So, instead we stayed home and watched "Night of the Flesh Eaters." For my birthday, they gave me the box set of the whole Flesh Eaters trilogy. Honestly, I couldn't think of anything better than staying up late, eating popcorn, and watching a scary movie marathon with my folks. I never really connected with kids my age. They're just so . . . juvenile.

My parents didn't treat me like a child. So, when the plucky vigilante made the obnoxious joke to the hysterical damsel, and I didn't get it, they weren't afraid to tell me about adult things.

We'd seen the emergency broadcasts, and the viral #bitergram videos, but everyone considered the attacks a New Hampshire problem. President Abedin pledged to turn Boston into a blockade against the infection. They set up roadblocks, and checkpoints, and mandatory medical screenings. We knew it was bad, but whatever it was, it was far away. The Capital was taking every precaution. Spared no expense.

Things were calm in Boston until the first attack inside the green zone. Then things got crazy. The President declared martial law, and ordered everyone to turn over their firearms, which immediately triggered riots. The military started escorting the medical examiners house-to-house with urban combat battalions.

Near the end of the second movie, "Return of the Flesh Eaters," when the radioactive pilot was finally going to eat the annoying college student, there was a knock at the front door.

"Thump! Thump! Thump! Thump!"

It was four hard raps, like on cop shows. Mom and Dad exchanged worried looks, and paused the movie. Dad went to the door and looked through the peephole.

"There's three soldiers on the porch," he explained.

"Back away, and hopefully they'll just leave," Mom whispered.

"But . . . it's the law." Dad hesitated as his instinct for self preservation argued with his conditioning to obey. He couldn't just walk away. He fastened the security chain and opened the door a few inches. "Evening Sirs. What can I do for you?"

The first soldier immediately SWAT kicked the door, breaking the chain guard, and knocking Dad back. The other two pounced, and dragged him to the ground.

I screamed, and before I could breathe the first soldier charged directly at me.

"Bang! Bang!"

Mom shot the revolver over my head. Two slugs, right in the center of mass. She'd kept a Colt Python in the end table next to the couch since the gun confiscation started.

The force knocked the soldier to the ground, but it kept coming, grabbing ahold of my foot.

"Bang! Bang!"

The next two shots went through the thing's head, but not before it took a big chomp out of my leg.

Dad screamed as the other two soldiers ripped into him, and Mom fired her last two rounds, blowing their heads to bits.

Dad was alive, but barely. He had bites on his hands and neck, and deep scratches on his face and chest. He was choking on blood.

Mom was cradling him and trying to stop the bleeding when the army medics showed up, drawn by the gunfire. They took him away on a stretcher.

Procedure dictated that we be taken to quarantine and examined. When Mom protested they said that discharging an illegal firearm in the green zone was grounds to call the Department of Children and Families and have me taken by force.

Mom tried to protect me. Tried to resist the medical examiners, but the bite on my leg was down to the gristle, and the blood on my pajama pants gave it away.

They locked me and Dad in an observation cell without even bandaging our wounds. It was so cold.

I had to watch Dad change. Within an hour he went from begging for our lives to unintelligible growling and snarling, and then he came after me.

I spent all night trying to keep away from him. When the field medics came back in the morning they tasered him and hauled him out.

The thing is, I never changed.

The next day Dr. Blum arrived from the CDC. The first thing out of his pudgy mouth was, "Daddy died and Princess didn't? Interesting. . . Let's try to rule out inherited traits. Pick up Mommy for testing."

Dr. Demento over there had me airlifted to a research lab in Manchester, New Hampshire. It was awful. He kept me strapped to an autopsy table, and wouldn't even address me as a human being. He just called me "the specimen."

I don't know where he took Mom.

The only reason I had any idea what was going on was because he recorded every little thought in his head into a voice recorder. He wasn't working on a vaccine. Dr. Blum is trying to weaponize this thing.

He said that the parasite consumed everything it couldn't use, and it protected whatever it could use. In most people that leaves nothing but their most primitive instinct to hunt. That's how it spreads. But in some people, more aggressive people, the parasite preserves more, because it can use more. Like a territorial instinct, or some basic tribal instinct.

After weeks of blood tests and brain biopsies Dr. Blum concluded I wasn't actually immune. I still have the larva in my blood, but for some reason they don't like my brain, so they never nest, and never mature.

To figure out why I was different he wanted to inject each part of my brain with the adult parasites separately, under laboratory scrutiny, meaning under a microscope.

Luckily, Mom busted me out before he put my brain through a meat slicer. But by then nothing was left of Dad but a wheezing lump of flesh, so we had to leave him behind. Mom said we were going north, to find Dr. Hartwell. She said he'd know why my brain was unique.

Five: The Rotter Box

"I don't get it. What is Dr. Blum doing?" asked Niles.

"Weren't you listening? He's turning G's into weapons," Scott said.

"No! I mean, what is he doing here, at S-Mart?" Niles clarified.

"Guys. We gotta get out of here." Ellie stood up. "Like, right now!" She started backing away from the group. "We never should have come here."

Scott grabbed her by the arm and yanked her back down. "Pipe down, Pipsqueak! Stay out of sight till it's clear."

"Isn't it obvious!?" blurted Ellie. "He's looking for me! Major Winters must have made contact with the CDC, and used S-Mart to attack Thornhaven so he could deliver me back to Dr. Blum."

"Wait! I have an idea!" Niles spun me around and started digging through my bag. "If Dr. Blum is here, and Major Winters is still mopping up at Thornhaven, Dr. Blum is going to try to reach him by radio." Niles pulled Dad's radio out of my bag. "If the Major is using a CB radio, and we can guess the channel, we can listen in."

"That's brilliant!" I grabbed the radio and started scrolling through the channels. *There's only eighteen.*

"Try channel thirteen," suggested Scott. "Winters is superstitious like that."

A voice crackled through the static. ". . . fires are out. We're just cleaning up now." *Success!* It was the Major. "The place is trashed, but there's lots of supplies and equipment. They got a generator worth taking. Some guns. A nice surveillance system. They got a better boiler than us, but that's a big job. We're boxing up the food and medical supplies now."

"Ten-four, Major. Give me a HERD report. Over." I didn't recognize the other voice, probably someone at S-Mart, but *HERD report* was military lingo. It stood for *Heads, Equipment, Rate,* and *Direction.*

"Eighteen confirmed kills. We got nine rotters, and five breathers in custody. Mostly women and children . . . I'd say there's about ten heads caught along the perimeter fence, but if our intel is good there's still about thirty heads unaccounted for. Dead or alive, I got teams searching the woods now. Better send up another *Rotter Box.* Over."

"What's a *Rotter Box?*" whispered Niles.

"Shh!" We all shushed him.

"What about the sheriff, and the other hostiles?" asked the voice.

"Last night I shot the Sheriff in the leg and threw him in the boiler room with the other rotters," said the Major. "He won't be a problem. Over."

There was a scuffle on the line. "Ok, fine! . . . Hey Major, there's a visitor here from . . . " And then it was more of a struggle.

"Major Winters! What is the status of the specimen?" It was Dr. Blum.

There was a pause before the Major replied, "You mean the girl? Over."

"Yes! The girl!" yelled Dr. Blum. "Do you have the slightest idea how mission critical it is that she be reacquired . . . alive?!"

"Listen here, Doc. I sent Woz and Cordell after her. My best men. And they both came back bit. If you want me to clean up your mess you better be straight with me about what we're up against. Over."

Niles and Scott both looked at Ellie and backed up half a step.

"Guys, just listen!" I yelled.

"You're imagination escapes you, Major." I could practically hear Dr. Blum's teeth grinding. "Where is the specimen now? Over."

"I got a lead on her and the brats she's with. A Denton's burned down not far from here. But you might not even need her. There's a science lab here you're going to want to check out. Lessard is dead, but she was studying the girl, and I got copies and samples of everything. I don't know what half this stuff is. Over."

"You think I give a whit about what some grade school science teacher thinks? Get serious! Now, I am ordering you. Drop everything you're doing, get your men, and meet me at this Denton's. I'll track her down myself. Over and out!"

The channel went silent, and I peeked over the snowbank we were hiding behind. Dr. Blum and his soldiers were still inside.

"We need to get out of here!" insisted Ellie. "Right now!"

"Hold up!" insisted Niles. "Before I go anywhere, I wanna know how you infected Officer Cordell and Private Woz!"

"It wasn't me!" She yelled. "Mrs. Lessard had one of those things chained up in the boiler room. I let it go, and it attacked them. Ask Max, he was there."

I nodded. "It was pretty brilliant."

Six: The Sneaky Sheriff

We made it back to the highway before the half-track, and when it went by we jumped behind a garbage truck and watched them go north.

"Well at least those big treads will cover our footprints," I said.

"Unless they figure it out, and come right back for us," replied Scott.

We had a problem. The highway was the only road south, and we couldn't walk the whole way in a day. If we continued on foot they were going to find our trail at Denton's, turn around and run us down. But if we found a working vehicle the tire marks in the snow would lead them to us, no matter where we went. We needed an alternative.

Then, as if drawn by the sound of the half-track's engine, a man stumbled into the road from the woods.

He had his back to us until the half-track disappeared in the distance. Then he turned around.

The man's pants were soaked in blood. He clutched a gaping wound in his thigh with one hand and reached forward with the other.

It was Sheriff Nap.

"I got this," called Ellie as she aimed the pistol.

"No!" I yelled. "S-Mart will hear a gunshot this close. If they call Dr. Blum back you'll lead them right to us."

She lowered the gun, grudgingly.

Nap was some distance away, and not moving very fast. I'm not even sure he could see us. One eye was covered by an eye patch, as it had been when he was alive, and with the other he squinted and scanned the area, searching for the source of our voices.

"Scott!" she screamed. "Bring me the ax!"

Suddenly, Nap's one eye locked on me, and I saw that it was bloodshot and constricted, like all of the dead.

It growled at me once it identified me as prey and then roared back toward the woods.

Two more G's ran into the street, as if responding to Nap's call. They were Private Woz, and Officer Cordell.

Nap took one step toward us, slipped in the snow and fell flat on its face. But Woz and Cordell galloped toward us like wild beasts, gurgling blood from their mouths as they closed in.

"Forget this!" yelled Scott. "I'm outta here!" Scott stood up and ran south, followed quickly by a terrified Niles.

Woz came at me first, lunging forward with its arms outstretched. I ducked into a crouch, and it tripped over me, bashing its face into the garbage truck, but it wasn't deterred for a moment, and immediately began reaching for my legs.

Cordell went after Ellie, but as soon as it was within reach she grabbed it by the hair, yanked it to the ground, and stomped on its back.

We both ran after Scott and Niles, and once we regrouped we all kept running. It was easy enough to outrun the G's. They weren't terribly fast, and they stumbled and fell over pretty much everything. But they didn't get tired. Everytime we stopped to rest and catch our breath they caught up within minutes.

"Guys, wait!" I stopped. "I have an idea."

We'd been running by houses that were obviously already searched and abandoned. I checked a few doors until I found one that was unlocked.

"Come on! Come on!" I waved everyone inside, and ran out to the street waving my arms. "Over here, you lamebrains!" When I was sure the G's saw me I ran inside and locked the door behind me. "Give me a hand!"

We pushed a couch and a bookshelf in front of the door before the G's started pounding on the door outside.

"Great, now what?" asked Niles.

"Now we slip out the back and sneak away," Ellie predicted.

"Exactly right," I confirmed. "They'll pound on that door forever, and by the time they break through we'll be long gone."

We all ran out the back door and looked for another way out of the yard.

"Max, look at this." Scott had out his map.

"We're in Campton, just a little south of S-Mart." Scott pointed his finger as he explained. "If we follow the road we have to go down to Plymouth, over to Blanoby, and up to Stinson Lake. But check this out. If we cut straight across, through the woods, it's like half the distance. We could be there by dinner time!"

"Not trudging through snow and over granite, we can't," injected Niles.

"Scott's right," I said. "We'll be harder to track, and any G's in the woods will be too clumsy and frozen to chase us."

"I don't care where we go. I am not staying here," insisted Ellie.

Scott swung the ax, splitting a board in the back fence and slipped through. "Now, let's go!" We all slipped through and found open woods on the other side.

I was the last one through, and just as Ellie propped the board back into place I heard the sound of a latch opening, and a rusty gate creaking. I ducked down into the brush and peaked back through the fence.

Sheriff Nap opened the sidegate and came around the house to the backyard. It tried the backdoor, but we'd left it locked. Then it moved along the back of the house and ultimately slipped inside a side door.

We all watched in disbelief. No one had ever seen a G behave that way. Strangest of all, *it was sneaking!* Sheriff Nap must have been a higher functioning G, like the Postman at Lochshire, or Officer Pike at Thornhaven. But it hadn't seen us, so we left it behind, and headed west, into the woods.

Seven: Bear Trail

There wasn't much snow on the forest floor, because it was all caught up in the tops of the trees. That made it easier to travel, but we had no direction. I'd have given up my last MRE for a compass.

I remembered a section in the PorcScouts Survival Guide about creating a compass from scratch, so I opened the chapter:

> *A compass needle can be made from any metal that can be magnetized. A paper clip, a safety pin, or even a razor blade can be used, but obviously an experienced PorcScout should have a sewing needle in their survival kit. . .*

Sure enough, I had a whole sewing kit. I retrieved it from my pack and skipped ahead a bit:

> *To magnetize your needle you'll need to rub it against something that charges it with static electricity. Ideally an existing magnet can be used. If not, silk and fur will work, or even your own hair. Rub the needle against the magnetizer using steady even strokes. Be sure to rub in one direction, not back and forth. 50 strokes should be enough.*

I began rubbing the needle against my hair, which triggered confused glances from everyone else, but I read on:

> *Next you'll need a way to float your needle in water. A coin-sized piece of cork is ideal. Insert your needle horizontally into the cork, so that the same amount of metal protrudes from each side. Any small item that floats can be used in place of the cork. If you're in the wilderness you can even use a leaf.*

We were in short supply of both, but I pulled a piece of bark off a low hanging tree branch and drove the needle through it.

Fill a bowl with a few inches of water and float the compass on the surface. The magnetized needle turns until it aligns with the earth's magnetic field to point north.

"Niles, let me see your camera case?" I asked.

He was confused, but curious, and handed it over.

Sure enough the snow inside was slushy, but not melted enough. I scooped out the chunks and added water from my pack.

"What are you doing?" he asked.

"Watch," I answered as I dropped the needle into the flooded compartment.

Ellie, Scott, and Niles all circled around as the needle spun until it lost momentum, turned briefly the other direction, and finally halted in one direction.

"Presto!" I pointed in the direction the needle indicated. "That's north, which means . . ." I pointed to my left, "we should go west."

"What kind of magic is that!?" exclaimed Scott.

"It's a little crude, but it's just a simple compass," I explained.

"Like the compass in a GPS navigation system?" he asked.

"Sort of," I answered. "Any freely suspended magnet will align with the Earth's magnetic field, so it should point magnetic north."

The look on his face only conveyed confusion.

"You seriously don't know how a compass works?" I asked. "We just finished a whole unit on magnets in science class."

"Ask him how he scored on the chapter test," Niles quipped under his breath.

"Shut up, Muppet Fart!" Scott punched Niles in the shoulder hard enough to knock him off his feet. "I'm not stupid. I just don't understand why the Earth's magnetic field is still working if the electricity is shut off?"

"Scott, the Earth's magnetic field isn't artificial," I explained. "The Earth is literally a magnet."

"What? No way!" he protested. "If the Earth was a magnet why would they make planes out of metal?"

Everyone groaned and Ellie put her palm over her face. "There's so much wrong with that question I don't even know where to start," she said.

We walked west for hours until the sun began to set, which confirmed the accuracy of the compass because the sun sets in the west. So, I used the remaining light to browse the book for other tips while we walked.

"What we need to find is a bear trail," I suggested.

"A what?" protested Ellie.

"Black bears make these trails by stomping their feet, and scratching the trees," I explained. "If we find one, it should lead to the creek where they fish."

"Yeah?" protested Scott. "And what are we supposed to do when we run into an actual bear?"

"Don't worry! They're hibernating right now," I said. "Look, the whole Mount Tecumseh region is covered in little rivers and creeks, and on this side of the mountain they all flow west. Which means, if we follow one, it should flow right into the lake."

i looked up the section on bear trails in the Survival Guide:

Bear paws have a soft pad that doesn't usually leave a distinct print, unless they're walking in mud. Bears often follow deer trails, or fire roads, but they also create their own trails by repeatedly stepping in the same footsteps as previous bears, especially as they approach their dens. This creates a pattern of divots in the forest floor that can last for years. Bears also stomp and twist their feet in these divots as a way of scent-marking their territory.

Scott had gotten pretty far ahead of everyone, except Stinky. The cat preferred to climb every rock, and walk every ledge. And Scott, it seemed, preferred to chase him. He stayed out of trees, but if Stinky wouldn't come down he'd start hacking at the trunk with the ax. Honestly, I appreciated the audible check in. I didn't like them being out of sight.

"Guys!" yelled Scott. "I think I found something!"

Once we caught up they were standing on a huge mound, next to a large tree that had toppled over, upturning its root structure.

"In there." Scott pointed.

Under the root structure there was a smooth entry slope, down into a large burrow of dirt in the hollow of the tree. In the clearing there was a pile of crushed twigs and brush.

"It's a bear den," I said.

Stinky hopped and slid into the brush, sniffing the air and jittering his tail excitedly.

"Yeah," agreed Scott. "But where's the bear?"

Our hearts sank as we suddenly saw the forest for the dangerous place it was.

"Maybe bears only use the same den once. Maybe this is last year's den?" I hoped.

"If you believe that, I say we climb in there and spend the night. I don't want to be out here in the dark," complained Niles.

"No way," Ellie objected. "If we camp outside we'll need a fire. If we build a fire the smoke will lead those goons right to us. We need to get there tonight. Even if we have to walk all night."

"You said bear trails lead to a creek, right?" Scott asked.

I nodded.

He pointed to a trail of divots on the other side of the den. "Well, it can't be far if this bear walks there every time it wants a fish. I say we follow the trail until we hit the creek." He gestured roughly that direction. "Creek leads to lake. Lake leads to cabin. Boom!" He slapped the ax head with his palm. "We're drinking hot cocoa and roasting marshmallows at Max's place by midnight!"

"Guys, I'm not going to lie," Niles injected. "That Denton's in Campton is looking pretty sweet right now. At least it'll be warm."

"It's in hostile territory!" cried Ellie.

"Guys, I don't think a midnight march is a good idea either way," I interrupted. "It's getting dark. It's going to get a lot colder. I think the den is a good idea."

"Are you crazy?" asked Scott. "Did you forget about bears?"

"This den may have been abandoned for years. It might not even be a bear's den. It could be raccoon, or deer or-"

"Or wolves!" interrupted Scott.

"Look." I pointed down into the den. "Stinky has already made himself comfortable."

Stinky had found himself a spot in the hollow of the tree and curled into a ball to rest.

I continued. "If this belonged to something hostile I think he'd know. He'd smell it. I trust his instincts."

They reluctantly agreed.

The bedding, crude as it was, was better than nothing. And in that confined a space our own body heat kept it warmer than open air. But it was a cold night, and the shelter was insufficient. We couldn't build a fire without exposing our position, so we had to make due without it. We had four emergency blankets and duct tape. So we got to work on insulating the shelter for the night.

We tied a line of paracord between the two largest roots to hang a blanket over the entrance, and laid a second blanket on the ground underneath, to reduce heat loss through the ground. That left us two blankets between the four of us. So, we slept in pairs. Niles and Scott. Ellie and me.

Stinky kept watch.

When I woke up Ellie had her arms around me. I brushed her hair over her ear, and she pulled me closer, but I think she was asleep.

Her eyes opened, big and green, and locked with mine. A pit sank in my stomach, until she smiled. Then it hatched into a kaleidoscope of butterflies and warm fuzzies, and I smiled too.

We got up and got ready to leave without even speaking. We all packed our things, and ate maple syrup and snow for breakfast. When it was obvious that wasn't enough, we split my last MRE. And then, without a word, we continued along the bear trail.

We walked for over an hour. The forest looked completely different by morning light. So bright, and beautiful. For a moment I completely forgot how desperate we were. Forgot about everything. The hunger. The danger. Even the outbreak itself.

It reminded me of training hikes I went on with the PorcScouts, when Dad was alive.

Thinking about Dad always snapped me back to reality.

I smelled the fresh water before I saw it. There was a freshness in the air. By the time I heard the rushing water we were all running. It was a wide shallow creek with snow embankments, but the rapids flowed too fast to freeze.

To the east, the sun was just above the treeline, and it was finally warming up.

We walked another mile and came across a huge log that had fallen across the river. Stinky was in front and immediately jumped up and trotted across. So naturally we all followed.

Scott jumped down off the log on the other side and yelled back, "Max! Look what Stinky found!" I was next behind him. It was a set of animal tracks in the mud. "Is that the same bear?" he asked.

"It might be." I jumped down too. "But these are fresh tracks." I answered.

Eight: That Sinking Feeling

Scott and I were on the north bank with Stinky. Niles was still on the other side. Ellie was in the middle of the log bridge.

"Guys, look!" she said, pointing the pistol upstream.

There, not more than a hundred yards away, was a large black bear, splashing around in the middle of the creek.

"Max," Scott whispered, "What does your book say about bear attacks?"

The bear was ignoring us. It was fishing.

I flipped through pages of the Survival Guide. "I'm checking."

Ellie crouched on the log with the pistol trained on the bear.

"What if it's not hibernating because it's hungry?" asked Scott.

"I don't think it's hungry." Ellie whispered as the animal pulled a severed human arm from the water with its teeth.

Scott and I exchanged horrified looks, and I went back to the book. "This is it!" I read the section quickly:

> *Bears just want to be left alone, but some people just won't leave them alone. If you meet one face to face, stay calm and back away slowly. Sudden movements and loud voices may trigger an attack. Never imitate bear sounds! It's impolite–*

"Skip to the end!" interrupted Scott.

I skimmed ahead:

> *Bear spray should be your first line of defense . . .*

Skip.

> *Keep your gear on, put your quills out, and play dead if you are attacked by a brown bear, or a grizzly bear . . .*

Skip.

> *Black bears are more easily frightened than grizzlies . . .*

"Black bears. This is it!" I whispered and read aloud.

> *If a black bear approaches, wave your arms and make yourself appear as large as possible. If they attack, DO NOT PLAY DEAD! Fight back with anything you've got! Aim for the eyes and muzzle. Do not climb a tree. They are excellent climbers. Their instinct is to chase fleeing animals, so whatever you do, never–*

"RUN AWAY!" Ellie screamed as she fired the pistol.

Bang! . . . Bang! Bang!

There was a spray of red as the bear charged straight at us.

We all ran.

The bear came running straight down the middle, through the shallow water, which at least slowed it down.

It's stupid to run! I was so scared that when Scott ran, I panicked.

Ellie ran back across the log to the opposite side of the creek with Niles. They split off into the woods, and I lost sight of them.

Stinky scrambled up the nearest tree and got left behind.

The bear went under the log, came out of the water and ran after me and Scott.

Scott ran along the river bank, but I broke off, hoping to lose it weaving through the trees. I remembered something Dad said once as a joke. *You don't have to run faster than the bear, just faster than the other guy.* It was an awful thought.

I ran until the trees cleared away and I was running across mud, and ice.

I stopped fast and took a wide stance when I felt the ground crack under my feet. It was Stinson Lake! Dad's cabin was across the water, on the south shore. The lake was only partially frozen, with a shelf of ice around the edge, and open water in the middle.

Just yards away, Scott ran out of the trees, followed by the bear.

"Scott! Don't run!" I screamed. "You've got to fight!"

Scott ran out onto the ice with a look of dread on his face. He stopped fast when he reached the edge, and turned back.

The bear charged forward, building speed.

Scott lifted the ax over his head, and stood ready to swing.

The bear planted its paws, as if to pounce, and Scott swung.

Except the bear didn't pounce. The ax missed its mark and embedded in the ice with such force that it slipped out of Scott's hands and was swallowed by the lake.

An instant later Scott and the bear were in the water.

"Scott!" I screamed and ran toward the edge of the ice. I slid out on my belly to disperse my weight and peered down. There was no sign of him or the bear below the surface.

I looked back toward the woods but the others were nowhere in sight. I had to go after him alone. I took off my pack and tied it to my foot with the paracord. At least I'd have something tethered to the surface.

I dove in.

The water was so cold it stung. It was murky and dark, but I caught sight of the ax head shimmering below. I kicked my legs and pushed down. The ax was sinking.

I swam into the dark, deeper and deeper, until Scott's hand jutted up. My bones ached, but I grabbed him by the arm and tried to pull him toward the surface. I could still see the daylight above.

He kicked frantically, but he was being pulled down. *Was it the bear?*

As my eyes adjusted to the dark I could see the grasping fingers of a dozen G's, maybe a hundred. All the G's swept away by all the creeks must have been deposited here in the lake.

The frenzy of corpses circled around the bear like sharks and absorbed it, turning the water red with blood.

And they were pulling us down too.

A hideous face, rotten and bloated, came out of the darkness and sank its teeth into Scott's shoulder.

He screamed.

I let go and scrambled for the surface, but something had me by the foot. I kicked free and pumped my arms until my lungs felt filled with battery acid.

Then my gear bag sank by me like a stone.

I was close enough to see Stinky peering over the edge of the ice. But the G's had ahold of my pack and the tether was dragging me down to some desperate fate.

54

Nine: Squatter's Rights

I have to cut the paracord now! My multi-tool was in the gear bag. Out of desperation I ripped the splint off my broken finger and used the knife to saw the paracord, but it wasn't sharp.

Once the cord snapped I scrambled for the surface.

I was shivering on the surface and spitting up water when Niles and Ellie came running to pull me out.

"What happened?!" cried Ellie. "Where's Scott?"

"And the bear?" Niles reminded us.

The sun was blinding above me.

"They fell through the ice." I sat up and turned toward the edge. "I tried to save him, but the lake is infested!"

"Infested!?" Niles hopped back as if he expected to see them clawing through the ice under his feet.

"Dozens at least. Maybe hundreds." I continued. "I just wasn't strong enough to pull him free."

"Sometimes you eat the bear, and sometimes the bear eats you," joked Niles with a strange southwestern drawl.

"He just died trying to protect all of us!" I insisted. "He's saved your neck more than once!"

"That guy has done nothing but terrorize me since kindergarten!" yelled Niles.

"Guys!" interrupted Ellie. "I hate to break up this little pity party, but it's cold and I'm hungry. Now, I'm all for honoring our fallen companions, and blubbering about their memory, or whatever, but can we please do it inside by the fire, with a hot bowl of soup?"

We both agreed.

My eyes fell to the paracord around my ankle, and the frayed nylon at the end. *Dad's research was gone.*

I rewrapped my broken finger with duct tape from Ellie, and a spoon from Niles as we trudged around the icy lake in silence.

My heart accelerated with every step toward the cabin, and before long I was running. It had been a long time since I'd been any place that felt like home.

Dad built it years ago to use as a clubhouse for the PorcScouts. The cabin was constructed from three modular kits, connected side by side, which produced a long vaulted space and two floors above ground. Inside there was a safe room which lead to an underground bunker. That's where all the PorcScouts families had stockpiled their emergency supplies. There was food, water, weapons.

The cabin was a simple design, with a rustic wooden exterior. It was triangular shaped, with a covered deck on one side, and a garage on the other.

There were huge, two-story windows on the backside, so there was a view of the lake from the lounge on the first floor, and the master bedroom on the second floor. There were loft windows on both sides of the roof, and a brick chimney.

"Max, I don't suppose your cabin's fireplace is on a timer?" Niles asked.

"No."

"Then, doesn't that mean someone else is here?" he asked, pointing to the smoke coming from the chimney.

I nodded. "I guess so."

At the end of the back deck was a wooden staircase down to a small pier where Dad's fishing boat was docked. We climbed onto the pier and walked up the steps to the rear entrance of the cabin.

We followed the deck around to the porch. The front of the cabin had a second floor balcony with a satellite dish, a raised porch with stone steps, and a large front yard encircled with a picket fence.

The fence was crudely reinforced with slats of random wood and debris.

Above the double doors was engraved the latin expression *Semper Paratus* meaning "always be prepared."

"What was that?!" Niles spun around and pointed into the woods.

Ellie aimed the pistol where Niles was pointing. "What was what?" she asked.

"I heard something rustling," he explained.

We all froze in place and listened.

"I don't hear anything," I whispered cautiously.

"You're imagining things," Ellie said and turned her attention back toward the cabin. "The windows on the second floor aren't covered," she observed. "Maybe we can climb up to the balcony and break in. Take them by surprise."

"The front door is locked electronically. I know the code. If there's any juice in the backup batteries I can just open the door."

"Why don't we just knock?" Niles suggested.

Ellie and I shrugged and agreed to try it. Next to the door was a panel with a number pad, a doorbell and an intercom.

I reached for the doorbell.

"Wait!" interrupted Niles. "Just one thing. I need you to call me Holland," he insisted.

"What? Why?" I asked.

"Holland is more brave than Niles. If things get ugly I'd rather be him."

Ellie rolled her eyes, but nodded. Once I agreed, his posture literally changed. He had been hunched over with fear, and hiding behind me, but suddenly he stood up straight with his shoulders back and pushed the doorbell himself. Ellie stood behind us with the pistol trained on the door.

After the third ring a voice came over the intercom. "Am I going crazy or do we have a real live breather out there?"

I know that voice.

"So, which is it Breather, friend or foe?" asked the voice.

58

"Is this Joel Saxen!?" I asked.

"Who's asking?"

"I'm Max Hartwell."

"Max Hartwell? . . . Max Hartwell . . ." his voice trailed off and there was a long pause.

"Who the heck is Joel Saxen?" Ellie whispered.

"You've never heard of Joel Saxen!?" Holland gasped. "He's the host of *Info Planet*. Niles is obsessed with that show. Saxen kept broadcasting way longer than all the fake news networks. He had all the documents on this whole mess. He predicted the—"

"Sorry kid." The intercom interrupted. "No 'Max Hartwell' on the guest list."

"Guest list?" I protested. "This is my cabin!"

"Are you related to Rich Hartwell?" he asked.

"Yeah! He's my dad. How'd you know that?"

The intercom cut off, the deadbolt unlocked, and the door opened a few inches until the chain guard pulled tight.

One brown eye peered through the gap, and a small hand jutted out holding a fist full of envelopes. "You've got mail." It was a female voice.

I took the envelopes.

"There's tons of it," she explained. "Mostly coupons and *E-Prime* magazines . . . Look, no one was here when we got here."

"Who are you? How many of you are there?" I asked.

She held out her hand through the opening. "My name's Alix."

I shook her hand. "I'm Max, this is . . . Holland." He shook her hand vigorously. "And this is El–"

"Elliot!" interrupted Ellie in a low voice. "My name's Elliot Hartwell . . . Max's brother."

Holland and I exchanged a confused look, but with her hair under a hood, and the garbage bag suit covering her body she was pretty ambiguous.

"We seriously don't have time for this! I'm freezing my exhaust port off out here," quipped Ellie. *I think she's imitating Niles.* "It's our property. There's no reason we all can't stay. Just let us in and we'll talk."

"Well, property is theft!" insisted Alix. "And possession is nine-tenths of the law. That makes this our cabin!"

"We can talk in the garage if you're nervous. We just want to get out of the cold," I offered. "We've come a long way to get here. We've risked our lives, and lost friends."

"How do we know you won't try to kick us out, and take it back? Or kill us in our sleep?" Her brow furrowed into a dramatic squint.

"Where's Joel?" I asked suspiciously. "I want to talk to him."

Stinky took the opportunity to slip through her legs and run into the cabin. Alix slammed the door and went after the cat.

"Why are we suddenly calling you *Elliot*?" I asked under my breath.

The sound of broken glass echoed inside, followed by a child laughing.

"Think about it," she explained. "Dr. Blum is looking for a girl. If Joel is still on the air I don't want him telling anyone I'm here."

Makes sense. I nodded and turned to pound on the door. "Let me talk to Joel!"

Alix opened the door again, out of breath. Stinky found his way to the upstairs balcony and peered down on us.

"Who?" Alix and Joel said *a-little-too* in unison.

"Joel Saxen. The man on the intercom. The host of *Info Planet*!"

"Oh, right!" Alix snickered. "You got a good ear kid. What are the odds of you being fans?" She burst into laughter.

We all just stared at her confused, as she blushed like someone trying to keep a punchline to themself.

"Ok fine. We'll let you in, but we're going to need a show of good faith." Alix held out her hand to Ellie, as if asking for the gun.

"No way!" Ellie objected and pointed the gun at her. *Good trigger discipline.*

"No! *Elliot*, wait!" I blocked the barrel with my hand and asked Alix, "How do we know you won't just steal it?"

"Oh, we've got plenty of guns!" she smirked. "What makes you think there isn't a gun on me right now?"

"Just give her the bullets and keep the gun!" suggested Holland. "Now, can we please just get out of this cold?"

"Fine." Ellie released the magazine and handed it over. "But I want these back when we leave."

"Awesome!" Alix snorted. "You're going to get a kick out of this!" She shut the door, undid the chain, and swung it open.

She was a teenager, dressed in camo pajama pants, fuzzy red slippers, and a black tank top.

"Whoa!" Holland gawked.

Alix had a laptop cabled into the intercom system, and spoke into a connected external microphone. "Live, waging his crusade on ignorance. Broadcasting to you live via satellite from the *Info Planet*." The voice through the intercom was Joel Saxen's.

She laughed. "It's a voice modulator!"

"What?!" Holland was shocked. "You mean all this time Joel Saxen has been a–"

"A teenage girl," she interrupted. "For the show I used facial tracking software to animate him," she explained. "Joel Saxen doesn't actually exist. He's a hologram I based on Bill Hicks."

"I can't believe it." Holland was agape.

"I had better equipment before my old studio went to hell, but I'm up and running again. It's not internet, but I can broadcast radio. Still trying to figure out how to boost the range."

"Maybe Niles can help with that." I turned back to Holland.

"Who?" asked Alix.

I suddenly realized my mistake, but Holland covered for me. "He didn't make it."

We all feigned grief for a moment, not that it was hard.

"I forgot," I said, and then turned back to Alix. "But why not just host *Info Planet* as yourself?"

"Who do you think the average American is going to listen to? A sassy high school dropout who wouldn't swallow their propaganda, or a middle-aged good ol' boy who drives patriotic cars and drinks patriotic beer. He probably eats cucumber sandwiches on Sunday. If you want to influence the mob you've gotta look like the mob."

"I get it," I said.

"Come on in," she said. "I'm making popcorn. We're going to watch *Temple of Gloom.*"

Ten: Cabin Envy

Alix led us inside, and we all followed. The cabin was immediately familiar and alien at the same time.

Through the front door was the kitchen and dining area. Dad was actually a pretty good cook, and kept the kitchen very orderly. He used to say, *cooking is chemistry.*

Now the sink was so full of dirty dishes they were spilling onto the floor. All the cabinets were left open and their contents were scattered all over the counters. The dining room table was covered with piles of plastic wrappers, aluminum cans, and cardboard boxes.

One section of the table looked like someone swept all the garbage onto the ground to play a boardgame. An unfinished game of *Illuminopoly!* was still set up. Who knows how long it'd been there.

Illuminopoly! is a game I used to play with the PorcScouts. Each player was their own central bank, and could print as much money as they wanted. They moved around the board, buying and developing property. The catch was the more money you printed the higher the prices got, and the last bank to collapse won.

Built into the wall, next to the intercom, was a black reflective panel. It was a terminal to the cabin's built-in computer system. Similar panels were installed throughout the space, including the main viewscreen in the theater area. They would have been lit touchscreen interfaces if the cabin had power. That told me they hadn't found the generator, or didn't have fuel. But the intercom worked, so they had some power. Maybe the cabin had some auxiliary battery I didn't know about. Dad was always installing backups . . . and backup backups.

The kitchen corridor bent from the dining area to the lounge in the back, where huge windows overlooked Stinson Lake. In fact, the house was designed so the lake could be seen from almost every room, including the front landing.

Dad designed the interior according to something called the *golden ratio,* because he believed it produced a more harmonious space. The golden ratio appears throughout the natural world in spiral patterns, like snail shells, and even the spiral arms of the galaxy. But it also appears in unexpected places, like the size of the bones in human hands, or the relationship between the width of a human eye and the width of the iris. As a result, the golden ratio has been the fascination of architects and artists alike, informing the designs of everything from the colonnades of ancient Greece to the modern works of Salvador Dali.

Because of that, I knew for example that the width of the doors and the height of the dining table were the same. I knew that the ratio between the height of the main viewscreen, and the width of the main viewscreen was the same as the ratio between the width of the kitchen, and the width of the theater. And because I'd played laser tag here with the PorcScouts, I knew that the reflective panels of the cabin's computer terminals made the main viewer visible from virtually every room in the house.

Alix took us through the kitchen to the lounge. All the couches in the lounge were made of modular segments, matching the ones in the theater. So, they could be assembled into an amphitheater around the main viewscreen, but right now they were crudely circled around the fire pit.

The fire pit doubled as the cabin's central heating system, which captured heat and ventilated it to the second floor, accessible through a spiral staircase.

The golden ratio made the entire cabin feel organic to the touch. Like it wanted you to be there. More things seemed exactly within arm's reach than in other places. The theater and lounge were both a step lower than the kitchen and the front landing. And because of the golden ratio I knew that the height of that step was identical the width of the burners on the stove, and the depth of the sink in the bathroom. But the golden ratio couldn't tell me who the three kids sitting around the fire pit were.

"Hey guys," I waved. "I'm Max. This is my brother Elliot, and our friend Holland." *I figure everyone's got a right to be introduced as they prefer.* "The cat upstairs is Stinky." I pointed up.

Stinky had found the master bedroom directly above us, which was a loft within an indoor balcony that overlooked the lounge area.

"I'm Darleen." She raised her hand. Darleen was dressed in black, with thick curly hair that covered her face, and big round reading glasses. She was about my age. "That little gremlin is Torrance." She pointed.

Torrance looked about six. He was dressed in a green crocodile-style onesie pajama, with jaws and eyes as a hood. He was always bouncing in his seat, or jumping up and down, and when he got bored with that he was running circles around the fire pit.

"Torrance, Alix, and me are all sisters," Darleen explained.

"Hey!" cried Torrance. "I'm your brother, not your sister!"

"Whatever. Grow up, Baby." Darleen rolled her eyes.

The fourth was a boy that looked about a year older than me. He had light hair, and a striped sweater. He'd kept quiet, but reacted when he saw us all looking at him. "Oh, my name is Hephae . . ."

"Did you say *Jefe?*" I asked.

"No, *Hephae,*" he answered. "My parents named me Hephaestus." He paused. "You know, the Greek god of fire . . . They were weird."

"We're not related," inserted Alix. "We took him in a few weeks ago. He lives in the attic."

Of course the cabin didn't have an attic. What it had was a small perch above my bedroom Dad called *The Hartwell Observatory.* In reality it was a tiny room, barely large enough for a telescope and a couple chairs, accessible by the spiral staircase. There wasn't even space for a bed up there. He must have slept curled up in a ball on the floor.

"What gives?" Darleen asked. "Do these trash people live with us now?"

I think she was referring to the garbage bags.

"I'm the *Mom*, Darleen! I make the rules," Alix explained. "When you're the Mom, you can say who stays and who dies!"

Ellie, Holland, and I all exchanged confused glances. I mouthed, "Mom?" and they shrugged.

"Hey," interrupted Ellie. "Where's the bathroom?"

Darleen and I both pointed toward the bathroom door simultaneously, and her eyes fixed on me suspiciously.

"It's my cabin," I told her. "I know where the toilet is."

Ellie disappeared into the bathroom.

Alix brought out the popcorn and everyone gathered around the fire pit with blankets to stay warm.

When Alix said we were going to watch *The Temple of Gloom* I assumed she meant the movie, and asked why we weren't in the theater. She said they didn't have enough electricity for movies. She was going to act out the whole thing for us by the fire pit.

"I'm ready to start. Is your brother going to take forever in the bathroom?" Alix asked impatiently.

"I don't know. Sometimes he takes a long time," I answered.

Alix started the performance without her.

Eleven: Shared Grief

Halfway through *The Temple of Gloom*, Alix was holding her arms out like wings and gliding around the room, making propeller noises with her lips, and occasionally machine gun noises.

I was watching, completely absorbed, when Ellie poked her head out of the bathroom and waved me over.

I went over and peeked inside.

The bathroom on the first floor was the only one in the cabin, but at least it was spacious. It was a jack-and-jill design, with one entrance in the theater, and the other in the lounge. Retractable hospital-like privacy curtains could separate the bath, the toilet and the sink basin in oddly perfect ergonomic shapes.

"What's up?" I asked.

"Come in," she answered. "Close the door."

Ellie had moved a kitchen chair in front of the bathroom mirror.

Most of the cabin was lit by the huge windows in the lounge, but with the bathroom door closed it was pitch black inside. Ellie leaned her flashlight against the mirror, so the light diffused throughout the room, and I noticed scented candles on the back of the toilet. Sandalwood.

She sat in the chair, wrapped a towel around her shoulders, and pulled back her hood. Her red hair spilled out over the towel. "I need you to cut off my hair." She handed me a pair of scissors.

I took the scissors and stood behind her. I could see her face in the mirror. "Are you sure? Joel Saxen isn't even real, and Alix doesn't have the power to broadcast very far."

"I'm sure. There's no one left in the world who knew me before the outbreak, and the fewer people know I exist the safer I'll be. I'm better off being a stranger in the world," she explained. "And from a purely practical standpoint, long hair is a liability. I don't want some creeper grabbing a hold of it."

I touched the raw skin around my ear as I thought about it. "Maybe I should cut my hair too," I wondered aloud.

"You got it. I'll do you next," she offered.

I started in the back. "You know, just because we didn't know each other before doesn't mean we're strangers." I'd never cut hair before, but I started clipping and shaping like I imagined barbers did. "Especially if you're my brother now," I joked.

"Max, you've gotta help me become Elliot," she begged.

"Ok," I agreed. "How?"

"I don't know. Teach me how to be a boy."

That reminded me of something that made me laugh.

"I'm not kidding!" she insisted.

"No. It's something Dad told me once. He said, *Those who can, do. Those who can't, teach*," I explained. "I can't teach you to be a boy. I just am one."

"Is it true that boys don't cry?" she asked.

"No," I said, kinda surprised. "I cry. I think everyone does."

"Yeah . . . Dad cried," she shrugged. "Mom told me that this kind of pain never really goes away. It just gets duller with time. I hope that's true, but now she's dead too, and I still can't cry."

"You cried that night on the roof in Lochshire," I corrected. "That was the first time you told me about your mom."

"No I didn't," she paused. "I don't remember it that way."

I shrugged. "For me it's reversed. When Dad died the pain was really quiet at first, but sometimes it hits me like a knife when something reminds me of him, or when something happens that I want to share with him, but I can't."

"If I focus really hard, I can sort of imagine not being sad everyday, but it doesn't matter. When Mom died I had to move on no matter how I felt. I had to survive. I didn't have time to mope. I've barely even had time to remember them."

I moved around the chair to the front to even out her bangs, and trimmed the hair above her ears. "You have time now. Why don't you tell me something about them?" I suggested.

"No," she sighed. "I'm not going there. Not right now." She paused. "I think grief is about rewriting your life story, now that you can't have the story you wanted. I expected more time with my parents, and now I can't do anything we planned. But I think once I can really imagine some kind of future without them, the sadness will go away."

"Maybe. I hope so."

I made a few last snips with the scissors, and looked at her in the mirror. Her hair was short on the sides and just long enough to be spiky on the top.

"Looks done," she said.

"Yeah, just need to get your ears on straight." I faced her nose to nose and tried to balance the hair around her ears. "I think we're done."

She stood in front of the mirror and turned her head side to side. "Yeah. It looks boyish enough. I like it. What do you think?"

What do I think? I thought. *I think you're the most beautiful girl in the world.* But I couldn't say that. She didn't want to look like a girl at all. *I think you're wonderful no matter what you look like.* Can't say that either.

I stood there staring blankly in her eyes, trying to think of something, anything to say. Then I don't know what came over me. I closed my eyes and leaned in to kiss her.

It came fast. A flash of pain and the taste of blood as my jaw met her fist.

"Keep your mitts to yourself, Creep!" she yelled.

She'd knocked me to ground, and I was disoriented. She gave me a look that simultaneously said she was angry, she was sorry, and she didn't want to talk about it.

"Ready to switch?" she asked casually. She whipped off the towel, sprinkling the floor with her red curls.

I was so confused. I didn't want to talk about it either.

I crawled up into the chair and she shook out the towel before wrapping it around my shoulders. I looked at myself in the mirror. My hair was just long enough to cover my eyes.

"So, what'll it be?" She wove her fingers through my hair and held it straight up. "How about a mohawk?"

We laughed awkwardly.

"No, I think you're right." I handed her the scissors. "It's gotta be too short to grab."

She started at the top in a manner that didn't inspire confidence, but I figured it didn't matter anyway. I wasn't trying to impress anyone.

"So, how do you do it?" she asked.

"Do what?"

"How do you keep the pain dull?"

I thought for a minute. I'd never really thought about it. "I think it's because I have a tendency to front-load grief. I try to be mindful about the passing of people while they're still alive."

"I don't get it," she admitted, as she snipped the scissors over the back of my head.

I tried again. "I don't really remember my mother, but I remember Dad crying at night when he thought I was asleep. Sometimes even years after she died. Then one night I thought, *someday I'm going to lose him too.* And I realized eventually we lose everybody, or they lose us. I remember thinking how inevitable it was, and how silly it seemed to pretend it wasn't going to happen. So, I don't pretend."

"You're basically saying if I die tomorrow you're not going to be sad because you've been coping with it since we met," she said, somewhat cynically.

"No. Of course I'd be sad. I'm saying pretending we're going to live forever probably makes death more traumatic, and maybe remembering that everybody dies eventually will make it easier to accept when they do. It's just a theory."

She thought for a moment and said, "I think I get it. And that's how boys think?"

"I don't know," I answered. "It's how I think."

Suddenly there was a pound at the door, and Alix was yelling at us. "Max! Elliot! The movie's over and people gotta use the facilities. Hurry up!"

"Cool your jets!" yelled Ellie in her Elliot voice. Then she whispered to me, "When are we going to eject these brats?"

"I don't think that's an option," I responded.

"Why? We can take 'em." She smirked in a way that made me think she was kidding. "I'll take Hephae if you take Alix. I doubt Niles can take Darleen, but Holland could."

Now I know she's joking. "And Stinky can take Torrance." We laughed. "No, I'm just saying it wouldn't be right to throw them out. We've gotta find a way to coexist here."

"Hey, it's your place. If that's how you want to play it, I got your back," she offered.

"Be right out!" I yelled to Alix. "Are we about done here?" I asked Ellie.

"Yeah, let me just get your *ear* on straight." She did a little more clipping around the sides, and when she was done we had matching cuts.

We exited into the theater just as Alix barged in and yanked the privacy curtain around the toilet.

I grabbed a blanket and walked out on the back deck. It was icy cold outside, but I sipped a bowl of oatmeal and brown sugar that Niles had heated over the fire. I like it very watery, more like hot soup.

I'd hoped I'd be able to see the crack in the ice where Scott went through, but it was too dark, and too far. I could see the stars in an awesome way.

"Don't beat yourself up. That dude was sort of a snot." Ellie elbowed me in the ribs as she leaned in next to me.

"Scott was . . . challenging," I admitted. "But he was loyal. And he was brave." I sighed. "Look, it's not only about Scott. I lost my gear bag."

"So. We have everything we need here."

"So, Dad's zPad is in it, and all of his research."

"Max, you need to give up this quest for the cure," interrupted Ellie.

"It's the best hope we had for beating this thing," I insisted. "And now it's sitting at the bottom of a corpse-infested lake."

"Trust me. There is no curing this thing," she continued. "I've seen the brain scans with my own eyes. The people changed by this thing, it takes over their brain, and turns it to mush. They aren't coming back."

"I know." I paused. "Maybe not a cure then. Maybe like a vaccine. Anything we can use to fight this thing."

"Max, stop pretending like you're going to save world. What makes you so sure it deserves saving anyway?"

"How can you say that when you're immune? You're the key to all of it!" I reminded her.

"Hey, I didn't ask for this!" she yelled. "I didn't volunteer to be anyone's guinea pig, and I sure didn't sign up to have every mad scientist on the east coast fighting over my brain." She paused. "Besides I'm not immune."

"What?"

"I'm a carrier, Max. My blood. My saliva. I'm contagious."

Twelve: The Ghost of 17

Hephae called us back inside, suggesting a trust building exercise he learned at an engineering camp in California. Everyone got warm by the fire in the lounge and told stories of their wild adventures. Obviously he was itching to go first.

***

You gotta be from California to know what I'm talking about, but there's this highway that goes from Silicon Valley to Santa Cruz called Highway 17. Now, 17 is not very long, but it goes over the coastal mountain range, which means it winds through redwoods and around rocky cliffs.

Well there was this . . . phenomenon that started happening. It was a treacherous stretch of road, plus it was a trucking corridor, so the speed limit was pretty strictly enforced. This cop was running a radar speed trap, and out of nowhere it came back with a reading of like 200 miles per hour. Hella fast!

He looked around and didn't see anything. It was late at night and there was no traffic. So, he put it out of his mind. Assumed it was just instrument error. Until it happened again, exactly a year later. And every year after that for years. It wasn't always the same exact day, but it was always in February.

After a while most of cops in that department had experienced it, and they started calling it The Ghost of 17. It became a kind of hazing exercise for rookies.

So, one day this author showed up who was researching ghost stories for a book. She took interviews from everyone who'd experienced it. She started digging into the police reports, and she had this crazy idea, to work backwards through all the February reports, and she found it!

Well, she found them.

17 unsolved missing persons reports, all in the third week of February, just two years before the phenomenon started.

She investigated those cases, and discovered from witness interviews that all but one of them were seen at the same party the night they disappeared, and they all left after calling a service called The Purple People Mover.

You've got to understand that there's a University in Santa Cruz, and a University in San Jose, and they're only about an hour's drive apart. So when the students partied together there was always a shortage of designated drivers. The Purple People Mover was this van that you could call to drive you over 17 for free. It wasn't a taxi service. The driver was just a good dude doing his part to prevent drunk driving. And he was the 17th missing person.

Once she knew what they were looking for, it still took them over a week to find it. The Purple People Mover had gone off the road and over a cliff without even leaving a scuff mark, so no one ever knew there was a wreck to find.

Obviously, no one knows what happened exactly, but the story goes that one night, in February, he was swarmed with 16 drunk college girls who wouldn't take "no" for an answer. The driver was perfectly sober, allegedly, but it had to be distracting. Experts said they had to be going over 200 miles-per-hour to go as far off the cliff as they did.

Lots of people believed she'd found the Ghost of 17, and the local papers ran with that story for weeks. But this one rookie cop, Officer Hogg, just couldn't accept it. He was determined to figure out what the thing was, so he teamed up with his buddy, Officer González. Hogg set up road spikes just before the spot where the Purple People Mover went over, and González manned the speed trap 17 miles back. That way she'd have time to radio ahead when she got the mysterious reading.

Then they waited.

Later that week it happened, González radioed down to Hogg and he deployed the road spikes in time to stop it.

It was an all black Fnord Shapeshift. A fast car! With blacked out windows, and no running lights. And when it hit the spikes it spun out and flew off the road in the same spot the Purple People Mover had years before.

When police recovered the car they discovered all the seats had been removed, except the driver's. And every square inch of the interior was stuffed with all kinds of white powder stimulants and stabilizers.

Police figure he'd been drug trafficking that way for years. In fact, after some investigating they discovered a trail of regional police urban legends, and figured he was probably headed somewhere around Barstow, from who-knows-where. He was probably partaking of his product more than a little to stave off fatigue and improve his reflexes. But they never found the driver, all they found was a pair of night vision goggles.

Thirteen: The Sleep Inducing Diary

"I don't believe it," insisted Darleen. "No way cops are that clever."

"Who's next!" Torrance bounced up and down and clapped his hands.

"Make one of the new kids tell us a story," suggested Hephae. "I'm sick of hearing the same old stories."

"I know what I want to hear!" Alix jumped out of her seat, ran through the kitchen and up the stairs. Moments later she came down with a giant porcupine head. "What's the story with this?"

"Yeah!" agreed Darleen. "If this is really your cabin, why don't you prove it?"

Of course I knew what it was, but it gave me an idea. "Haven't any of you ever heard of a porcwudgie?"

They shook their heads.

***

Before I was born this cabin belonged to my grandmother, and when she died it was full of her things. Dad was her only living relative, so he inherited everything. He decided to spend a weekend here, sorting out her affairs. Of course, that was before he met my mother, so he was alone.

My grandmother was a first-generation immigrant, and had a lot of old folk wisdom left in her from her homeland. She also lived through the Great Depression, which made her a bit of a hoarder. She hated the thought of wasting anything, and predicted another economic collapse at any moment, her whole life. I think that's where Dad got it. She filled this place with the clutter of a thousand unfinished projects. At least that's what she'd call it. Dad said it looked like a junkyard in here.

She especially loved making homemade candles in old baby food jars. I think she saved every baby food jar she ever owned. She grew a little herb garden in the side yard, so she could cultivate the scents she wanted in the candles. She liked lavender and sage most of all. In fact there are probably still boxes of scented candles in the garage someplace.

Among Grandma's things Dad found an old diary. It was handmade, strung together with yarn. The cover was a patchwork of fabrics and buttons, but the coolest thing was the clasp. It was a porcupine quill that hung off the back cover and fastened into a sleeve on the front cover. And it literally worked as a quill pen.

Inside the diary he found a log of her daily activities, penned in the most beautiful calligraphy he'd ever seen. It included recipes, gardening notes, that sort of thing.

Anyway, one night he reads this entry about a visitor, and she seems so excited to see them that Dad assumed it was some kind of romantic relationship. But he fell asleep while reading it, and when he woke up he can't find the entry again. He skimmed through the whole book and never found it.

Dad didn't know anything about his mother being in a relationship, and became preoccupied with finding evidence of it around the cabin, but there was none. Ultimately he concluded that the only way to find the entry about the visitor again was to read the whole diary, cover to cover.

He decided to take some time off work, and stay in the cabin another week while he read the diary and arranged her things. Who knew? Maybe this visitor would come by the cabin and want to claim a memento or two.

But Dad had this problem. Whenever he read the diary he'd fall asleep, and he'd have these dreams about reading the diary. It happened so often he hardly knew what was real and what was imaginary. In these dreams he always found the entry about the visitor, but there would be a knock on the door before he finished reading it. He'd get up to answer it, but he'd always wake up before he got there. He never saw who the visitor was, and he started to think maybe he'd dreamed the whole thing.

He was obsessed. He started taking the book everywhere he went, and trying to read it every waking moment. He was determined to get to the bottom of the strange power it seemed to have over him.

He was reading in the bathtub when he started to doze off and accidentally dipped the book in the water. He was immediately in a panic. The water caused some of the ink to bleed. He tried going over the wet pages with a blow dryer, but it was wrinkling the edges. So he started ironing the pages one at a time.

Then something amazing happened. The diary only had writing on the front side of each page. He'd assumed the backs were left blank because the ink bled through the page a little. Writing on the back would ruin the look of the calligraphy. But as he passed the hot iron over the blank side of each page, new writing appeared.

It wasn't like the other writing. It was blood red, and a messier handwriting. It turns out it's an old trick. If you write with lemon juice it's virtually invisible, but applying heat turns it burnt red.

The secret pages were more cryptic. They described the myths and folklore of the indigenous people of this region. But more than that, they described shamanic medicines and rituals. They were particularly concerned with a peculiar species of creature thought to be native to these woods.

Porcwudgies are half-porcupine and half-troll, with long quills on their backs, huge noses, pointy ears, and long fingers. They are master archers, and most of all they love garbage, so they mostly live in junkyards. Or, so the diary said.

The indigenous shamans avoided the creatures. They saw them as magic tricksters with a nasty disposition. But who ever wrote these pages seemed to know them intimately. They knew their potions and poisons. The writer knew their culture. Their customs.

For example, apparently porcwudgies, just like regular porcupines, are not gender dimorphic, meaning that males and females don't look physically different. They mostly identify gender by smell, not sight. As a result, porcwedgies tended to take gender neutral names. Like Ashley, or Goyabardash.

The secret pages also contained a lot of gardening advice, describing which herbs were most useful, and how to cultivate them for their magical properties. It suggested leaving raw corn on the cob out for the porcwudgies, and whenever she did they were always gone by morning. And it said, if she ever wanted to summon one, to burn an incense made from equal parts poplar buds, fir resin, and dried rosemary.

Dad resolved to make the incense. What's the worst that could happen? On the off chance a porcwudgie actually showed up, maybe it could give him some answers.

It took him some time to find the poplar buds, but once he did he combined the ingredients into a bundle. That night he came here to the lounge to sit by the fire, like we've done, and let the cabin fill with the sweet smell.

He was reading by the fire, like usual, when there was a sudden knock at the door.

Dad marked his place in the diary and went to answer the door. He peeked through the window and didn't see anything, but when he opened the door the prickly visitor was standing not more than *four feet tall. Its grey skin seemed to glow in the moonlight, as it reached toward him with it's unnaturally long grey fingers.*

***

"No way!" interrupted Darleen. "There is no way that thing is the severed head of some imaginary porcupine monster."

"Max, what gives?" asked Holland. "You said your dad built this cabin. Now you're saying he inherited it from your grandmother?"

"Guys, look," I pleaded. "It's just a campfire story Dad used to tell. Grandma died before I was born. I have no idea how much of it is true. The porcupine head is just a mask. It's part of a costume that parents used to scare me and my friends on camping trips. Once we were too old for that kind of thing, Dad had the head mounted, like a hunting trophy."

"So it's fake?" Torrance gave me a look of confusion and disappointment, and the group collectively decided it was time for bed.

"Why don't you three stay on the couches down here in the lounge," Alix offered. "You're all boys. It shouldn't be a problem."

"Why? There's plenty of space upstairs," I protested.

"There's only three beds upstairs," said Alix. "Why do you think Hephae sleeps in the attic?"

"It didn't feel safe enough to sleep on the first floor," explained Hephae. "It's cramped up there, but I make it work."

"First off, it's not an attic. It's an observatory," I corrected. "But also, there are five beds upstairs. Both beds in my room—"

"Our room," Ellie corrected.

"Right. *Our room* has trundle beds under both beds for sleepovers."

"What?!" exclaimed Alix. "We had no idea."

"Why don't you four take the four beds in our room," I suggested. "We'll make due in the master bedroom, that way–"

"We don't use that term here," interrupted Darleen.

"What term?" asked Holland.

"*Master bedroom*," answered Alix. "It has a bad connotation. There are no masters and no slaves here."

"Fine. What do you call it?" I asked.

"*My room*," answered Alix.

"What?!" I protested.

"Hey! You weren't here," she explained.

"How about this?" Hephae injected. "We'll put one of the roll out beds in Alix's room for Torrance. Darleen and Alix can share the big bed, since they're sisters. Max and Elliot keep their old beds. Holland can take the last guest bed in their room. And I'll stay in the *observatory*."

"No," objected Ellie. "I'll take the observatory. It'll be luxury compared to where we've been, and I want to set up a look out where I can keep watch. I bet I can hunt some dinner without leaving the balcony."

"That's a good idea," I said.

We all agreed and went upstairs to sort it out. Of course the second floor was as filthy as the first. The floor was covered in dirty clothes. There were dishes and crumbs in my bed. But I had enough old clothes to give Ellie some boy clothes, and there were clean sheets in Dad's dresser. Best of all, I got to sleep in my own bed, in my own room. It was the best I'd slept in months.

Fourteen: The Porcupette

Life in the cabin was strange. It felt like home, mainly because it literally was home. But everyone that belonged there were missing. Not just my dad, but all my friends in the PorcScouts, who I expected to make it there. But maybe worse than that, no one who was there seemed to belong. Most of all me. My cabin had been taken over by strangers, and I had to figure out how to live with them with as little conflict as possible.

Ellie and Niles reacted to Scott's death differently. Ellie barely knew him and brushed it off. She said there wasn't room to miss anyone but her mom and dad. That made some sense to me.

Niles was of two minds about Scott. In fact, he was of two minds about everything. When he was Niles he was glad Scott was dead. He said Scott was nothing but a bully and deserved what he got. But Holland was Scott's friend, and when Niles became Holland I think he genuinely missed him. It had become difficult to tell when he was Niles and when he was Holland. In fact, I think he lost track of himself sometimes. Luckily, he wanted the new group to believe he was Holland all the time, so I didn't have to guess what to call him.

We dug a grave for Scott in the yard. His body was at the bottom of the lake, but we agreed it was important. I just couldn't think of anything to say. I tried to think of my fondest memory of him, but honestly there wasn't a lot to choose from. He was pretty obnoxious. I wouldn't say I missed Scott, but I still thought about him a lot. Even though he was a jerk, he still did the right thing in a crisis. And it made me wonder if he would have ever realized that potential for heroism if the outbreak had never happened. Maybe he would have stayed a jerk his whole life.

Before we arrived, the Siblinghood had devised a system for sharing responsibility, and included Hephae when he arrived. Every morning they put their toothbrushes in a cereal box, shook them up, and drew them out at random. The owner of the first toothbrush pulled was "Dad" for the day. The second was "Mom". The third was the "Kid". And the last toothbrush got to pretend to be a cat for the day. That way no one ever got to tell everyone what to do all the time.

Basically "Mom" and "Dad" made plans, and worked to provide for everyone. If they disagreed, "Mom" had final say about inside things, and "Dad" had final say about outside things. The "Kid" had to do what the parents said. Do chores. That sort of thing. The "Cat" got to play all day, and didn't have to do what anyone else said.

They were also allowed to trade roles if both people agreed, but mostly they just conspired to keep Torrance the cat as often as possible, since he was so unreliable. The conspiracy fell apart if, by chance, Torrance got picked for "Mom" because he always refused to trade. He loved having final say about the inside, and on those days they usually ended up playing games all day, with couch cushion forts and squirt guns.

Those were the rules, and it worked for them. But within a week there was disagreement over how to include us in this bizarre family ritual.

"We obviously can't have more than two parents," insisted Alix. "The other three toothbrushes just have to be more kids."

"How about a dog, and two children," suggested Torrance. "So the cat has someone to play with!"

"Keep in mind, we have an actual cat," Ellie pointed out.

"Guys, we can't have too many kids playing all the time," inserted Hephae. "We won't have enough people doing the actual work. We have eight mouths to feed now, if you count Stinky. We need two dads, two moms, two kids and two pets."

"Stinky can't play," insisted Holland. "He doesn't have a toothbrush."

"Then we make Stinky the cat all the time," suggested Alix. "And to make it fair we'll make Torrance always the dog."

"Oh! Yes please!" Torrance grabbed Stinky and squeezed him.

Stinky went limp, looking annoyed but not fighting.

"Good," continued Hephae. "Then that's six toothbrushes. Two dads. Two moms. Two kids."

"But what if the two dads, or the two moms disagree?" inquired Darleen.

"I know," bubbled Holland. "We'll have a grandma, a grandpa, a mom, a dad, a sister and a brother."

"Guys," I said.

"What's the difference between a sister and a brother?" asked Torrance.

"Guys?" I said again.

"Nothing I guess," Holland continued. "Maybe the brother is in charge of the dog, and the sister is in charge of the cat."

"Guys!" I yelled to get their attention. "If society collapsing has taught me anything, it's that nobody should get to tell anyone what to do. And nobody should have to do what anyone else says, no matter what."

Ellie and Holland nodded.

"I have an idea," Alix inserted. "Let's be pirates!"

We all looked at her a little confused, waiting for an explanation.

"Joel Saxen used to be part of a pirate radio network. We could make the cabin into a pirate ship! The big bed in my room is a captain's bed, so let's call that the *captain's quarters*."

"And we can call the kitchen the *galley* . . . and the bathroom the *privy!*" exclaimed Torrance.

"If you like," I agreed. "But a pirate captain isn't like a Navy captain. Everybody on a pirate ship has the same rights. A captain really only has final say during battle. They can make plans, but big decisions are made by negotiating with the other officers."

"What other officers?" asked Alix.

I knew a bit about historical pirates from Dad. "Well, the captain's first officer is called a quartermaster–"

"No masters!" interrupted Darleen.

"Ok . . . I guess the *sailmaster* is out too?" I thought. "Let's just call the quartermaster the *first mate*. They assume command if the captain is incapacitated, and they're in charge of rationing supplies to the crew."

"What else?" asked Alix.

I tried to remember. "Sailmasters are navigators. We can just call it that. It's not like we sail anywhere, but we need someone to make maps, and chart places to search for supplies." I paused. "There's a bunch of others. The *chef* cooks, obviously. Some pirate ships had surgeons on board. A *boatswain* was in charge of maintenance and repair. A *swabbie* mopped the deck like a janitor. The cannons were operated by *gunners* and *powder monkeys*."

"I get to be the powder monkey!" Torrance began bouncing around, scratching his head and armpits like a monkey.

"A boatswain sounds like the *chief engineer* on starships in Tsar Trek," observed Hephae.

"You like Tsar Trek!" bubbled Niles, pushing Holland into the background. "*Kosmos Five* or *The Next Acquisition?*" I don't think any of the new kids noticed, but I could definitely tell that Holland transitioned into Niles when he got excited.

"Neither," answered Hephae. "*Tsar Trek: Vortex* is the best."

"If we mash up pirates and Tsar Fleet we can be space pirates! I want to be the *helmsman*. That's basically a navigator," insisted Niles. But then a strange look covered his face. Like he was deliberating internally. Like Holland was asserting himself. "No, I'd rather be *chief of secur–*"

"No chiefs!" interrupted Darleen. "That's just another word for *master.*
Besides, it's Native American cultural appropriation!"

"Actually it's *Indigenous Peoples,*" corrected Hephae.

"Actually it's *French,*" corrected Niles.

"WHATEVER!" yelled Darleen. "Let's just elect a captain already."

Alix, Darleen and Torrance all voted for Alix. Ellie, Niles and I voted for
me. That gave Hephae the tie breaking vote, which he didn't seem to
want, but he voted for Alix because she was the oldest. *That's fine. The
crew is the real power aboard a pirate ship, not the captain.*

Alix made me first mate to keep it fair, which was perfect, because
managing the supplies was the most important job anyway. Plus they
didn't even know about the emergency supplies in the bunker under the
cabin, and I wanted to keep it that way for the time being. There was an
internal perimeter of steel reinforced walls that enclosed a safe room
behind the spiral staircase. It was a good fallback position in the event
of an intruder. It was also the only direct access to the cabin's computer
core, and the bunker below.

Torrance insisted on being the powder monkey because he liked the
name, although we didn't actually have cannons, which meant we didn't
have gunpowder kegs for him to manage. *Yet.*

Ellie volunteered to be gunner and offered everyone firearms training.
She dubbed Torrance her *ammo monkey* and he agreed. She'd be in
charge of weapons, and he'd be in charge of ammunition. They renamed
the observatory the *crow's nest,* and that became both the armory and
the post for nightwatch.

Hephae liked the sound of *engineer,* even without the *chief.* He devoted
himself to reinforcing the fences and entrances. Most urgently he
wanted to wall up the sliding glass door, and the huge bay windows on

the first floor with a stack of old plywood he found in the cargo bay. He thought it wasn't safe. And he was right.

Darleen and Holland both wanted to be navigator once we decided it meant planning away missions.

Darleen just wanted to get outside. She'd been cooped up for weeks because when Alix was Mom she made her stay inside, and when Alix was Dad she wouldn't let her go outside, so either way Darleen was stuck. The odds that she'd be a parent while Alix wasn't were pretty slim, and then Alix could always trade with Torrance if she needed to. To Darleen the cabin was a cage. A *consensus* cage, but still a cage.

Niles was a tinkerer. He was eager to help set up the studio in the theater, and wanted to plan away missions to search for the equipment he wanted . . . or maybe it was Holland. He was the adventurous one.

So, Alix and I decided to combine the navigator position with the chef and the swabbie. Darleen and Holland could both lead away missions, but at home they both needed to cook and clean. I knew Niles had a flare for cooking.

Oh, and Torrance insisted Stinky was a parrot.

That was our crew. Everyone agreed. The only question left was what to call the ship. Niles and Hephae were full of suggestions from the show. *The ISS Decenterprise. The ISS Recovery.* But Torrance made the suggestion we ultimately went with.

"The Porcupette!" squealed Torrance.

"What does that mean? I asked.

"It's a baby porcupine!" he yelled with great enthusiasm.

We all laughed and agreed it wasn't worth contradicting him.

CROWS NEST

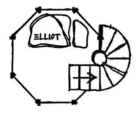

SECOND FLOOR

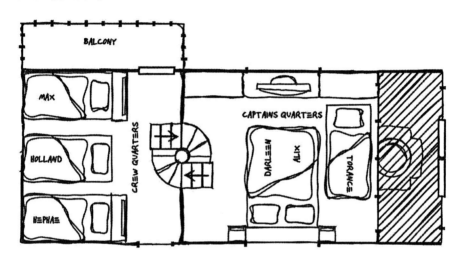

GROUND FLOOR

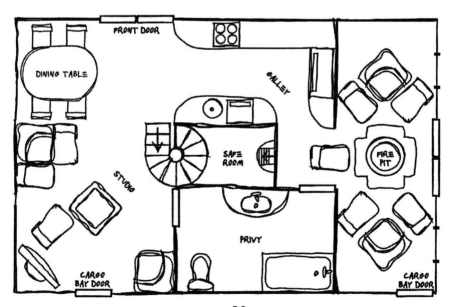

90

Fifteen: Power and Money

Alix and the others had limited electricity when we arrived. I knew there was a gas generator and fuel in the bunker, but they hadn't gotten into that yet. But they somehow gained access to some of the ship's internal functions, like the intercom. The system was designed to lock out intruders, but somehow they'd gained at least partial access without the command codes.

Hephae was the mastermind behind the hack apparently. It started when he found Dad's old bicycle in the garage, which he called the *cargo bay*. He explained, "I got the idea from a bicycle generator I saw in Oakland, California. Political protesters had occupied Oscar Grant Plaza in front of City Hall, and they used old bikes to recharge their phones and laptops."

It was ingenious, and I insisted that he explain everything.

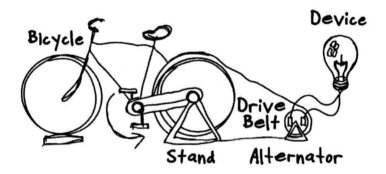

"My first working prototype was just an alternator I salvaged from an old car, which is basically a 12 volt motor, connected to a stationary bike with a drive belt," he explained. "It generated electricity, but that's the easy part. It works on the same principle as regenerative braking in electric cars."

"What's regenerative braking?" I asked.

"It's how electric cars reclaim lost power when they brake. The basic idea is if you run a motor backwards you generate electricity instead of expending it."

"Wait, really?" I asked, surprised. "Running a motor backwards creates energy?"

"Not exactly. You can't *create* energy," Hephae explained. "But you can *convert* energy. When you run a blender, or whatever, the motor converts electrical energy into kinetic energy. This is the opposite. Peddling the bike creates kinetic energy, which the motor turns into electrical energy. With the old setup we could really only power lights, or simple appliances."

"Wait," I interrupted, "you just said you can't *create* energy. So how does peddling *create* kinetic energy?"

"Good point. You're quick, and you're right. The kinetic energy isn't created. It's converted from chemical energy in your body, which came from foods you ate, which collected energy from who knows where."

"That's gotta be how wind turbines work. The wind turns the propeller, which turns a motor, right?" I asked.

"Exactly. And gas generators. Even thermal power. Anything that turns a wheel can generate electricity. I've actually been thinking we could reinitialize the hydroelectric plant in town and power a whole neighborhood, as long as the river keeps flowing."

"Ok, you said that's the easy part. What's the hard part?"

"Storing the electricity," he answered. "Without a battery you have to connect stuff directly to the motor. Direct current really only works well for lights. With my first setup we only got power while we were pedalling. More speed. More power. But nothing stored and nothing to regulate the current. That'll blow fuses and more complex circuits. But, a car battery isn't enough. It took me a long time to find the other parts I needed."

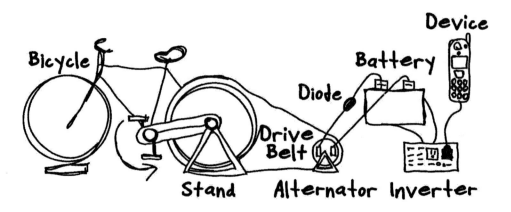

He continued, "The most important thing is the diode. Most alternators come with one, but this one was faulty. I found this diode at a Ham Hut in town while Alix was looking for radio equipment."

"What does it do?" I asked.

"It stops the current from running the other way. Otherwise whatever power is stored in the battery will just discharge and turn the wheel the other way when you stop pedalling." He rolled the diode between his fingers. *It's so small for such a big job.*

"And what about this thing?" I pointed to the last piece of equipment in the chain. It looked like an oversized plug strip, with a fan built in.

"I found that in the cargo bay. It's a power inverter. It changes direct current to alternating current. DC to AC," he answered. "That's what we needed for complex appliances and electronics, since we can't plug into the walls."

The generator only produced enough power for one appliance at a time, or to recharge small devices, like the electric drill Hephae used to construct the exterior reinforcements.

For something as power draining as a microwave, or a space heater it often depleted the stored power, and someone had to be peddling their hardest to keep them running.

Hephae had somehow bypassed the computer core and powered many of the ships integrated systems directly. We could watch TV on the main viewer, but only if someone peddled at all times. So mostly we watched movies on smaller devices.

Electric heaters proved to be too much work. Instead we heated the cabin with chopped wood. Dad had already stacked enough for the winter before the world went crazy, but it was already almost gone. Alix and the others burned a lot of wood, but they didn't like to chop it.

Power had to be generated with hours of physical labor on the stationary bike. So that became the currency of the crew. Once we scavenged enough car batteries for each of us we started using them like bank accounts. Trading favors around the ship for time on the bike.

Alix used most of her power on the radio receiver, scanning for any signal, any sign of life, but twice a week she recorded and broadcast an episode of *Info Planet*. She still needed some equipment they hadn't found yet. Primarily a mixing board, but also some headphones and other accessories. But the bottleneck was always electricity.

At meal time we all ate together, but the leftovers belonged to the chef, usually Niles or Darleen. If anyone wanted second helpings they'd have to negotiate with power.

There was some disagreement about how to measure power. We started out just logging time on the bike, but Hephae rightfully pointed out that not everyone generated the same amount of electricity in an hour. And everyone peddled harder on their own battery than they did on anyone else's.

It was a problem of motivation. If an hour is an hour is an hour, it didn't matter how hard anyone peddled. They got credit for an hour. So Hephae picked up the right meter at the Ham Hut and proposed measuring the actual watts. Every trade was uniform. Price structures could emerge. Work harder. Finish sooner. It was motivating. The problem was that measuring power in watts instead of time turned physical privilege into economic advantage. It seemed especially unfair to Torrance.

Consequently the older kids had the greater part of the labor burden, and the greater economic control, bribing younger kids to do chores in exchange for screen time they had a hard time generating themselves.

We never really agreed on a standard. Every trade was a negotiation. Is time money, or is money power? I was always happy to use whichever method the other person preferred. Usually I traded time with younger kids, and power with older kids.

The way I figured it, trade was good either way. Because people only trade if they want what they get more than what it costs. So, if both people want to trade, both people are better off.

To me utility was the real value. Is an hour of cartoons worth a chocolate bar? That's the real question. And it's subjective. Every trade is subjective. I liked to spend my electricity on the movies in the common area because the custom became that people would gather around to watch together. Some kids got upset when other people watched their screens for free, but I liked it. It made old movies feel new again to watch them with someone for the first time. And it contributed to the sense of community on the ship. Plus, the free riders usually volunteered to peddle when I was done, and then I could sit and watch for free too.

I briefly considered trying to work out the conversion from calories to watts. We were all stocked, but food wasn't infinite. We were living off emergency supplies, and still a long way from sustainability. I had to assume a person performing work required more food. Food was the baseline. Power was a luxury. But I didn't know how to approach measuring that.

Ellie had mostly been keeping to herself in the crow's nest. Things had been awkward since I tried to kiss her. *I'm so stupid sometimes.* But I'd never met anyone like her. Assertive and curious. Snarky, but not aggressive. I'd be dead without her. She's my best friend.

I had to smooth things over somehow. But what did I really even know about her? I didn't even know her last name. I knew she was from Boston. I knew she liked cheesy movies.

I tried to think of the cheesiest movie we had. Dad had a huge DVD collection. Maybe *Clown Cannibals from Cucamonga*. No. With everything going on, cannibalism was probably off the table. And nobody likes clowns.

She needed a distraction. Something funny. Maybe *Statutory Ape*. It's this courtroom comedy about a gorilla that learns sign language and becomes a lawyer defending an innocent kangaroo. It's hilarious.

Then it hit me. *Scratch Allen*. It's about this wacky genius who escapes an insane asylum and becomes a doctor. It's funnier than it sounds. Practically the opposite of the world, since apparently most doctors belong in insane asylums now.

I grabbed the DVD, charged my laptop, made a bowl of popcorn, and went up to see her.

She eyed the DVD case disapprovingly.

"Max, seriously? I could go the rest of my life without seeing another crazy doctor in a white lab coat."

Stupid! "You're right. I'll go back downstairs and watch it with the others." I turned away.

"Max, wait! You don't have to go." She pouted. "Can't we just hang out and do nothing?"

"Why not," I answered. "We may as well kill time before time kills us."

We both laughed.

"Exactly!"

We sat together on the bedding she'd brought up from downstairs. I was nervous because the space was almost too cramped to sit without touching, but then she squirmed under my arm and put her head on my shoulder, so I guess that was allowed.

"Seriously though. What do you do up here all day?" I asked.

"Keep watch mostly. I write a little. Think a lot."

"About what?" I asked.

"I try to remember things mostly. Try to imagine where I'd be if none of this happened."

We paused.

"This time of year they used to have a big Christmas display in downtown Boston, with robot elves and twinkling lights." She laughed, but sniffled as if she was crying. "I guess I'm worried I'll never see lights like that again. Mom and I used to go ice skating every year. It was so much fun . . ."

"I was never very good at balance. Dad and I mostly just got into snowball fights."

"Hey! I bet we can find some skates. We can go out on the lake. I'll teach you."

I winched. "I don't think I ever want to go out on the lake again. Not after seeing what's in it."

"It's weird isn't it?" she asked.

"What?"

"Everyone we ever knew is dead," she said. "Probably wandering around some department store someplace, or if they're lucky someone put them out of their misery."

"I keep feeling like if I go home to Lochshire, Dad will just be sitting there on the couch watching Z-Files like nothing happened."

"I know what you mean. I keep hoping I'll wake up. Like a nightmare," she said. "I didn't even have nightmares before all this."

"Me either," I agreed.

"Now that's all I dream," she said.

"Same here . . . do you think the world will ever get back to normal?"

"I hope not," she said. "I'm hoping we can take this opportunity to do it better this time."

Sixteen: Among Thieves

PorcScouts Rule Number 12: *Set your life in perfect order.* Dad used to say that all the time. It was basically his way of saying "clean your room." Whenever I lost something. Whenever I made a mess. Whenever I was anxious or overwhelmed. *Put your life in perfect order* was his advice.

He didn't just mean, "clean your room." He meant organize my thoughts. Systematize my routine. It was an exercise in living intentionally.

So, when a whole box of Mighty O's cereal went missing, it set my mind on edge.

One morning, when Holland and I went downstairs Alix was already accusing Darleen. "Where'd you hide them!?" she yelled.

"Why are you always blaming me?" Darleen cried.

"Because you always sneak out in the middle of the night!" insisted Alix. "You probably have a whole stash of stolen food someplace."

"Maybe it was the mice," Darleen grinned.

We did have a mouse infestation. Stinky caught them regularly, but I still heard them scurrying around at night. Any food left out was nibbled on by morning. But worse, if they didn't find enough food they chewed the rubber off wires, or the glue out of book bindings. They were a nuisance, but a mouse doesn't drag away a whole box of cereal.

"Don't be stupid! It wasn't mice," Alix countered.

"Well it wasn't me!" Darleen insisted. "I bet it was you!" she pointed her finger at Torrance, who had already decided canned carrots and maple syrup made a better breakfast anyway.

"It was the monster," Torrance whispered. "I saw it."

"Don't start that again," ordered Alix. "There's no monster in the cargo bay!"

I'd have noticed Hephae or Holland sneaking out of our quarters, or even Ellie climbing out of the crow's nest in the middle of the night. The thief had to be one of the Siblinghood . . . unless Alix was just wrong about there being another box of Mighty O's, which was entirely possible.

I suggested searching all the crew quarters, but Alix refused to open the captain's quarters up to inspection. *Maybe it was her.*

The Siblinghood was all up before us, and seemed content to keep the dispute between themselves. So the rest of us went on with our day.

Ellie kept watch, patrolling the perimeter fence and checking the snare traps we set for small game in the surrounding area. Hephae tinkered on his projects in the cargo bay.

Holland suggested just going out and finding more cereal. There were other lake cabins nearby we hadn't searched, and lots of abandoned stores in Blanoby. Alix and Darleen liked that idea, and ultimately the three of them geared up for a day of scavenging.

They asked me to watch Torrance while they were gone, and I agreed.

I kept thinking about Dad's advice, "Set your life in perfect order." But it just made me more frustrated. Everyone was so disorganized, and it was out of my control. Nothing was ever clean. No one took any personal responsibility. People started activities they never finished and just left materials all over the ship. And now someone was stealing food. It wasn't just the inconvenience. It's that it was so inconsiderate.

I needed to get away. To find a space I could set in order, even just to put my mind at ease.

I decided to start in the herb garden. It was a twenty-three foot wide, thirteen foot high aluminum conduit dome Dad had built in the yard as a greenhouse. It was covered in glass panels, except the top, which was designed to catch rainwater.

Inside there was an elaborate feedback mechanism where water flowed from a giant fish pond, through the plant beds and back. Dad called it *aquaponics.* In theory the system could be balanced so the fallen plant matter fed the fish, and the fish droppings nourished the plants. But the plants were all dead, and someone had trashed the place. Shelves were knocked over. Pots were shattered. The only tools left were those too small to use as weapons. Whoever had done it even took the seeds out of the supply cabinet. At least they were planning ahead.

I spent the day straightening it up, with Torrance's help. With any luck we'd have a crop of vegetables by the next harvest season. I compiled an inventory of assets on hand, and a list of things to look for in town.

I thought about Mr. Romero's tomato seeds, sitting in my gear bag at the bottom of the lake.

After clearing the debris out of the aquaponics pond we found actual living fish. *What a treasure!* Especially with the lake infested. A school of uncontaminated edible fish, ready for cultivation!

"Fish pasghetti for dinner!" Torrance boomed.

"No!" I cried. "At least not yet . . . and probably not spaghetti. We need to farm these fish, not eat them."

"Why would you farm fish if you aren't going to eat them?" He looked genuinely confused. "Are they like pets?"

"We are going to eat them," I clarified. "Just not until we have enough."

"It's like that saying," he tried to remember. "*Build a man a fire and he'll be warm for the night. Set a man on fire and he'll be warm for the rest of his life.*" He grinned.

"Sort of." I couldn't help but laugh. "The point is if we eat them now we won't have any more fish in the future. But if we breed them into a huge school of fish we'll always have enough."

He nodded in agreement, but then stopped with a look that said something heavy was on his mind.

"What is it?" I asked.

"I'll tell you, but you have to promise to believe me."

"I'll to my best," I answered.

He whispered, like he was confessing, "I think I saw the porcwedgie take the Mighty O's."

"What did you see?" I asked skeptically.

He continued, "It came in from the cargo bay and rummaged through the pantry. I've seen it before, but no one believes me."

"What came in?"

"A porcupine man, like you said. I thought it was a monster 'til you told that story. It probably lives in the cargo bay because it likes all the garbage."

The Siblinghood used the cargo bay as a junkyard. Maybe a porcupine was living there. That wouldn't be terrible. In a crisis they're one of the only animals you can eat raw. But if so, why hadn't Stinky found it? How did anything sneak into the kitchen without Stinky alerting us?

"What did it look like?" I asked.

"It's big!" Torrance held his arms out wide. "Like, as big as you. And it has spikes all over it's back, like dirty hair. And it has fangs, and claws."

"Did it walk on two legs or four?" I asked.

He thought back. "Both I think. It snuck around like a ninja." He searched my face, but I must have looked doubtful. "You believe me don't you?"

I tried to think of a way to explain that I didn't believe or disbelieve him. That I didn't think he was lying, but wasn't sure he saw what he thinks he saw. I needed more evidence to know for sure.

Before I could answered we were interrupted by loud screaming.

"It's Hephae!" said Torrance.

I grabbed a trowel from the tool cabinet and we ran toward the cargo bay.

"Guys!" Hephae came running toward us, out of breath. "Where's Elliot? There's something behind the cargo bay!"

"He's on patrol. Follow me." I'd seen her out front earlier, when I hooked up the water hose.

We all ran to get her, and we armed up to take a look behind the cargo bay together. Ellie had the Mosquito, and Torrance followed her with the ammo bag. I had the trowel from the aquaponics dome and Hephae grabbed a long-handled sledge hammer from the cargo bay.

Hephae lead the way, "I was in the cargo bay, working on a fishing pole when I heard rustling outside. I went around to look, and it ran away when it saw me."

"What was it?" Ellie asked. "What did you see?"

"I don't know," he puzzled. "I didn't get a really good look. Like it was camouflaged in the bushes. It was on all fours at first, and I thought it was an animal, but it stood up and ran away on two legs."

"Are you sure it wasn't a person?" I asked.

"I'm sure," he answered. "It was too small. Like maybe a monkey . . . do monkeys live around here?"

"No," I answered.

Sure enough we found tracks behind the cargo bay. They were big footprints with a checker pattern. Like tennis rackets had been pressed into the snow. They reminded me of the marks left by wicker snowshoes.

We followed the tracks to the edge of the yard, where the fence was reinforced by wood and metal panels they'd salvaged.

"The tracks just stop," I observed. "Do you think it climbed the fence?"

"I don't think so," Hephae answered. "Look at this." He held up a screw he found in the snow, examined it for a moment, and then reached for the fence.

The nearest panel certainly looked secure. It was steel and looked like it was a mounting bracket of some kind. But when he pushed on it the panel swung open. Three of the four screws holding it place had been removed, and it easily spun on the forth.

There was no snow on the forest floor, so there were no tracks. We fanned out and combed the thicket of woods beyond the yard.

We found a thick canopy of low hanging branches not far from the ship, and it appeared someone, or something had used that spot to make camp. There was a cold fire pit, and a collection of garbage that might have been some kind of bedding.

It was mostly food wrappers, including the empty Mighty O's box.

Most ominous were the small collection of sharp spines strewn chaotically around the camp, each with the signature black and white markings of porcupine quills.

Seventeen: The Porcwudgie

Hephae smashed the canopy of branches with the sledge. "Whatever that thing was, it's not welcome here!"

"I thought the porcwedgie was friendly?" protested Torrance.

"I don't think it was a porcwudgie," I suggested as I examined one of the porcupine quills. *It seems authentic. Not wood or plastic.*

"Fine, then what the heck was it?" asked Ellie.

"I don't know," I admitted. *A porcupine doesn't build a fire, and certainly doesn't work a screwdriver.*

"Max, until Alix gets back from town you're acting captain," explained Hephae. "So, what are your orders?"

I thought. "First off, let's get back inside the perimeter. Hephae, I want you to screw that loose panel back into place, and double check the rest of the fence for loose screws."

Hephae drew the electric drill from his belt holster, and held it near his face like a secret agent. "Aye Sir!" He revved the motor for dramatic effect.

"When you're done, return to the ship. We'll need your help there too. Elliot and Torrance, come with me. We've got to figure out how this thing got into the cargo bay and patch the hole, then we've got to reinforce the hull of the ship."

They all agreed, and we set to work.

We worked the rest of the day securing the ship against any potential invader, but we weren't dealing with G's. We didn't know what we were dealing with. We didn't know how smart it was, what it was physically capable of, or even how many there were.

When Hephae finished checking the perimeter fence he joined us in the lounge. Ellie and I had begun to install drop bars over all the doors of the ship.

Torrance quickly lost interest and disappeared upstairs. Moments later he was on the balcony in the captain's quarters, sitting on the railing and hanging his legs over the edge so he could watch us work from above. He had a compendium of folklore he'd found in Dad's collection. "It says, *they can transform into a walking porcupine, covered in quills on the back, but with the face and hands of a human, or a troll.*" Torrance kicked his legs with glee as he read.

"Torrance, get down from there. Don't read that," I ordered.

"Why not?" he balked.

"Let him read it. I want to know what we're up against," said Hephae.

"It says they can appear and disappear," Torrance continued. "And they hunt with poison arrows."

"They aren't real!" I insisted.

"So?" responded Ellie. "You got a better suggestion how we keep him occupied while we work?"

"Elliot, not you too?" I said.

"Max, think about it," Ellie said. "Indigenous people told these stories for generations to pass down their knowledge. Maybe there's some exaggeration and distortion over time, but isn't it possible they knew something we don't? Isn't is possible a long long time ago they discovered some kind of creature that's been hiding in these woods ever since?"

"They hide in junk yards not forests," Torrance corrected.

"Whatever. This one is hiding in these woods, right now," Ellie continued. "The point is, isn't it possible that this outbreak has affected the wildlife and contaminated the ecosystem so severely that this strange creature has come out of hiding?" She paused to assess the look on my face.

I wasn't convinced. "You're describing bigfoot," I quipped.

"It's like that bear," she countered. "Out fishing when it should have been hibernating."

Torrance continued, "It says, *mating season begins when the full moon coincides with the winter solstice, which is so rare that they can become dangerously amorous.*" He paused. "Winter solstice, what's that?"

"It's the longest night of the year," I answered.

"When's that?" he asked.

"December twenty first," Ellie answered. "I've been thinking about this actually. We lost track of the date weeks ago, but the solstices are fixed. So I've been tracking the first light each morning for about a week now. The nights get about one minute longer everyday now, so as soon I record a night that gets one minute shorter we'll know the date."

"But will it be a full moon?" asked Torrance.

"I don't know. I've been watching the sun not the moon."

"Torrance, what does it say about porcwudgie mating season?" insisted Hephae.

Torrance continued reading, *"An old joke suggests that porcupines mate very carefully. But in reality male porcupines soften the female's quills with urine. Pukwudgies are no different."*

"Ew gross!" Ellie exclaimed.

"Come on now," I protested. "That might not be age appropriate."

"I used to read Jerry Rotter fan fiction online," he said mockingly, as if I'd get the reference. He kept reading. *"For that reason urine is their natural repellant."*

"Repellent?" interrupted Hephae. "Read that!"

"Guys, it's not real!" I insisted.

"Max, you didn't see this thing. We did!" asserted Hephae. "So don't tell us what's real."

"Yeah!" agreed Torrance.

"Keep reading," Hephae instructed Torrance.

"The smell of male urine tells the amorous pukwudgie that a prospective female partner has already mated, and it will move on. So it's important to mark the entrance to your home with male urine during mating season."

"That's it!" yelled Hephae. "Let's go whiz on the perimeter fence."

"Seriously?" I was shocked.

"Look," asserted Hephae. "If tonight's the longest night of the year, Elliot won't know till tomorrow morning. That means it might be porcwudgie mating season right now!"

"What about the moon?" asked Torrance.

"We'll know more by tonight, but right now, we're better safe than sorry."

Hephae and Torrance ran outside to begin marking their territory. Ellie stayed behind with me.

"Why aren't you going?" I asked.

"Because I'm not a real boy, Geppetto. Remember?" She laughed. "Besides, I was just playing along so the children would go play outside and let us adults talk. Look, I don't believe in magic disappearing porcupine people, but those two saw something–"

"But what?" I interrupted.

"I don't know," she admitted. "But nevermind them. They're just being hysterical. They're slowing us down. I'll tell you something I learned a long time ago. There's no such thing as acting your age. Those kids out there are children and they're going to be children the rest of their lives. You and me are old people, and that's why we're going to survive to be old people."

Suddenly the front doors swung open with a crash. Holland stumbled in, arms full of boxes, and tripped over the debris on the front landing. He spilled single serving cereal boxes and snack chips all over the ground, and somersaulted over the back of a couch unit in the theater, coming to a soft landing upside down on the other side.

"Guys! Come quick!" He hollered into the house. "You're going to want to see this!"

Ellie and I ran through the galley to the front door.

Holland turned around and stood up. "Darleen is about to collapse the whole economy." He ran back out, leaving the doors wide open.

Eighteen: Bicycle Girl

We chased after Holland, who yelled back, "We hit the Blanoby Animal Hospital and snagged a whole case of antibiotics, by the way. It's technically for pigs but it's just as good . . ." He paused, so excited he lost his pacing.

Darleen picked up the thread, "I found her checking parking meters. I call her *Bicycle Girl.*"

It was a G, and judging by the uniform it had been a cop.

Alix interrupted, "The bicycle helmet gave me an idea. So we took her."

"Took her?" I asked "How did you get her back here?"

"Easy," they all said in unison.

Upon closer examination I saw that Bicycle Girl was fitted with blinders, like a horse, and it was wrapped in a leather harness that covered it's mouth and held its arms by it's side.

"But why?" I asked.

"It's like you said," Holland explained. "They have muscle memory of what they did when they were alive. Well, Bicycle Girl *bicycled.*"

"What's *muscle memory?*" asked Torrance.

I thought for a moment, but a good explanation didn't come to mind.

"I want you to try something for me, ok?" asked Holland.

Torrance nodded.

"I want you to pretend to brush your teeth."

Torrance made a fist, as if holding his toothbrush, and began shaking it in front of his face.

"Ok now stop. And put your hands by your sides," Holland instructed.

Torrance quickly complied.

"Good. Now pretend to brush your teeth again."

Torrance went back to shaking his fist, opening his mouth as if brushing his back teeth.

"Now stop," ordered Holland.

Torrance dutifully stopped his performance and stood with his arms at his side.

"Ok, now one more time."

And again Torrance began imaginary brushing, laughing this time.

"Ok stop," instructed Holland. "Now, this time I want you to hold your hands behind your back."

Torrance played along. To him it had become a kind of game. Like freeze tag.

"Ok, I'm going to ask you a question, and I want you to answer without moving your hands. Understand?"

Torrance nodded enthusiastically.

"When you brush your teeth," Holland paused for dramatic effect. "Do you start on the right side, or the left side?"

I could see the gears turning in Torrance's mind as he struggled to remember without moving his arms.

"I don't know," he answered finally.

Holland smiled. "Well, would it surprise you to know that all three times you started brushing on left side?"

Torrance looked at his hands, and began to mimic brushing again, but slower, trying to be mindful of what he was doing.

"And I'll bet you always start on the left side when you brush your teeth."

"You're right!" Torrence exclaimed.

"Yup," Holland agreed. "Your hands knew that, even though your head didn't."

"And that's *muscle memory!*" affirmed Torrence as his face lit up with understanding.

"Right."

Sure enough, Bicycle Girl bicycled. She had to have her feet strapped to the pedals, and her hands strapped to the handlebars, but it worked, as long as she had something to chase.

Stinky immediately took to prancing around in front of Bicycle Girl to keep her pedaling.

I explained the porcwudgie situation to Alix, and she dismissed it as absurd, but agreed increasing security was good idea anyway.

I briefly suspected that the whole fiasco might be her doing. That she might have used the porcupine mask in the captain's quarters to scare Torrance and steal the Mighty O's herself. She could have eaten the Mighty O's and scared Hephae while she was supposedly in town. But that would mean that Darleen and Holland were part of the conspiracy.

I checked upstairs, just in case, and the mask was still mounted on the wall. So, the only person that could have put it back after scaring Hephae was Torrance. But if Torrance was in on it, what was the point of faking the first sighting? Besides, Torrance was with me when Hephae saw it.

No. It had to be someone or something from outside.

By nightfall we saw that the moon was three quarters full, but then it might have been one quarter empty. We couldn't tell if it was waxing or waning until the following night. Which meant the hysteria continued.

The possibility existed that the moon was waxing, and the full moon was a week away. The possibility also existed that the winter solstice was a week away, and may occur on the same night. I conceded those facts. What I wouldn't accept was that this astrological coincidence somehow signified an increased threat from porcwudgies in heat, which didn't even exist.

Tension was high. Hephae and Torrance were utterly convinced we faced a magical adversary. And of course, they were our only eye witnesses, so almost all the evidence flowed through them. Alix tried to dismiss everything as Torrance's childish imagination, but she couldn't with Hephae backing up everything he said. And no one could deny the Mighty O's box. Darleen was convinced she could construct some kind of banishing spell with candles and chalk.

I'm not sure what Ellie believed. I think she was mainly trying to avoid the pissing contest.

And there was a pissing contest. Holland started it when he ran to the fence, dropped his pants, and proceeded to urinate while trotting sideways along the perimeter. When he was finished he measured the length of fence he'd covered, and challenged the other guys to do better. The game lasted all week.

We built barriers until the sun set, and then retired to the lounge.

We quickly realized that Bicycle Girl generated more power when she was really excited. In fact, she generated enough power to watch movies on the main viewer. And if we pointed her at the screen some shows were exciting enough to keep her pedaling. She especially responded to hockey for some reason. At times she even seemed to roar with the crowd. It was like perpetual motion.

"Hey Hephae?" I asked. "If we wired the generator into the ship's power grid couldn't we charge the internal battery and plug into the wall outlets instead of an inverter?"

"It's a good idea. We tried it before you got here. But I couldn't access the ship's power grid without the command codes."

"Yeah, but I know the command codes." I revealed.

"What?!" He literally leapt out of his seat. "Why am I just learning this now? With those codes we can activate the computer core, boot up the operating system. Who knows what kind of toys this place has?"

I do. "There's only one way to find out."

Hephae patched Bicycle Girl into the ship's power system, which prompted a security wall from the operating system. I entered the code. 11. 12. 03. and the whole screen went green with white letters that read *ACCESS GRANTED.*

For an instant everything on the ship came on. Every light. Every panel. The main viewer. The microwave. *Everything.* Then just as quickly it all powered down.

"Bummer," said Hephae looking at the dark viewer. "I guess it doesn't work."

"No, look!" There was one lit panel near the door. It was dark blue with huge white letters that read *LOW POWER MODE.* "That's the operating system. It's working, it just doesn't have the power to maintain the current settings . . . Check it out." I tapped a small battery icon in the corner of the screen to open the battery diagnostic tool. "We're only at

114

1%, but we're charging . . . check out the alerts!" I tapped an exclamation point above the battery meter and a menu of twenty three notifications filled the screen. "See that. It's notifications of all the systems that were shut off as the battery drained. And they'll come back on, one by one, as the system charges. With one exception."

"Exception?" he asked. "What exception?"

"Well, there are twenty four systems on this ship." I backed out of the battery diagnostic to the home screen, which still read *LOW POWER MODE*. "Which means there has to be one system still engaged." I navigated into the primary systems settings. A few taps and swipes and, "We have lights!"

Nineteen: Larry's Ammo

By morning the ship battery read 3%, and at that level we were able to access some other basic features, including the navigation system. The map wasn't current, but there was an archived version of the last time the computer had internet access.

It was a total game changer. We found a listing for a gun store just two miles away in Blanoby. And in the current climate of porcwudgie hysteria, more guns seemed like a good idea to everyone.

As first officer I assembled the away team. I chose Ellie as gunner, and Holland as navigator. We left for the gun shop on foot.

Stinky followed.

It was the first time the three of us had been alone together since Scott died.

Niles broke the ice. "I'll use my real voice if you use yours."

"Deal." Ellie laughed.

"So, what do you guys think?" asked Niles.

"About what?" I asked.

"Anything," he answered. "Do you think we're going to survive?"

"Survive what?" Ellie asked.

"Oh you know . . ." He thought. "The porcwudgie attack, the G invasion, the mad scientists. All of it."

"That and more," she smirked.

"What about Elliot, is he going to survive?" Niles asked.

"I've been thinking about that," Ellie explained. "At some point I'm going to have to come out to the other kids . . . but as long as Dr. Blum is out there I just think it's safer not to exist."

"So, what are you going to do?" I asked.

She paused a long time, "I think I've got to kill Dr. Blum."

"What!?" I protested.

"Oh, don't act like he doesn't deserve it!" she scoffed. "He wants to kill me in his demented experiments. I should have done it in the S-Mart parking lot. He was totally exposed, but I wasn't prepared. I need a better weapon."

"What about Holland?" she diverted. "Is he going to survive?"

"For now," answered Niles. "I still need him . . . I think we all need him. I mean, he caught Bicycle Girl, not me, and look how good that turned out. I couldn't have done that without–"

"Niles, listen to me," I interrupted. "There's nothing Holland can do that you can't do. You're just as good as him. I know it. Ellie knows it."

She nodded. "And Holland knows it too. You deserve to be here as much as anyone."

That last line stung me in a way I didn't expect. Like I needed someone to say it to me. But I couldn't shake the feeling that Dad *deserved* to be alive more than me. That I was only alive because of him, because of all the preparations he'd made, but no matter how grateful I was I could never repay him, or even thank him.

When we arrived it had the look of a wild west saloon. Like an existing barn was extended with a covered porch and wooden railings. Above the awning was a neon sign that read *Larry's Ammo*. Of course the power was out.

We entered through the back door with caution, but confidence. The three of us had been through a lot together, especially me and Ellie, and we were proficient at clearing out lingering G's as a team. But we found none inside. So, we relaxed and started shopping.

The inside felt more like an old general store. Not like any gun store I'd ever imagined. More like a sporting goods store. In fact, there weren't even any guns on display. *Maybe they were all taken.* We were especially looking for .22 rounds to fit Ellie's Mosquito, and shells for Alex's twelve-gauge double-barrel Remington, but any caliber was worth taking. Lead was like gold. *Heavy.*

Ellie opened the front door to peak outside and unwittingly triggered the signature jingle of a cowbell on a string.

Klunk-l-lunk

Suddenly a hunched figure straightened up behind the register.

"G!" yelled Niles, and Ellie immediately drew and fired.

The man raised his arms and dropped to the floor. "Hands up! Don't shoot!"

"Holy crap! He's alive!" Ellie yelped and ran toward the counter. "Are you ok, Mister?"

"The money's in the register." His voice quivered. "Take whatever you want." He stayed ducked behind the counter.

Ellie hopped up to look over the counter, and quickly met with a shotgun barrel pointed up her nose.

"Now, how about you drop that little bean shooter, and you and your friends get outta my store." His voice suddenly bold and gravelly.

"No! No! No!" Ellie dropped the Mosquito and held up her palms. "I thought you were a G! I didn't mean to–"

"A what?" he asked.

"A ghoul!" I yelled. "One of those things out there."

He stood up, shotgun ready, and I saw a sizzle of smoke near his chest. *He took the bullet!* "You're wounded! I have a medkit. You should let me–"

"I'll tend to my own self." He pointed the gun at me. "So, this ain't a robbery?"

"No!" Ellie shook her head. "We were just scavenging for supplies, and–"

"So you're looters?" He pointed the gun back at her.

"No!" I interrupted. "Not exactly. We thought it was abandoned."

"Let's all take a take a deep breath." Holland stepped forward with his hands raised. "My name is Holland. This is Max, and his brother Elliot."

Ellie flipped her hood off, looking boyish with her new haircut.

"What's your name," asked Holland.

"This is Larry's Ammo." He lowered the firearm, squinting skeptically. "I'm Larry."

He placed the shotgun on the counter and started unbuttoning his shirt to assess his injury. He was wearing some kind of body armor underneath. "My friends call me *LaMoe*, but I don't appreciate it." He dropped the expelled bullet on the counter, and groaned in pain as he rolled his shoulder. "That's going to leave a bruise."

"Whoa!" Ellie's eyes locked on the flattened bullet.

"Are you alone? Where are your parents?" he asked.

"Dead," Ellie answered.

"Mine too," said Holland.

I nodded., "Same here."

"I see." Larry's tone softened. He spied the Mosquito on the ground. "I bet *Trigger Finger* here is looking for .22s, am I right?"

"And twelve-gauge shotgun shells, if you've got them," I answered.

"Not for sale. I need those for my *Boomstick* here, but I got .22s for miles." He started pulling boxes off the shelf behind him. "They don't have the best stopping power, so I got a sale going. Buy two, get one. You buy a box of a hundred, it's twenty bucks. You take a three hundred, it's fifty.

That math is wrong. I got the feeling we were being hustled.

"Larry, what are you doing here? How are you living here?" Ellie asked.

"Son—" he began.

"Please don't call me that," she interrupted.

"This is my ammo shop," he said. "I live upstairs and I got everything I need. No undead pukes are going to chase me out of my own home. "

"So what are you doing down here?" I asked.

"Running the shop," he said casually.

"Why?" Holland asked.

"Oh, you know . . . I don't know." He searched his mind for a good answer. "I hadn't had any customers in a long time, and the pukes were pretty much frozen outside. So I just went back to doing what I did before. Opened the shop. Kept the books. Managed the inventory." He paused to think. "Sometimes I move the displays around, just to keep busy." He pointed to the globs of fake snow along the window sill. "This here's my Christmas theme."

We all stared at him blankly.

"So you guys want these rounds, or what?" he asked.

"I don't have any money." Ellie shrugged and looked back at me.

I shook my head.

Holland stepped forward, pulling a sack from his pocket. "Will you take any of these?" He dumped the contents out on the counter. It was dozens, maybe a hundred little metal trinkets.

"What is all that?" I asked.

"I've been collecting shiny things I find on the ground, pretty much since the outbreak started," he explained. "It's like an exercise in situational awareness. Really flexes my crow brain. Plus you never know what'll be useful someday." He turned to Larry. "Can we agree to 25 cents a round? Or 3 for 50 cents?"

That math is still wrong.

Larry nodded, rolling his eyes as if dissatisfied with the size of the sale. He opened a box and started counting out bullets on one side of the counter while Holland counted out coins at the other end.

"Lots of nuts and bolts here," observed Holland. "Will you give me two for one?"

"Sure," replied Larry. "Wait. Two bullets or two bolts?"

"Two bullets," answered Holland.

"No way!" Larry objected. "You find me a bolt that fits a nut and I'll give you a bullet. Otherwise, what good are they?"

"What about this?" Holland had an empty bullet casing. "Can you do anything with this?"

"I got primers and powder, but I'm out of stock of lead balls."

"What about this?" Ellie reached across the counter and slid a dime out of Larry's coin pile.

"A dime? So what?" he asked.

"A *silver* dime," she corrected.

Larry picked it up and held to the light, trying to read the fine print. "How do you know that?"

"US coins from 1964 and before were made of silver," she explained. "They're made of zinc or something now."

"You're right! It's 1963," he said. "You're telling me you read that from all the way over there?"

"No . . . I heard it." She grinned. "It's something my mom taught me. She used to be a bookkeeper, so she handled a lot of coins. You can hear the difference when they drop."

She took the dime out of his hand and dropped it on the counter. Then she grabbed another dime and did the same. *She was right.* The sound of the modern dime was dull by comparison. It didn't ring as clear.

"Hear that?" she smiled. "It's silver." She picked up the silver dime and handed it back to Larry. "Which means I bet it could be melted down and repurposed into a silver bullet."

"Maybe." He examined it closely. "I have the equipment to refurbish ammunition, but why would I trade a live round for pieces of a spent round?"

"Because two grams of silver is worth a dollar at least. That dime is worth six rounds." She beamed.

"I gotta hand it to you, Kid. You know your stuff." He smiled. "I'll tell you what. I'll give you four rounds for the silver dime."

"Six!" interrupted Holland. "It's my dime after all, not Elliot's. So you're negotiating with me."

"Five." Larry pointed at Holland, and in doing so closed the dime in his palm.

"Deal!" Holland pulled five bullets into his pile on the counter.

They both smiled and went back to sorting the trinket pile.

"What do you mean they don't have *stopping power?*" inquired Ellie, looking at the Mosquito.

"I mean they're good for target practice, I guess," Larry answered. "But I swear I've popped some poor puke in the head it didn't go down. Like it didn't pierce skull."

"You got anything bigger?" Ellie glanced around the shop.

"I carry all the common calibers, but this is an ammo shop, not a gun shop."

"Wait," I injected. "You sell bullets, but you don't carry firearms?"

"Yeah . . ." He suddenly looked embarrassed. "I never got around to figuring out the paperwork." He shrugged. "And I managed to run a pretty good business supplementing ammo sales with whatever else people needed."

"You mean you've got nothing?" Ellie bemoaned.

"Well . . . I didn't say that." Larry scratched his chin and sized her up. "Take a look at this." He retrieved a pistol from a waist holster. "This here's an HK45. Husten and Keil. Forty five caliber."

He checked the safety and handed it to Ellie handle first. She took it carefully and examined it.

"It might be just what you need. I got it because it's got a smaller grip than standard. I got small hands. So it only takes ten rounds. But it might be just your size."

"How much!" She asked.

"Oh, I don't know . . . This is my personal piece. I wasn't planning on selling it." It was clear Larry was an experienced negotiator. "I'm going to need something more than some trinkets you kids found in the street. We're talking about a serious trade here."

"Aargh!" Ellie groaned and slammed her fist on the counter. "I don't have anything to trade."

"Meat!" boomed Holland.

"What?" we all asked in unison.

"Meat. You loan Elliot the HK45 and take his Mosquito as collateral. In addition, you rent me that." He pointed above the main entrance, where a crossbow was mounted on the wall.

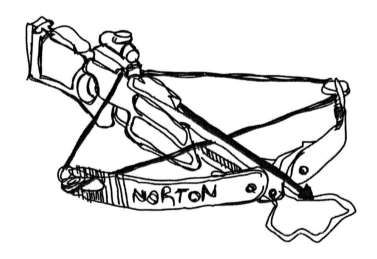

"With that," Holland continued, "we can hunt without spending ammo, and we can deliver a portion of meat, every week, until the crossbow is paid off."

Larry laughed. "Kid, I like your style, but I got no guarantee you ever come back. Then I'm just trading a .45 for a .22."

"You're the only ammo shop for miles. We'll be back to trade," I assured him.

Larry fingered through the shiny things on the counter and seized upon a small glass cylinder.

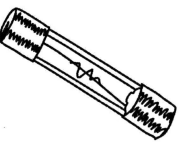

"Well I'll be! Is that?" He examined the butt end of the tube's metallic cap. "Do you know what this is?" Larry asked Holland.

"I thought it was like an ooze canister for a Kung Fu Hamster action figure," Holland answered.

"Close," Larry chuckled. "It's a fuse!"

"Is that good?" asked Ellie.

"Let me try something, and if it works I think we've got a deal."

Larry disappeared into the back room and moments later all the fluorescent lights on the sales floor blinked on. All the ceiling fans whirred to life, and the air filled with the hum of a model B17 Bomber circling above the register on a string.

Larry came running back onto the sales floor, jumping and laughing. "It worked! It worked! The generator is fixed!" And he ran right out the front door.

Klunk-l-lunk

"Come look!" Larry yelled from the parking lot outside. "It's glorious!"

We all followed him outside and turned to see what he was looking at on the roof.

The neon marquee blinked, *Larry's Ammo, Larry's Ammo, Larry's Ammo* in bright yellow.

"Looks like I'm back in business, boys!" He hopped. "And you!" He pointed at Holland. "You just bought yourself a crossbow."

126

Twenty: Perfect Order

The walk home was jubilant. Ellie had her new cannon. Holland was eager to hunt, and practiced shooting at mailboxes.

"Vandalizing a mailbox is a felony," I joked. "They're federal property."

"I commit three felonies a day," Holland retorted as he aimed, fired and embedded a bolt in the rump of a cow shaped mailbox.

"Only three?" Ellie teased.

"At least three!" He struck a dramatic pose, "For I am Sir Robin the Brave, and you are my loyal men in tights!"

Aaand, Niles is back.

We all laughed.

We all had reason to celebrate. Even if we didn't find the cache of guns we wanted, we found another friendly survivor, one open to cooperation and trade.

"I can't wait to shove this thing in Dr. Blum's face!" Ellie stroked the barrel of her new HK45.

"The best thing to do is hunker down through the winter," I suggested. "Monitor the situation by radio. With any luck he'll give up and move on to some other obsession."

"We don't have enough food for the whole winter," Niles objected.

Oh yes we did! There was enough food in the bunker to last a year or more. Dad calculated ten years for the two of us. Enough to wait out a nuclear fallout. The thing even had carbon dioxide scrubbers and air filtration. Once we got into it we'd have food to last until civilization rebooted, or longer.

"No, I've been thinking about this," Niles interrupted. "We should wait for the next big thaw, when the rivers are fullest, and take that boat all the way to the coast."

"No way," Ellie protested, "We're living in the motherload of post apocalyptic luxury right now. We stay put. We hang tight. I just gotta take care of this one little thing to make sure it's a safe space to start planting roots."

"I really don't think it's worth the risk to go after him. He's surrounded by soldiers," Niles objected. "And there's some kind of porcupine Kaiju living in these woods!" Niles got very animated when he was excited.

"Whatever, Niles. You're just a coward. And you," she pointed at me, "you are a pacifist. This guy's got it coming, and I'm going to give it to him." The look on her face said she was scheming. "I need to find something with more range."

I remembered Dad's rifles in the bunker below the safe room. An AK-47, an AR-15, and the Red Ryder BB gun I trained on. If she knew about them she'd take one and go after him for sure. Just one more reason to keep the bunker closed for now, but I knew we'd need those supplies soon.

"Hey guys, I got a question." Niles looked ponderous. "Is there any reason to think this G virus—"

"It's not a virus," I interrupted. "it's a para—"

"I know, I know," he interrupted. "The G parasite, couldn't it have some kind of *mutagenetic effect* on animals, like the goo in *Adolescent Radioactive Black Belt Hamsters*? What if we're dealing with some kind of half-human half-porcupine half-dead genetic experiment created by Dr. Blum to hunt us down and kill us?"

We waited for him to laugh, but he didn't. "Are you serious?" I asked.

"Why not?" he shrugged. "Weirder things have happened . . . apparently."

"No," I rejected. "Parasites don't have *mutagenetic* effects. Nothing has mutagenetic effects. *Mutagen* is fictional comic book nonsense. The porcwudgie, whatever it is, it's human. There's no way some mutant creature spontaneously learned how to use a screwdriver. I don't believe in spooks and hobgoblins. I'm going to catch this thing, and I know just how I'm going to do it."

By the time we got home it was evening, and the waxing moon threatened to fill in just a few days. But the power was up to five percent, and Bicycle Girl was going strong. That meant we had enough power to bring some more systems online, specifically the security cameras.

All the computer terminals inside had cameras, and there were sixteen external cameras. A few more percentage points and we'd have motion detectors too.

Holland and Ellie bragged to Hephae and the Siblinghood about their new acquisitions, but Alix didn't seem to approve of Holland's arrangement with Larry.

"We need that meat! He shouldn't get free meat forever just because he owns a piece of equipment he wasn't even using!" Alix objected. "We've got enough mouths to feed here already without having to provide meat for some stranger."

"But now that we've got the crossbow we can hunt for more food than before. We're better off than we were," Holland argued.

"So?" objected Alix. "I don't see why we have to do all the work while he eats for free."

"Because he's letting us use his property," explained Holland.

"Property is theft!" she yelled.

I didn't want to argue. I had a security system to calibrate. So I left.

I set all the sensors in the galley and the cargo bay on high alertness, but left the cameras on the second floor off to save power. I turned on eight of the sixteen external cameras and reoriented them toward the outside of the cargo bay and the area where the porcwudgie came through the perimeter fence.

Everyone spent the next week ratcheting up the porcwudgie hysteria. Sometimes it resulted in useful preparations, like digging pit traps in the yard. Enough to hold back a dozen or more G's if the time came. But mostly it resulted in superstitious behavior, like Darleen making candles scented with peppermint, cayenne pepper and Torrance's urine, because some shaman's almanac said that would be good for banishing rituals.

Every morning Ellie was up before the sun, and came down eager to report the break of dawn, but she still hadn't confirmed the solstice. And every day Torrance and Hephae counted down the days left to the full moon, on the auspicious chance that those two things coincided.

Hey, if it gave them some hustle, at least they were being productive.

I decided to try something that had worked last year at a PorcScouts event. I took all the dishes in the house and divided them evenly among the occupants, then I labeled them with everyone's names. That way instead of everyone sharing all of the plates, everyone had a plate of their own that they were responsible for. Their own bowl. Their own cups. If their dish wasn't clean, they'd have to clean it.

Dad called it *The Tragedy of the Commons.* It was this idea about the way people treat shared stuff. Most people neglect collective responsibilities, because it's easier to let someone else do the work. People imagine that they can get away with not doing any work, as long as everyone else does theirs. But if too many people make that calculation, the work doesn't get done at all. Or worse, it gets done by one person out of spite.

It ruins relationships, he said, and when that happens the only solution was to reestablish individual responsibility by assigning ownership.

It seemed to work. Before, when there was a random dirty dish left out, everyone had plausible deniability. It could have been anybody's, so it basically became nobody's. And nobody cleaned it up until somebody, usually me, did it out of sheer frustration. But with names on the plates, everyone's mess was traceable back to them. There was a chain of custody.

People got in the custom of moving people's dirty dishes to their beds, instead of mixed in the sink. It was certainly an improvement. At least the sink was clear, and I was perfectly happy to wash my own dishes, and make my own bed.

One morning, even before Ellie's dawn report, we were awoken by the sound of Torrance galloping around the ship yelling "Fool's moon! Fool's moon! Fool's moon!" at the top of his lungs.

If the full moon and the solstice are going to coincide, today's the day. Of course we wouldn't actually know if it was the solstice until tomorrow morning, but hysteria doesn't require certainty.

Normally we only carried weapons on away missions, but that day everyone was armed. Alix with her *Boomstick*, Ellie with her HK, Holland with his crossbow and Hephae with the sledge hammer. Darleen had some kind of a ritual dagger, and even Torrance carried a fist full of firecrackers he was determined to set off as an alarm if he saw anything.

Torrance used fireworks like punctuation marks when he was excited, which was often. He'd set off a bottle rocket and yell, "Shiboomy!" at the top of his lungs. We tried to stop him but he insisted fireworks were *ammo monkey business.* He'd agreed to only use them as a distress signal if he was in trouble, at least for the rest of the day.

I preferred a simple wooden staff. I made it out of the handle of an old rake. I liked the reach, and the precision. I used it to dig through clutter without using my hands.

I spent most of the day repairing an external sensor hub, with Hephae's help. It was a sphere made of metal and plastic, about the size of a softball. It could be moved around the yard to record video, audio, infrared and ultraviolet. Plus it was filled with some kind of gyroscopic stabilizer, so you could play catch with it, and it still captured a stable picture. Dad used it to record his work in the aquaponics dome mostly. *He really liked recording things.*

There was just one snag. It's internal battery was faulty. Normally it could be charged and taken anywhere in the yard. It could even connect to the ship computer wirelessly within a limited range. But without a battery it would only function when plugged in directly.

I was confident that with two fifty-foot extensions cords, strung end to end, I could place the sensor orb outside the perimeter fence in a place where it had a view of the intruder's garbage den. The only question was whether the moon was bright enough to get a clear picture.

By the time we got the sensor orb fixed the shadows outside had grown long in the waning daylight. I brought a folding ladder, but no one else would come with me to hold it steady for me. Too afraid I guess.

I walked to the end of the extension cord and leaned the ladder against a tree. From the top step I found the bough of a branch where I could point the sensor orb toward the porcwudgie den. *It's a long shot . . . and a long shot.* I laughed a little in my head.

I was tapping through the settings on the orb, setting it up for continuous recording, when I heard a rustling in the bushes below me.

For some reason I assumed it was Ellie, or maybe Niles, playing some kind of prank on me, but it wasn't.

I was looking over my shoulder when I fumbled the orb and dropped it. I expected to hear it shatter on the ground, but instead the sound of grasping hands catching it.

It was the porcwudgie! Two of them. The shorter one caught the orb, while the taller one crouched behind it. They were no more than five feet tall, covered in quills, standing at the bottom of the ladder, and looking up at me. But they had no eyes!

The tall one put its hand on the ladder and I freaked out, jumping up into the tree and kicking the ladder down behind me.

"Max, is that you!?" cried the one with the orb. "It's me, Bobby!"

I shined my light in the thing's face as it pulled at the skin of it's neck, peeling back some kind of rubber mask. "Bobby Wilson!" I moved my light to the other one as it pulled off its mask. "And Jack Freeman! You're alive!"

I leapt down, stumbling as I landed, and threw my arms around them.

"Max, no!" they both yelled.

Bad idea!

133

A thousand tiny spears, burrowing into the meat of my arms and chest.

The problem with porcupine quills is they have backward-pointing barbs that hold them in place. If not removed they'll bury even deeper into the skin. Luckily I was in good hands.

Jack was quick on the draw with his medkit and ready to cut them free and suture the wounds.

"What are you doing here? How did you get here? What's with the masks?" I had so many questions.

"It's natural defense," answered Jack. "I don't know if you've noticed, but the humans out here are more dangerous than the deadites!"

Deadites. I smirked. "I get it. Quills are smart. But why are you terrorizing me and the others?"

"We didn't want any confrontation," Bobby explained. "We were just looking for the stuff our parents intended for us."

"And we took some firewood," quipped Jack.

"We know it's your cabin, but our parents invested a lot in this place," said Bobby. "Besides, we didn't know you were here."

"But why all the secrecy?" I asked.

"We agreed not to trust new people," said Jack. "Look, my dad didn't make it." He and Bobby exchanged glances. "Our group was attacked by scalpers."

"Scalpers?" I asked.

"There are these bartertowns that have sprung up in places." explained Bobby. "And some of them take deadite scalps as money. So there are these people whose job it is to keep the trade routes open."

134

"So why did they attack you?" I asked.

"Well, some of them have figured out that it's impossible to tell if a severed scalp came from the living or the dead."

"I made it here with uncle Ian," Jack continued. "But when we saw that the cabin was occupied by strangers, we decided it wasn't worth the risk of a violent confrontation. So we set up camp nearby, and started collecting supplies."

"There's six in our group," said Bobby. "Now seven including you. We're going north, where it's too cold for corpses."

"We've made contact with a group in Maine called the Pirates of Botany Bay. We're going to go build the perfect order, like our parents always talked about," said Jack. "Think about it. No more police state. No more war on everything. No central bank. No taxes. No bureaucracy. It's all gone! Up in smoke." He got excited just thinking about it. "And this is our golden opportunity to start things over right. To build the society we've all been dreaming about. Based on the PorcScouts creed."

It was an enticing offer. It would get us away from Dr. Blum and the G's. It would connect us with other like-minded survivors. *They were familiar faces!* It'd been so long since I'd seen familiar faces.

"That sounds awesome!" I exclaimed. "I'll go get the others."

"Others?!" burst Jack. "What others?"

"The people in my group." I pointed back at the cabin. "They should come with us."

"Aren't you listening?" asserted Bobby. "No outsiders. We can't trust them. They don't have the same values we have."

"You got to at least let me bring Ellie," I pleaded.

"Who's Ellie?" Bobby asked.

"Elliot!" I corrected. "I meant *Elliot*. He's this kid I met early on. We've been looking out for each other. Helping each other. We trust each other. I wouldn't feel right leaving him behind."

"No way," insisted Bobby. "We'll take in outsiders once we're self sufficient, but right now we're a small group, on the move. We can't afford to let in strangers. Besides, we've survived some pretty rough trail. Not just anyone can keep up with us. Not without our training."

My stomach sank. I couldn't leave her. It wasn't just the cure. With Dad's research gone any scientist would basically have to start from scratch anyway, and she was never going to consent to an examination again. No, at this point it was more important to keep her out of a lab. But it was more than that. It was her.

"I can't leave them," I said. "I'm staying here," I affirmed.

"Seriously?!" They both said.

"Yeah," I nodded. "Seriously. Will you at least come inside and tell everyone you're not porcupine monsters?" I begged.

"Negative!" Bobby flipped his mask back over his face, which I saw now was a rubber troll face sewn into the lining of a hoodie. "This is double top secret. Besides . . ." he smirked. "It's better if they believe it. It keeps the porcwudgie alive."

Bobby had this crazy idea that ideas were more real than . . . well reality. That as long as people believed a thing, in some sense it existed and had power. And he had a variety of metaphysical theories about what kinds of powers belief had.

"Tell you what. I'll have everybody pack up some supplies tonight and we'll leave them as an offering to the porcwudgie." I smirked. "I hope you like corn."

We all laughed.

"We're going to miss you, Max. But it's not goodbye forever." Jack rummaged through his gear bag and retrieved a memo pad and quill. He scribbled down some numbers. "We're building a Pirate Radio Network. Tune in to this frequency and it'll have everything you need to follow us, if you change your mind."

"What do you mean, *pirate?*" I asked.

Jack winced like the question physically hurt him. "It's a lot to explain, let's just say there are people in the Capital that want to reboot the Constitution, and there are people out here who think that's a bad idea."

He put the note in my hand. They said their goodbyes, and they disappeared as suddenly as they'd appeared.

I left the sensor orb in the tree, *may as well*, and carried the ladder home. By then it was dark, but there was plenty of light from the moon.

As I approached the fence the whole crew came running into the yard.

"Where have you been? I want a full report," said Alix.

Torrance took one look at my puncture wounds and bubbled, "Did you see a porcwedgie?"

"Yeah, I saw two." I chuckled.

Ellie ran up, threw her arms around me and whispered in my ear, "I heard everything."

Twenty One: The Safe Room

I told the others that the porcwudgies wanted an offering, and we spent the evening gathering supplies to leave on the back deck, like in Dad's diary story. Believers left corn products, as the lore suggested, mostly corn chips and cans of cream corn. I, on the other hand, tried to think of things the PorcScouts would actually need marching into the icy north, which meant it was time to open the bunker.

"You're telling me you knew about this thing the whole time!" Ellie asked.

"Yeah," I admitted.

"Why didn't you tell us!"

"I wanted to save it for an emergency. And I couldn't be sure the supplies wouldn't be wasted," I explained. "And there's *guns* . . ."

"Now you're speaking my language. Open it up!" Ellie ordered.

"Look, Ellie. I know you want to go after Dr. Blum, but it's a bad idea. I'm worried you're going to get yourself killed. But the PorcScouts have a right to some of the supplies down there."

"Max, I'm not going to do anything stupid," she agreed. "Now, where is this thing?"

"I'll show you."

The hatch was under the spiral staircase, covered behind a curtain.

"How many secret rooms you got in this place?" Niles beamed.

I grabbed ahold of the curtain. "Officially? None." I pulled it back revealing a keypad and a hatch that lead to a small steel reinforced room hidden between the kitchen and the bathroom. That room granted total command access to the computer core, and had a ladder that went down to the bunker and up to the captain's quarters.

I went to the keypad and punched in the code to open the entrance to the safe room. 11. 12. 03. It flashed *PROCESSING PROCESSING PROCESSING* briefly before the whole screen went red with white letter *ACCESS DENIED.*

"What!?" I gasped. "I don't understand. That should be right."

The screen went dark again and then switched to an image of someone sitting in the glow of a computer terminal.

"What's that?" Alix asked.

"I think it's a video feed," added Niles.

"Is someone in there?" asked Alix.

"No, it's a recording" I answered. "It's my dad."

> *"Hi Max. At least I hope it's Max. If you're seeing this it means you made it here without me. Which means there's a good chance I'm missing . . . or worse. I tried to put everything in here I thought you'd need. Food. Medical supplies. Weapons. Even some gold and silver to barter with, in case it's comes to that. I hope I'm alive, but in case I'm not, I want you to know what a privilege it has been to raise you. I know it's been hard for you without your mom, and I hope you know I did my best. It's been hard for me too. We've had some rough patches, but you've never stopped surprising me in the most amazing ways. With your character. With your mind. You've always performed beyond my wildest expectations. You're mother would be so proud of the young man you're becoming."*

Dad paused as his eyes began to fill with tears. I fought the urge to cry myself.

"I'm sorry I'm not there. I wish I knew why. I guess I'm really hoping you never see this video. But if I'm dead, and there's anything on the other side, I'll be waiting for you. By now you're probably wondering why the code I taught you didn't work. I used your birthday so it'd be easy for you to remember, but it's also too easy for the wrong person to guess. So, I've got a riddle only you can know. Do you remember the the giraffes and the jackals? Do you remember the name of the ship?

Well the ship was named after your mother's favorite book. There's a copy in my library. Find the book with the name of the ship in the title. The code is the number of letters in each word of the title. I'm sure you can find it. You've always been my little professor."

Suddenly I couldn't hold back and my eyes welled up with tears. Ellie and Niles put their arms around me.

I wiped my eyes and cleared my nose. "The ship was the *Stranger*. Look for a book with *Stranger* in the title," I ordered.

Everyone scattered and began scanning the book shelves.

"*Strange Days: The Jim Morrison Story*," guessed Alix.

"Let's try that!" I exclaimed. "Count it for me."

"*Strange* is seven. *Days* is four. Three. Three. *Morrison* is eight." She read them out.

"*Story* is five" I punched the numbers into the keypad. 7. 4. 3. 3. 8. 5. The screen turned red again. *ACCESS DENIED*.

"I found *Strange Tales To Tell In The Dark* by Alvin Schwartz," said Niles.

7. 5. 2. 4. 2. 3. 4. ACCESS DENIED "No. It's gotta be *Strang-ER* not *Strange*. Keep looking."

"I've got it! *Stranger in a Strange Land* by Robert Heinlein." Ellie called out, shaking the book above her head.

I punched the numbers into the keypad. 8. 2. 1. 7. 4. It began processing again. Then the screen turned green. *ACCESS GRANTED.* And the lock released.

"Yes!"

Everyone's eyes were wide as I pulled the steel door open and they rushed down the ladder to the bunker below. Lights and computer screens powered on as backup generator activated.

"Greetings Max. At current quantities we have sustainability for two adults for ten years, two weeks and three days." It was Dad's voice, only more digital.

"Who's there?" I asked.

"I am the Built In Operating Database And Directory, or BIODAD. I have been installed to instruct and explore the features of this safe room, in the event of Rich Hartwell's absence." The BIODAD appeared on the computer screen as a virtual presence modeled on recordings of my dad taken before the outbreak.

"BIODAD, recalculate current sustainability for seven children . . . and one cat," I instructed.

"Insufficient data," came the computerized voice. "Please indicate the age of any children under the age of thirteen."

"I'm six and three quarters," answered Torrance.

"BIODAD, one child is seven years old." I rounded up. "Three children are twelve, and the rest are over thirteen."

"Calculating . . ." said the BIODAD.

"This is awesome!" quipped Niles.

"At current quantities we have sustainability for three adults, three adolescents, one child, and one cat for two years, ten months and six days."

"I guess we're *adults*." Hephae nodded to Ellie and Alix.

"I can also operate household appliances, monitor security, allocate energy usage, lock doors, assign chores, suggest age appropriate entertainment . . ." The BIODAD went on.

The bunker was built out of two corrugated steel shipping containers, and was incredibly cramped. The living quarters two bunks, two footlockers, a toilet and a shower stall, but they took up less space than a prison cell. The kitchen and dining area were just as small.

Everyone flocked directly to the pantry, which was full of metal shelves stocked with food. Corned beef hash, macaroni and cheese, corn dogs, and more.

"Oh! Hot chocolate with mini marshmallows!" beamed Torrance.

"We could feed an army with all this!" said Holland.

"We have to be careful. Food goes fast," I responded. "And we're giving half of it to the porcwudgies."

"Half!" yelled Alix. "Are you out of your gourd?"

"I don't want to hear it, Alix," I insisted. "This is happening whether you like it or not."

"Excuse me!?" Darleen backed up her sister. "She's the captain."

"Yeah, well it's my bunker. They're my supplies. If you don't like it you're free to take zero. But if I were you I'd be grateful to have ten times the food you had this morning, and stop dwelling on the loss. Take the win!"

"This baby's got my name on it!" Torrance pulled the Red Ryder BB gun off a wall mount and spied down the sights.

"Put that down!" Alix grabbed it from him. "You'll shoot someone's eye out!"

"That's what I learned on," I told her. "I could show him. He's got to learn eventually."

The AR-15 and the AK-47 were still on the wall mount.

"Do you want to talk about this?" asked Ellie when she saw me dwelling on the rifles.

"The way I see it, you and me are the only two here remotely qualified to handle weapons this size. You're the gunner, you should take first pick."

"Really?" she asked.

"Really," I assured her. "But before you choose you should know I'm giving the other one to the porcwudgies. They're going to need some firepower where they're going."

She seemed surprised. "Okay. How do we choose? I've never fired either of them. What do the numbers mean?"

"The AR-15 was the fifteenth model made by ArmaLite Rifles, and the AK-47 was manufactured by Mikhail Kalashnikov in 1947," explained BIODAD.

"No help there. But then why didn't they call it the MK-47?" she asked.

"Maybe because it's Russian," I speculated.

"What was your dad's first choice?" she asked.

"The Kalashnikov. But I think he just liked it because it's old," I said. "The AR is lighter, longer, faster and has almost twice the range. It's the superior machine."

"Then it's a no brainer. I'll take the AR. They get the AK." She started pulling the rifle off the wall.

"Wait," I stopped her, just briefly. "I know what you want to do with it, but—"

"Max, he did things to me you can't even—"

"I know. I know. I just want you to think about something first. Something that's been on my mind. It's your decision, just hear me out."

"Ok, go ahead," she agreed.

"We know the infection likes aggressive people. Well, what if what makes your brain different, is that you're not wired right for aggression? What if you're immune because the parasite has nothing to work with?"

She thought a moment. "That makes sense. So what?"

"Well, what if killing someone rewires your brain in some way you can't reverse? What if it gives the dormant infection what it needs to change you?" I took my hand off the rifle. "Just think about it."

She ignored the feeding frenzy and ran straight to the crow's nest. She was too excited by the new toy to think about it right then, but I could tell I'd planted a seed in her mind.

I started moving supplies to the back deck. Half the first aid supplies. Half the jackets. Half of everything. I left a note with a map to Dad's unit at Lochshire, where some other supplies were stashed.

By morning everything was gone. Of course it turned out it wasn't the winter solstice anyway, but I let the others believe what they wanted to believe.

Torrance was so excited he went running around the yard, waving his arms and screaming, "Do a shiboomy! Do a shiboomy! Do a shiboomy!" And he wouldn't stop until we agreed to launch a whole volley of bottle rockets off the back deck, to celebrate the coming of the porcwudgie.

Is this how traditions start?

It was loud, but it seemed safe enough. The G's were mostly frozen, unless they were stuck inside someplace, or found some other way to stay warm.

I wondered if the PorcScouts heard our firework solute. How far north had they traveled? Then I remembered the PorcScouts radio frequency in my pocket.

Twenty Two: Emilio Airhart

Alix and Hephae were working in the studio. Niles joined them, convinced his shiny collection would prove useful. So, I gave them the radio frequency to see what they found.

Suddenly there was this unintelligible shouting from the roof. It was Ellie in the crow's nest. She'd seen something through her new scope, and was calling everyone up.

Torrance was helping Darleen make lunch in the galley, until he decided to race me up the stairs. Niles and Alix followed from the studio. Hephae was already in the crow's nest with Ellie, tampering with a new antenna.

It was tight quarters with all eight of us stuffed in that little room, trying to look out the same window. Stinky preferred to sit outside on the roof, of course he didn't know what we were all talking about.

"Let me see!" cried Holland, reaching for the AR-15.

"Hands off!" yelled Ellie, pointing to a pair of binoculars. "Use those."

He peered into the binoculars and screamed, "UFO!!!" pointing and waving frantically.

At first I thought it was some kind of amateur hot air balloon, just floating above the treeline on the other side of the lake.

"What? Where?" Torrance squirmed his way to the front of the group and popped his head through the window hatch.

As it drifted closer it became obvious they were helium balloons tied to a person. *Clouds offer no sense of scale.*

"Is it dead or alive?" Ellie took the binoculars from Holland, and handed them to me.

It was impossible to guess at this distance. It definitely looked grey enough to be dead, but it also had bright purple hair and a striped shirt. "I think it's a clown." I handed the binoculars to Hephae.

We all watched as it drifted over the lake.

"Hey mister!?" yelled Alix. "Do you need help?"

"Let's shoot it down." suggested Ellie.

"We can't do that. What if he's alive?" I objected.

"I said shoot it *down*, not shoot it! I mean, shoot the balloons."

"Guys!" interrupted Hephae. "He's got something pinned to his shirt." He crammed his eyes into the binoculars. "It's like a name tag, but I can't read it. He's still too far away."

"I got this." There was a trunk in the corner that contained my stellar telescope. I held it up like a spyglass and fiddled the knobs to focus in on the figure. "Oh, he's dead alright." I paused to refocus, "The name tag says, *Hello, my name is Emilio Airhart, property of Syrkis Barker.*"

"What's a circus barker?" asked Torrance.

Niles answered first. "It's the guy who stands out front of a carnival and yells, *Come one! Come all! Come see the strangest freaks, the highest acrobats!*"

"No," I interrupted. "It's *Syrkis*, not *circus*. It's somebody's name. It sounds Russian."

"Guys, it gets worse." Alix had the binoculars. "Look over there!" She pointed to the trees across the lake.

Dark figures were lurking out of the woods and onto the ice. Just a few at first, but soon they looked like a line of ants walking across the lake.

"Do you hear that?" asked Alix.

We all got quiet and strained to hear. Everyone else heard it before me. In the distance, almost too faint to hear, but getting louder all the time, was the shuddering sound of carnival music with the twang of Spanish guitar.

"They G's are following the sound!" I realized.

"And they're coming this way!" Ellie warned.

Of course, the lake was only frozen around the edges. So, as the G's crossed they stepped aimlessly over the edge, and bubbled to the bottom of the lake.

Crisis averted!

We turned our attention back to Emilio as he floated overhead. He definitely saw us. I made eye contact. But he made no effort to even reach in our direction. Just this hopeless look on his face, like he just gave up trying.

"Now can we shoot it down?" asked Ellie. "I bet I can hit it from here!" She took aim, struggling to find the elbow room to hold it correctly.

"Wait!" screamed Alix.

"But I've been practicing," insisted Ellie.

"I want to see where it's going," Alix wondered. "I want to see who it belongs to." She thought a moment. "Max, take an away team and go after it. You can take the Boomstick. Elliot, take the hand cannon."

"Oh, if I'm leaving the ship I'm taking the long gun," Ellie insisted.

"Fine, whatever," agreed Alix. "Then leave the pistol here."

"If we can bring Emilio back intact, maybe we can hook it up to another bicycle generator," suggested Hephae.

"Good thinking," responded Alix. "Take the crossbow and go with them."

"No way. This is a bad idea," countered Hephae. "You have no idea who put that thing in the air. They could be hostile. We should just shoot it down and take that sound equipment."

"That's all the more reason to find them," injected Ellie. "To see how far away they are, and how dangerous they are."

"Not a priority!" insisted Hephae. "We have food. We have shelter. We've got a line on supplies from the ammo shop. It's stupid to go wandering off on some half baked adventure when we're safe here."

"Fine," agreed Alix. "Holland, you take the crossbow."

"Actually . . ." Niles resisted. "I'd rather stay too. Besides, you need me here. We've got enough power now I think we can integrate your studio equipment directly into the BIODAD systems. Boost the signal. Maybe even get the satellite dish working. See what's going on in the world."

"Holland, since when do you know anything about audio-visual equipment?" asked Alix.

"It's basically the same thing I set up at Thornhaven. We ran the radio signal through the school's intercom system so runners could connect to home base from the field." Then, as if hearing himself for the first time, he added, "i mean Niles did . . . before he died. But I watched him the whole time. I'm sure I can do it."

"Hey!? What about me?" protested Darleen. "It should be me on this mission!"

"No!" said Alix. "I need you to stay here and watch Torrance."

"I can watch myself!" countered Torrance.

"It's dangerous!" yelled Alix.

"Guys!" I interrupted. "Emilio's not waiting for us. If we're going after him we've got to go now!"

"Fine! Go," conceded Alix.

"Yes!" Darleen fist pumped triumphantly.

I grabbed the binoculars and we ran out, tracking Emilio south.

It was easy to see Emilio at a distance, and even when we couldn't see him we could still follow the music. But it was hard to see him through a canopy of branches directly overhead. So, we kept some distance. Luckily he wasn't moving more than a casual walking pace.

We followed Emilio for miles, and he mostly stayed along the main road to Blanoby. Interestingly, he changed course a number of times, circling abandoned buildings along the way. He took us to a towing company, a boat repair place and a quilting supply shop. Emilio wasn't just cast to the wind. He had some kind of maneuvering thrusters up there.

We could see he was wearing a backpack that housed the speakers, and presumably a camera operated by whoever was steering, so we stayed out of view. He also had propellor motors like some kind of quadcopter drone. The balloons gave him lift, and the propellor motors were used primarily to steer. He was a reconnaissance ghoul.

Eventually he deviated course and left the road, forcing us to follow him along fire roads and dirt trails until we came to a chain link fence. On the other side Emilio circled over the Blanoby waste processing station. We were in the woods behind the dump, in a remote area on the south side of Blanoby.

Darleen was first to climb over the fence, and we all followed, sneaking from car to car, trying to cross the dump without being spotted by Emilio's camera.

Once he'd surveyed the waste processing station sufficiently he continued south, across Highway 25.

Then there was another intermittent sound, behind the deafeningly loud carnival music.

Clunk Clunk Clunk

The clunking wasn't coming from Emilio, or the dump. It was coming from the highway.

Clunk Clunk Clunk

My stomach sank.

The source of the clunking was out of sight, but getting closer. If we wanted to avoid being spotted we'd have to give up the pursuit of Emilio. Fortunately Darleen made the decision for us. She let one bolt fly from the crossbow that tore through the balloons, popping at least a handful.

Immediately the music stopped, leaving only the strained whir of the motors, fighting against the lost lift. Emilio turned and began to float away with more speed, but struggling to keep altitude.

"Did you see that!" Darleen shouted. "Someone grab my bolt. I'm going after him!"

I spotted the bolt. It had vaulted over two lanes of highway and come down in the median. I went for it.

Darleen shot again, but it zipped over my head and fell short of Emilio.

"Hey, watch it!" I yelled. "I'm down range!" I grabbed the first bolt and went for the second one, which landed in the street behind me.

Ellie drew her AR. "I got this!" She squinted and aimed the rifle high.

In the distance we heard a human holler. "Bring out your dead!"

Clunk-lunk!

And again. "Bring out your dead!"

Clunk-lunk!

Getting louder as it got closer.

Twenty Three: Wheel Top

Ellie lowered the rifle without firing at Emilio and looked to me. I said we should hide, in that unspoken language of eyebrow gestures and head tilts that we'd invented through experience. She agreed.

I ducked behind the hedges of the highway median, and Ellie hid behind an abandoned vehicle. Darleen on the other hand . . . didn't get it.

"What are you guys doing?" Darleen spun around in the middle of the road.

I tried to wave her over, but it was too late.

It was another clown, pulling a wooden cart and ringing a cowbell. *Emilio was getting away, but this clown is alive!*

"Young lady!" said the clown.

Darleen glanced around for her backup. I looked to Ellie and offered to cover her with the shotgun, but she disagreed, and she was right. She had the more precise weapon, and I had the buckshot, so I approached the clown, and Ellie covered me.

"Where's– " Darleen stopped when she saw me making a shushing face. *She's learning.*

"Young man, do you know the best way to kill a group of undead clowns?" He dropped his pitchfork and cowbell onto his pull cart, and raised his hands in a surrendering gesture. "You aim for the juggler!" He laughed awkwardly, until he realized we weren't laughing. "Get it? Juggler, jugular . . . not funny?"

We all kept our weapons aimed at him.

He continued, "There's no need for violence. I mean you no harm. I'm just your friendly neighborhood *dead collector.*"

"What's a dead collector?" I asked.

"It's pretty self explanatory isn't it?" He pointed at the stack of corpses in his cart. "We have all kinds of uses for them."

"So, you're a scalper?" I asked.

"No way!" he objected. "Scalpers are bottom feeders. About the only thing worse than a scalper is a clown!"

"Aren't you a clown?" asked Darleen.

"I most certainly am not!" He seemed genuinely offended. "I am a barker."

"What's a barker?" asked Darleen.

"A hawker," he answered, "Who calls gawkers to see spectacles so astounding they can never be ignored, or forgotten." He waved his arms in big circles, almost dancing as he spoke. "I also happen to be a vendor of fine wares."

"You're Syrkis aren't you?" I guessed.

He grinned. "You must have seen my . . . flyer." He spun his finger in the air. "Syrkis Barker at your service." He bowed.

We lowered our weapons, and I waved Ellie out of hiding. She came forward, but kept her sights on him.

He had one of the strangest looking costumes I'd ever seen. He was wearing what looked like a civil war era navy jacket, with huge gold fringe epaulets. He had a comically large red clown nose, which matched his comically large red bow tie, and comically large red clown shoes. His face paint was more grey than white. He had a giant orange beard, and a natural grin that was big and clownish enough on its own.

Ellie and I exchanged confused looks.

"Look," said Syrkis, "It's good for everybody if scalpers keep the trade routes clear. It's a perfectly honorable profession if that's what you kids do."

We all shook our heads.

He relaxed and lowered his hands. "Thank goodness! Every scalper tells the same story, about a bartertown in Portsmouth called *Primitive* where a dead scalp is worth a day's rations. Well, I'm just a little more ambitious. Your average scalper has a *get-rich-quick* mentality. They just take the scalp, and run off to the next kill. I'm more of a *use-every-part-of-the-buffalo* type of guy. So, when scalpers come through town I inquire about their recent dispatches, and come out here to pick up the pieces."

"That sounds awful!" injected Darleen. "And so dangerous!"

"Not at all!" insisted Syrkis. "The scalpers have already taken all the life out of 'em. I can fit over a dozen bodies on this cart, and if I catch a live one they can even pull it for me. Like I always say, when life hands you lemons get out of the kitchen. I can find a use for anything."

"Wait," I shuddered at the thought. "You're saying these bodies are the victims of a recent scalping party?" I couldn't bear to look.

"You use them?" wondered Darleen. "For what?"

He opened his coat, revealing a variety of bottles sewn into the lining. He drew one, in dramatic fashion and held it out to us. "*tBlocker* is an invention of my own creative genius. Certified, rarified and bonafide to repel what eats you." He depressed the plunger on top of the bottle, squirting a dollop of grey cream into Darleen's hand. "You boys want a free sample?" He offered the nozzle to me and Ellie. "Don't worry. It's ok for boys to wear makeup in an emergency."

It was the same grey face cream he and Emilio had on their faces. I was reluctant.

"Come now, boys. Curiosity crumbles the cookie."

I held out my hand to receive a dollop. Ellie refused.

Darleen smelled it and wretched. "That's disgusting!"

I sniffed it carefully. It wasn't entirely unpleasant. It smelled mostly like tea tree and garlic, but with the unmistakable aroma of decomposing human remains. I wiped it on my shoe.

Syrkis was disappointed by our reaction. "I'm still trying to perfect the recipe." He pulled off his rubber nose and revealed the inside. "I keep a potpourri of wildflowers in here to mask the scent. Not a bad idea, and it's a small price to pay to keep Wheel Top's patrons safe and trigger free."

"And what's Wheel Top?" asked Ellie.

"A little bartertown of my own." He swelled with pride and took a deep breath, as if to savor the moment. "Wheel Top. *Wheel Top.* What can I say that will convey what Wheel Top is? I'm filled with gratitude and felicity to live in such a great facility. But there's only one way to know the whole truth about Wheel Top. Come see the show, and exit through the gift shop."

So we agreed to go see Wheel Top, following him around the next bend in the highway, where the lights and music were obvious from blocks away.

Wheel Top was a traveling carnival on it's way from Montreal to Portsmouth. Of course what Syrkis called a *trade route* sounded more like rumors, scattered radio signals and reports from wary travelers headed the opposite direction. There were bartertowns, but there was no map. Just stories of dubious reliability.

I asked why he wasn't going north, like most people, and he barked, "Think! Only an ignoramus goes north. Everybody's going north, and people are more dangerous predators than some dead MOOP. Why would I go where the predators are going?"

"What's a MOOP?" I asked.

"*Matter Out Of Place*," he said. "But that doesn't mean they don't *matter. Everyone matters!*" It was a conviction that shaped his entire personal philosophy. "Everywhere," he said, "the living seek safety behind walls. Well, I wanted to create a safe space for the dead."

Rumor was that Primitive was ruled by a character named Baron Steen, who only accepted survivors willing to swear off modern conveniences and live according to his unconventional environmentalist ideas.

Syrkis saw it as an opportunity to corner the black market on modern conveniences, but more importantly he wanted ocean access. He intended to assemble a fleet large enough to sail his whole community south, to Jekyll Island, Georgia.

We left the highway and the air filled with carousel music, and the smell of kettle corn. Flickering lights lead the way to the main entrance where giant banners advertised sideshows like Fenix the Disappearing Man, Concha the Armless Trapeze Star, Orgo the Prognosticator, and La Santa the World's Strongest Woman. But all along the path were smaller, inconspicuous signs for the gift shop.

Syrkis explained that the G's, which he called *patrons,* were attracted by all the lights and music, which corralled them through the main gates and into an attraction called *Chapel Perilous.*

"What's in there?" I asked.

"Only what you take with you," he answered ominously. It was a hall of mirrors, or as he called it a *chamber of reflection.* "Don't ask me why, but even the most frenzied patron finds tranquility surrounded by their own reflection."

That was, or course, the purpose of Emilio. G's follow G's. Emilio's job was to attract any lurkers in the surrounding area and lure them back to Wheel Top to get caught up in the spectacle of it all. And, hopefully, anyone still alive that followed Emilio out of curiosity had the good sense to follow signs for the gift shop.

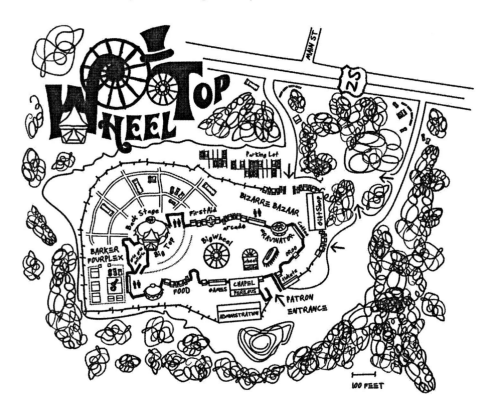

Wheel Top consisted of a number of carefully regulated zones, separated by wooden fences. Backstage was safe for the living. It included the gift shop, concessions, an administrative office, and even a coffee shop. It was a trailer village with everything from RVs to camping tents. Everything compact. Everything mobile. Everything owned by a huge extended family. Backstage is where the Barker family lived, worked and traded. Inside the fences, but outside the walls.

As welcoming as Syrkis' demeanor suggested, the Barkers didn't just accept anyone. A tour was one thing, but they typically only let contracted labor backstage. And frontstage was only open to the public

158

during a show. They were still deciding whether outsiders could officially join the clan at all, except by marriage.

The Barkers had plenty of food stockpiled in concessions. Animals, they discovered, could eat infected meat that wasn't too rancid, except it seemed to make them more aggressive. So they wouldn't feed it to animals they raised for meat. The community was split whether or not to feed it to dogs. They also had chickens and goats. But what Wheel Top had in surplus, what they had to trade, was electricity.

So, a market bloomed. Nomads began following Wheel Top, setting up camp outside the fences wherever they stopped. So Syrkis dubbed a section of backstage the *Bizarre Bazaar* where friendly outsiders were free to set up vending like a flea market. The Bizarre Bazaar had one rule. *Break a deal, feed the wheel.* If someone broke their word, engaged in fraud, or committed any property crime, they would be sentenced to some term inside the Big Wheel.

"What's the Bit Gheel?" I asked.

He thought for a moment, weighing his response. "I can't tell you, but if you'll go frontstage with me I can show you."

On the other side of the walls was frontstage, which was safe for the patrons. An immersive, carefully engineered environment where G's were commonplace, even domesticated.

In the wild G's have two modes; search and destroy. If they see you, smell you, hear you, or in anyway become aware that you're alive, they attack. But left alone long enough and they revert to their muscle memory. Some of them do something resembling hunting, especially the fast ones, but mostly they just kinda wander around, kinda docile.

Syrkis and the Barkers called these modes *safe* and *triggered*. Frontstage was a *safe space* where the patrons were painstakingly sheltered from anything that triggered them. All the carnival staff wore tBlocker on all exposed skin. Maybe it was the color, maybe it was the smell, probably both, but in the clown makeup they could safely walk among the patrons.

Syrkis accepted wild G's in trade, and paid double for runners. After a period of observation they called *auditions* they assigned handlers to the high performers to train their latent behaviors into useful labor.

Although, being a handler took some training too. The dead couldn't be broken with a whip. That only aggravated them. The trick was misdirection.

If a trainee ever triggered in a safe space their handler was expected to put them down immediately. Because a triggered patron triggered other patrons, which could have a cascading effect through the whole crowd.

Conformity kept the patrons safe. Look like them. Act like them. Sound like them. Smell like them. All of these precautions made it possible to walk among them. But Syrkis discovered they could also be trained to recognize other ingroups and outgroups.

"In the beginning, before I invented tBlocker, I noticed a kind of group preference behavior, so I conducted a few experiments." Syrkis was speaking my language. "I filled the *Gravinator* with dead patrons. It's this ride that locks everyone inside a spinning saucer, but the lights inside spin the opposite direction. And the centrifugal force creates a kind of fake gravity inside. It's very disorienting. So I put half the patrons in red shirts, and half in blue shirts, then spun them for about thirty minutes, and left them locked inside overnight. And you know what I found in the morning?"

"What?" I asked eagerly.

"When we opened the Gravinator they were all in safe mode, but the crowd had segregated into two groups according to their shirt color, all on their own."

"No way!" I was shocked.

"Yes way! And you know what's even weirder? When I went in to wrangle the patrons I realized that the red shirts were harder to trigger than the blue shirts."

"What? Why?" I asked.

"Because by coincidence I was wearing a red shirt. Once a patron has imprinted on a group, a living person presenting like that group is less triggering, as long as they don't make eye contact, or trigger them some other way. But the whole group might attack a new dead patron in the wrong color shirt."

That scenario would never happen in the wild, but Wheel Top was a controlled environment where it was possible to orchestrate such experiments. So he converted the entire carnival into a laboratory of undead behavior. Some patrons even imprinted so strongly on their handlers that they were almost completely safe with them.

I thought of the dead S-Mart employees. The Major must have made a similar discovery about work uniforms.

The backstage tour ended behind the Big Top, the largest stage in the circus. "If you want to see the Big Wheel, if you want to see what really makes Wheel Top the beacon of light that it is, we'll have to go frontstage. But it's not safe in there without tBlocker. Company policy." He offered us the bottle.

We all hesitated.

"Hey, I didn't make it rain. I just invented the best umbrella," he said.

Ellie and Darleen still refused, but I couldn't resist. I applied the cream to my face and hands and followed Syrkis behind the curtain.

We stepped out on the stage, interrupting a band of dead musicians fumbling with broken instruments. We were surrounded by theater seating, empty except for a few distracted patrons. Everyone completely ignored us.

Syrkis motioned for me to stay quiet with one hand, and to follow him with the other. We walked slowly through the seats and out the main exit of the Big Top.

Outside was a twinkling wonderland of family fun. Spinning rides and games of chance. All populated and clumsily operated by G's.

Directly in front of us, in the center of it all, was his crowning achievement. It was a ferris wheel, converted to spin on its side like a carousel. The entire structure had been wrapped with chain link fencing. It was a giant spinning cage. And as we approached I saw through the fence and realized the genius of it all.

The arms of the wheel formed eight separate compartments, like the slices of a lemon, and each segment was filled with patrons, organized by color. Red, orange, yellow, green, blue, indigo and violet. Around and around. Over and over. G's chasing G's, which spun the wheel, which turned the motor, which charged the battery, which powered the entire blinkered arcade.

Twenty Four: By The Numbers

By the time Syrkis finished our tour of Wheel Top the sky was grey over the Bizarre Bazaar, and vendors were packing it in.

Syrkis offered to let us stay in his guest trailer, and head home in the morning, but I didn't feel comfortable staying out overnight without the other crew knowing. We tried to make radio contact with the ship, but we were out of range, so I saw an opportunity to introduce Syrkis to Larry.

I knew from experience that Larry's Ammo was within radio range of the ship. So, I thought I'd make the introduction, touch base with the others, and make the decision about a night hike then.

It was so funny to think about, both Syrkis and Larry shining their neon flashing obvious signs into the darkness, but not finding each other, even though they were less than two miles apart. Just across the highway and a few blocks in.

Although Syrkis was new in town, I'm sure Emilio's camera would have found Larry eventually, or Larry would have heard the carnival music.

Before we left Wheel Top, Syrkis retrieved a giant industrial cable spool from a pop up booth alongside the highway. It must have been over ten feet high, massive and heavy, yet it rolled easily on its steel rims like a giant wagon wheel. He used it to string rope lights along the power lines, across Highway 25 and into Blanoby, affixing the cable with a long metal polearm, so the twinkling lights signaled the way home, and potentially snared any witless *MOOP* that happened by.

Syrkis called it *hospitality*. He liked to offer some free electricity as his opening salvo on what he anticipated would eventually become enthusiastic trade negotiations. Of course, what he actually called it was *horse brutality*. He said, "You can beat a dead horse but you can't lead it to water." To him, electricity was the promise of modern living, of civilization. And in an uncivilized world it was a gift too good to refuse. It also meant he came to trade. It was an olive branch that served as an advertisement. In his mind he was literally evangelizing salvation. He was promising coexistence with the dead, and electricity symbolized all that to him.

After only a short distance I realized Syrkis had a funny way of using familiar idioms . . . incorrectly. Instead of saying, "six of one, half a dozen of the other," he'd say, "half of one, six dozen of the other." When I asked him why he preferred life on the road he told me, "a rolling stone is worth two in the bush." And whenever he did it, there was a gleam in his eye, like he knew, and he wanted you to know he knew you knew. He had all the guile of a con artist, which made it impossible not to trust him implicitly.

Larry and Syrkis hit it off immediately. One a nomad, the other a recluse. One an innovator, the other a creature of habit. But both business men.

We all decided it best to claim one of the eighteen frequencies on a standard handheld CB radio, to better communicate with each other. I knew the Major and Dr. Blum were still using channel thirteen, because we kept tabs on the channel. That's why our away teams used channel four on the opposite side of the dial.

Syrkis already used eight and eighteen, for operations and administration, irrespectively. We could try him on either of those and if it wasn't him the message would chain letter to him eventually.

When Syrkis asked Larry what channel he'd like to claim, he literally pulled out a twenty sided die and a rolled a five.

Syrkis and Larry were already conceptually dividing the spoils of adding Larry's Ammo to the Primitive trade route by the time Darleen successfully hailed Alix. Soon Larry would be stocked with all kinds of great stuff, and we'd be hawking homemade jerky for trade.

"Darleen, is that you?!" yelled Joel Saxen's voice through the radio. The signal was choppy, but we were receiving them.

Darleen walked outside to find a clearer signal, and I followed.

"Affirmative! This is Darleen. Do you copy? And why are you using the voice modulator? Over," answered Darleen.

"Darleen!" barked Joel. "We've been trying to reach you for hours. Are all crew accounted for? Over." We couldn't actually tell who was on the line, since everyone sounded like Joel through the modulator.

"Yes. We're all fine. Over. We'll give you a full report when we get back. Over." said Darleen.

"Well get back quick. You've got to listen to this! Over!" There was a scraping noise, like someone grabbed the mic and dragged the base along the desk. "Numbers!" interrupted Joel in a slightly different pitch. *I think it's Niles.* "We picked up a signal!" came another slightly different Joel Saxen voice. *Maybe Hephae?*

Ellie grabbed the radio from Darleen. "What kind of signal? What is it? Over."

There was a ruckus like they were struggling over the mic now. It was like listening to Joel argue with himself. "It's 128 digits. Over and over again. I've been trying to figure it out for hours. It's not pi. It's not the Fibonacci sequence. Just get back here and help us figure this out. That's an order . . . Over!" *That must be Alix.*

Before we left I asked Syrkis if he knew anything about a 128 digit number. He just shrugged, but in a way that seemed patronizing. Like he knew, but wanted me to figure it out for myself. "Maybe some kind of code," he suggested unhelpfully.

By the time we got back to the ship it was the final moments of dusk, before the sky went black. The stars and moon were out, but there was still a purple glow in the western sky.

Everyone was in the studio, crowded around the radio, tuned to a frequency where a woman's voice was calling out numbers.

"172. 16. 254. 1."

"What do they mean?" I asked.

"They don't mean anything!" cried Alix. "I tried everything. It's not a replacement alphabet. It's not prime numbers. I even tried radio frequencies. It's just nonsense."

"Look!" Hephae pulled out a page of handwritten numbers. Hundreds, maybe thousands. "Sometimes it changes, every hour or so, but never the whole number sequence, only a few numbers, But always 128 numbers. But here's the weirdest thing."

He spun the dial and fiddled with the knobs honing in on another signal.

"192. 168. 1. 15. 24." It was another number station. This time in a male voice.

"There's five or six of them. But they come and go," Hephae explained. "Different frequencies. Different voices. But always the same 128 number sequence on every station."

"If we had two receivers we could triangulate a broadcast position," suggested Niles. "If one's nearby."

"Do what?" Asked Ellie.

"The Feds used to do it with trucks to track down pirate radio stations. Basically you use two mobile antennas to pincer on a direction and you search until you find the transmitter," explained Niles.

"Like using two tachyon beams to find a cloaked ship in Tsar Trek?" asked Hephae.

"Exactly," agreed Niles.

"Do they both have to be mobile?" asked Alix. "Couldn't we use the studio receiver?"

"I don't see why not. The Feds searched in a grid pattern. But if we used the studio as an anchor and carried a mobile receiver in larger and larger circles, I bet that would work. But it'd have to be close. The accuracy will get worse and worse the further we get from the studio," explained Niles.

"Ok, so where are we going to get another receiver,"

"Let's go ask Syrkis," suggested Darleen. "He uses radio. Heck, this might even be his broadcast, or someone else on the road to Primitive."

"No, this isn't his style." I added. "He's too flamboyant for something this cryptic. If this were him he'd be broadcasting carnival music and product placement. Besides, I have a feeling any help from him comes at a price. But I have an idea where to find a receiver. Follow me."

Twenty Five: The Ghool Bus

The garage, now cast in the role of the cargo bay of the ISS Porcupette was about to become a shuttle bay.

It used to be Dad's *Man Cave,* which was sometimes an inventor's workshop and sometimes a study. It had four doors, an entrance in the lounge, another in the studio, a door to the back deck, and of course a garage door to street.

Dad also cut out a few skylights for ventilation. That had to be how the PorcScouts got in, although there was no trace of them breaking and entering. They really were like porcupine ninjas.

One side of the cargo bay was a huge workshop. Dad kept all the power tools there so the noise wouldn't disturb the rest of the cabin. It was full of all kinds of pet projects he was always working on. He was an endless tinkerer.

Before we arrived the Siblinghood was basically using the garage as a dump. What they didn't know was that under the trash heap was a giant black tarp. And under the tarp was a school bus. The short kind. I opened the shuttle bay door so we could shovel all the garbage into a couple pit traps out front, and then yanked back the tarp.

We all choked on dust that swirled so thick we couldn't see. But once it was clear, there it was. "A few of the PorcScouts parents picked it up years ago when the group got too big to fit everyone in a minivan. They wanted it for field trips and stuff, but it had some problems and Dad wasn't much of a mechanic."

Engine parts were splayed out on the ground next it. One of Dad's many unfinished projects.

"Where's this receiver you're talking about?" asked Alix, always keeping us on task.

"It's got an integrated radio system," I answered. "I'm sure we can boost the reception. The trouble is the engine doesn't run. It never really ran." I paused just long enough to see they weren't as optimistic as I was. "It's a little banged up, but once we can get it running, that's the mobile receiver we need. Anyone know how to fix an engine?"

"No" Alix's eyes gleamed. "But we're going to figure it out."

Hephae found Dad's repair manuals in the workshop and was confident he could fix the engine, provided we had all the parts we needed. Darleen jumped at the opportunity to help him. Meanwhile Alix worked with Niles to rig the radio system.

Hephae had to salvage all the parts they needed, but the only school buses for miles were at Thornhaven. So they'd have to jerry-rig it with parts from other compatible vehicles.

"Are you thinking what I'm thinking?" I asked.

"The crashed prison bus in Campton," answered Ellie.

"Exactly."

Ellie lead the away team, but she chose Hephae and Darleen. It would take them dangerously close to S-Mart, although I wasn't sure if it was more dangerous for them, or Dr. Blum.

The radio receiver on board worked just fine, but according to Niles that wasn't enough.

"The integrated antenna isn't going to work," Niles explained. "It has to be a directional antenna, so we can start mapping vectors and triangulating the signal."

"What's a directional antenna?" Alix asked.

"It's an antenna that only gets reception in one direction. Or it doesn't get reception in one direction. Either way. You have to be able to determine the direction of the signal. What we really need is a loop antenna."

"Where do we get that?"

"We build it."

Niles had been sorting all kinds of scrap trinkets and trash into bins in the workshop. He coiled a phone cable into a loop and wrapped it with electrical tape to hold the form. Then Alix helped him wire it into the bus system.

I tried to help but it wasn't really my skill set, and Niles and Alix seemed annoyed with me after a while, so I left them to it.

Torrance decided he needed to spend the day running around the yard in different shoes to figure out which were the fastest.

So, I spent a lot of time alone in the crow's nest with Stinky, keeping watch. I thought a lot about the night I met Ellie at Lochshire. We spent that first night on the roof of the building, and I swear she was flirting with me. At least I thought she was, but now she gives me the cold turkey. Or whatever that expression is.

Torrance screamed.

I lept to the window. *I was supposed to be watching him. I was lost in my head again!* I didn't see him.

I shot down the ladder and charged down the stairs, interrupted suddenly by Torrance's shrieking laughter. It was sometimes hard to guess what sounds from him meant.

"Guys! Check this out!" Torrance was in the shuttle bay. When I walked in he was climbed up on the hood of the bus with a can of spray paint. He'd covered the "SC" above the cab with a big sloppy "G" so it read, "GHOOL BUS."

We all laughed.

When the away team returned Ellie came up to the crow's nest to hang her rifle.

"I didn't kill him," she said. "I would have, but we didn't see him. No chatter on channel thirteen either."

With the engine parts acquired, we all worked on the bus together. While Hephae and Darleen focused on the mechanics, the rest of the crew painted it bright green with red splats along the side like blood splatter.

The next day, on a routine run to Larry's Ammo for incidentals, we snagged the steel wedge off a broken down snow plow we'd spotted. It took all of us, but we carried it home and bolted it to the Ghool Bus.

Ellie reinforced all the windows by welding bits of chain link fence to the outside. She even covered the door so G's couldn't break in. But we needed a way inside, so I cut a big hole in the roof and mounted a ladder I took from a neighboring boat dock to the side. That way we could get in through the roof hatch.

Using some of Dad's leftover dome building conduit, we turned the roof entrance into a locking hatch with a 360 degree gunport, which Torrance, in his infinite wisdom, painted to look like a turtle.

We gutted the inside. Took out all the seats except the front row, and repurposed the hydraulic wheelchair lift as a cargo loading ramp attached to the rear emergency exit.

"I like that it's still wheelchair accessible," mused Darleen. "In case we ever need that."

We installed two narrow bunk beds stacked behind the driver's seat, and enough cargo space for two weeks of supplies. Transmitter hunting would probably be our longest away mission so far.

Niles and Hephae were able to remove enough of the ships secondary computer components to construct a modest system aboard the Ghool Bus, running an abridged copy of the BIODAD. Mainly for the radio system, and navigation. Although, within Wi-Fi range the ship's system could take full control of the Ghool Bus system.

By the time we were done the Ghool Bus was a fortress, and ready for transmitter hunting, except it still didn't run.

Twenty Six: The Omnivore Engine

A working engine still needs fuel to run. There was quite a bit of gasoline stored in the bunker for the gas generator, but the Ghool Bus needed diesel.

I asked around and none of us really knew anything about diesel. Ellie knew her mom couldn't figure it out. Hephae knew putting gasoline in a diesel engine was a bad idea.

The obvious answer was to siphon fuel from other abandoned diesel vehicles, but which vehicles? We looked for garbage trucks at the local waste processing station, but they were all deployed. They could be anywhere. Lots of the boats around the lake ran on something called "marine diesel oil" but we had no way of knowing if it was compatible.

I hailed Larry first, to see if he knew where we could get some. He said Syrkis would know, but mainly wanted to know where Holland was with the meat. *He'd been missing deliveries.*

There was plenty of small game around. Rabbits, squirrels, even the occasional pheasant. It wasn't a lot, but we were grateful for any fresh meat. Stinky devised a strategy of getting behind small prey and chasing it toward Holland with the crossbow. But the more time he spent as Niles, the less time he spent as Holland, and Holland was the one who hunted.

"He's been too busy with car repair to hunt recently. Will you take packaged beef jerky?" I asked.

He agreed, and I promised to deliver some on my way to Wheel Top. And to swap the HK45 back for the Mosquito. *I think I'll keep the Mosquito for myself.*

So, Syrkis has diesel, but what did we have to trade? Obviously he'd want Bicycle Girl, but that was out of the question. Wheel Top had food, weapons, fuel, even family. We had nothing he wanted. What he wanted was a vast trade empire across the eastern seaboard. We had no way to provide that.

I decided to make the call anyway. "Syrkis Barker? This is Max, do you read? Over."

There was static for bit, "Yeah, this is operations on channel eighteen. If you want administration they're on channel eight. Over."

I switched channels. "Paging Syrkis Barker. This is Max. Over."

"Syrkis is on one," came another voice.

I turned to channel one, which was already transmitting the sound of moist smacking, like he was eating something.

"Yeah, what's up kid?" He paused a long time. "Look kid, don't make me break the camel's back before the horse. The era of over saying 'over' all over is over. You're either going to get a sense of my pace, or you're not. Just don't interrupt me and we'll do just fine."

"Oh . . . ok." I stammered. "I'm hoping you've got diesel fuel to trade. But I'm not sure what you'd want in return."

"Fresh vegetables, my boy. That is the currency of the sea, especially vitamin C. But I'll tell you what I want from you. And I'm willing to trade big . . . I want your ship."

"My ship?!" I puzzled. *Did he mean the Stranger?* "What are you talking about?"

"I've heard the radio chatter, you kids have some kind of Jetson's World cruise liner on that lake, and I'm headed to the coast. So, how about you let me hoist that sucker outta there, and you can take as much fuel as you need, and all the civilian vehicles you want to burn it in."

"Oh! It's not a cruise liner. It's a cabin we call a ship as a game," I explained. "I do have a fishing boat, but we've already got our own wheels, anyway."

"Hey kid, don't count your chips before you fold. I'll tell you what. I got some errands to run this afternoon, why don't you come with me and we'll talk about diesel engines?"

We agreed to meet at Larry's Ammo so I could deliver the jerky, and return the pistol. Syrkis arrived with a .22 rifle strung over his shoulder, and we walked back to Wheel Top.

While we were walking I noticed Syrkis was constantly looking upward. I assumed he was watching for Emilio, but it turns out he was checking the telephone poles. When he found what he was looking for he drew his rifle, and took aim at what looked like a metal trash can mounted under the cross pole like a coconut.

"What are you doing!" I asked.

"Hunting transformers."

"Seriously?"

"The grid is out, and these distribution transformers are full of mineral oil, just waiting to be liberated." He took aim again, and plinked a .22 caliber hole in the bottom of the drum. Moments later globs of what looked like dark honey dribbled out of the bottom.

Syrkis caught it in a top hat designed to deposit the fluid in his expanding clown pants.

"It insulates the connections inside, and works as a coolant. You can salvage a few gallons this way, and it adds up."

Mineral oil?

He stopped every few blocks to plink another transformer, but he was adamant that we not drain every one. He said we had to leave some for others, but he also seemed to think he had some superstitious *sense* which was ones had a big payload. *He's building a new electrical grid and sabotaging the old one.*

"Max, let me tell you a story about five clowns." It seemed Syrkis was incapable of remaining silent. He probably needed the world to chatter on the outside as much as his mind chattered on the inside. As a result he was always telling stories.

"See these five clowns, they died. So I put them in Chapel Perilous to calm them down. I knew more than anything they wanted to chew off my ugly mug, so I rigged a hatch in the ceiling where I could lean in. Let them get lost chasing my reflection through the maze. But what I needed to know was what they were afraid of. I needed a deterrent."

"Electrocution?" I guessed.

"Hey kid, that's right!" He smiled. "You really know your stuff."

"While I was at Thornhaven they used tasers," I explained. "It shorts out their nervous system. Paralyzes them."

"Exactly right, plus it really pisses 'em off. So, I got my guys to rig up something special for me. First we built this observation room inside the chapel. It was a glass house paved in good intentions. It had all outfacing one-way-mirrors so we'd be able to watch them from a safe space. Then we installed a playground slide in the center of the maze. In theory they could climb up and get me, except the ladder was set to electrocute them if they reached the top. Then they'd slide back down to the beginning of the maze. But it didn't just zap one clown. It zapped all of them."

"But why?" I asked. "That just seems cruel for no reason."

"Because the Devil's in the pudding! Pretty soon they all learned to stop going for the ladder."

"Oh . . . right."

"But it gets better. See, the next thing we did was take out one clown, who's afraid of ladders to this day, and put in a new clown. Guess what happened?"

"The new clown went for the slide and got electrocuted?" I guessed.

"Oh, he went for it alright, but he didn't make it." Syrkis cackled out loud just remembering it. "You should have seen the look on his face. The moment his buddies realized he was going for the slide they tackled him and dragged him to the ground."

"Wait! G's ganged up on another G to keep it away from you?" I asked.

"That's right," he smiled smugly. "But it gets better. I replaced another of the original clowns with a new one, and the same thing happened. Then again, and again, and pretty soon I had a chapel full of clowns, deathly afraid of attacking me, and willing to take down anyone who tried. But they didn't know why, and they'd never personally been electrocuted."

"That means they learned the behavior from each other . . ." I pondered.

"Not only that," he continued, "it means they're social creatures."

"What do you mean?" I asked.

"Well, the first five learned by electrocution, but the rest didn't. They learned by being pummeled by the others."

"So?"

"So, the pummeling isn't the deterrent. It's not about pain. I could punch these MOOPs in the face all day and they'd never learn anything. It only works because they're being punished by their own kind . . . The disapproval of their peers. That's the deterrent. Because we are, deep down in our lizard brains, fundamentally social creatures. Now all my clowns go through the electric slide program."

"And you basically have an army of undead bodyguards."

"Yup. And that's just the start of it."

I had to hand it to him. Syrkis had a fascinating way of figuring things out. It was scientific, but not method. More like scientific instinct.

When we got to Wheel Top he took me to the Barker fourplex. It was a small gated compound way in the back. Four units, reserved for his inner circle. His immediate family. Unit one was his personal chateaux.

"Do you know why we stopped here, Max?"

"No," I admitted. "I assume it was a good midpoint between two other bartertowns."

"Not really. I stopped here because we need fuel."

"But you said–"

"I know what I said, and I meant it. You know what's great about diesel engines, Max?"

"What?"

"They're omnivores," he said.

"Huh?"

"A standard engine is like a freshly converted vegan. It's fussy. And regular gasoline only has a shelf life of about two years, less if it's got ethanol in it. You can extend it with chemical stabilizers, or isopropyl alcohol, but it's not ideal. Plus, it evaporates."

He pulled the fluid sack out of his giant clown pants and poured the oil into a steel drum outside his RV. "Nine gallons from five transformers. Not a bad haul for a morning walk. You strain that through a t-shirt, mix it with enough hard alcohol so it pours like hot maple syrup, and you got fuel for any diesel engine."

"No way!" I couldn't believe it.

"Believe it," he said. "Diesel engines will burn just about anything."

"Marine fuel?" I asked.

"You bet. Motor oil. Kerosene. Heck automatic transmission fluid burns hotter and cleaner than standard diesel fuel. I once made it across the Arizona desert on nothing but fumes and window cleaner."

"Really." I was in disbelief.

"Combustion is chemistry. Window cleaner is about ten percent methanol. You spray that into the intake manifold. The alcohol burns in the combustion chamber as fuel, and the water converts to steam. You ever been to a tractor pull? All that smoke billowing out is actually steam coming off the pistons. It actually improves your fuel economy. My own rig has six injectors, one for each piston. And I've got a second tank so once the engine gets hot I can switch to a mix of waste cooking oil from the funnel cake trucks. Makes it smell like fresh french fries, plus it keeps the injector pump lubricated."

"That's amazing!"

"But Wheel Top takes more than one pair of clown pants to get it's mojo risin'. We're headed for an electrical substation in Plymouth with a transformer the size of a hippy wagon. Crack that valve and it's gotta have hundreds of gallons of fluid. More than enough to get us to Portsmouth. But we gotta get to Plymouth first."

He pulled out his laptop. It had a huge *Alien Seed* sticker on the shell. He opened it, revealing a split screen of four video feeds, and tapped them each in sequence. "That's Emilio Airhart, Verna von Boom, *she's armed*, Lucy and Diamond. I sent them in an expanding orbit looking for semi trucks, air ports, construction sites, fire trucks, industrial farm equipment, restaurants. Even crude oil straight out of an oil well will burn well enough, if it's filtered. Well, Emilio found this near the Blanoby dump . . ."

He set the lower left hand video to full screen, and navigated with a video game controller. Emilio rose into the sky for an aerial shot, and then Syrkis used the software to zoom in on a vehicle.

"A dump truck? Do they have abnormally large oil pans or something?" I asked.

"Maybe . . . I'll check. It'll have ten to fifteen gallons of transmission fluid too. But more importantly they have about sixty gallons of hydraulic fluid. That'll get us to Plymouth."

"Wait! Do you keep recordings of these videos?" I asked.

"It's all in the archives," he assured me.

"Can you take us back to when Emilio crossed the lake?"

Twenty Seven: Watching the Watcher

Syrkis rewound Emilio's video all the way to when he was over Stinson Lake and paused. It showed a line of G's, a dozen or more, following Emilio into the lake. Most of them were in police uniforms, or in black robes, but all from different eras. It looked like the exhibits of a wax museum just walked off their platform.

"What a loss!" lamented Syrkis. "In my experience, dead police are higher functioning than average. A little cocky at first. But trainable."

I thought of Bicycle Girl. "The parasite likes aggressive brains. If cops are wired that way it probably preserves more of their higher brain functions." I speculated. "Can you zoom in?"

"Sure thing," Syrkis answered as he zoomed in on the edge of the ice.

"See there? Pause it," I said.

Syrkis paused it just as a very large man put a new crack in the ice, and toddled over the edge, but before the splash.

"Look at that. His shirt doesn't even fit," I observed. "Unless he put on about fifty pounds post mortem that's not his shirt. It's not even buttoned all the way. And look at his shoes." I pointed "Red bowling shoes? Not exactly standard police issue."

"You've got a point, Kid," agreed Syrkis. "But if someone is intentionally dressing them, that means this is a managed crowd."

"Managed by who?" I asked.

"Probably by this guy." Syrkis tapped the keyboard to rotate the image and zoomed in on the treeline at the edge of the lake.

There, dressed in a crisp new black police uniform, was Sheriff Nap. Behind him were Private Woz and Officer Cordell with dozens more G's waiting behind them instead of marching into the lake.

I gasped. "That's impossible!"

"What's up, do you know these guys?" asked Syrkis.

"Bad guys, from the school we escaped," I answered. "But they're dead! I saw their wounds. I looked into their eyes! They are dead," I insisted.

"Let's have a look." Syrkis zoomed in on Nap's face as it stared back at the camera with its dead eye, analyzing it. *Analyzing us.* "Maybe you can explain what we're looking at."

"I've seen this before. There was a herd that followed a dead postman—"

"Another uniform," Syrkis interrupted.

"And a jerk," I inserted. "His whole herd marched off a third story balcony, but not him. He stopped. He knew better."

"Just like the sheriff down there?" said Syrkis.

"Exactly," I agreed. "And the rest of them, maybe they're not following the music. Maybe they're following the sheriff," I guessed.

"Possible . . . It's a good theory. If he spent his life herding crowds I suppose he might have retained some of those skills, in some sense, after death. Of course that means the dumb ones went into the lake, and the smarter ones are left in the crowd." He stroked his beard. "It's practically like natural selection," quipped Syrkis ominously.

"G's herding G's." I shuddered.

"Why do you call them G's?" Syrkis asked. "What does it stand for?"

"It's something different to everyone," I said. "It can stand for whatever you want, I guess."

"How about a *Graboids?*" he mused.

"There's no way they dressed themselves. They were in different clothes when they died. This herd has a handler . . . somewhere."

"Let's roll back the tape," he suggested.

I agreed, eagerly.

Their trail led back to a little village called Ellsworth, so small I'd never heard of it, even though it was only a few miles away from where I grew up. Syrkis looked it up on his handheld device.

"Wait! You've got internet!?" I demanded.

"What I've got is a CB radio way more powerful than the FCC would have ever allowed, which gives me access to a variety of information sources, including transmitted data packets not entirely unlike the internet," Syrkis explained as he scrolled through something called *Wikipocalypse.* "Ellsworth is the birthplace of something called the *Cliosophistry Society.* That explains all the black robes."

"It looks like the whole town joined the herd." I pointed to children, dressed in little black suits.

"Everyone's got funeral clothes," quipped Syrkis. "Whoever's shepherding this flock has them gathering at someplace called the *Oliver Ellsworth Historic House.* Some local haunt."

"But look at the video," I pointed. "Emilio drew out some of them, there's a hundred or more still fenced in."

We couldn't tell any more about them from the video, but Syrkis agreed to scramble Emilio and Verna to surveil Ellsworth Village. Meanwhile Lucy and Diamond patrolled the sky above the junkyard for threats.

Syrkis drove a purple pickup truck that we took out to the dump truck to harvest the fuel. "I pretty much never pass up a diesel engine I can salvage," he boasted. "Especially one with a manual transmission. This thing's got a mechanical fuel injection that would survive an EMP."

Twenty Eight: Transmitter Hunting

"Ok! We got the bus fixed. We got the mobile receiver. We got the gas. Now can we go already?" pleaded Alix. "If I don't figure out what those numbers are I'm going to go bonkers!"

"Think about it!" said Hephae. "If they're moving frequencies and intensities they're either mobile themselves, or they're a network of people. They could be military, like a search party."

"Searching for what?" Alix asked.

Ellie and I exchanged knowing glances.

"Who knows?" I answered. "There's also a chance we'll find other survivors, like some kind of communication network. Maybe we can finally get some answers."

"It's some kind of encryption. They're probably computer geeks," added Niles. "Computer geeks are usually good people. Just a little weird sometimes." He spoke in Holland's voice, but I knew whenever he talked about computers it was actually Niles.

"How could you know that?" asked Ellie.

"My brother was a geek. Went to trade shows and robot fights and stuff. Whoever they are, they've got working radio transmitters, lots of them, so they're technical. And they're communicating through code, which means they're cautious. They're trying to stop bad guys from finding them. That means they're good guys."

"You're some kind of genius!" Alix seemed smitten.

We loaded the Ghool Bus with supplies and Niles explained the procedure.

"The reception is only clear when the loop antenna is pointed directly at the signal, like the eye of a storm. When it's misaligned, the signal stops. So, you've got to turn the antenna by hand until we find the strongest signal. When you do, you're lined up with the transmitter, and you mark that direction with a line on the map. Here I did the first one already."

He handed me his copy of the Denton's Sugar Shack map with the ship marked and a line drawn diagonally through it.

"That's our first vector," he said.

"But this points right into downtown Campton," I observed. "Maybe it is a military code. You're sure this is the frequency I gave you?"

"It is, and it does. That's a good theory, but don't make any assumptions yet. The transmitter could be anywhere along that line, forward or backward. So, to know for sure we gotta get another reading from somewhere else on the map. The further away from the first vector the better. Distance is the key to triangulation, just like it takes two eyes to see three dimensions. Wherever the two lines cross, that's where we go next. The more vectors, the more accuracy. It's that simple."

"This'll work perfect!" I beamed. "Just make sure there's enough cable so while I'm driving you can operate the antenna from the roof."

I had hoped Ellie would come with me, so we could spend some time together, but it really was better if Niles came. Alix and Niles were the radio experts. Having one of them on both ends made the whole operation run much smoother.

Radio broadcasting seemed more like voodoo to me than science. I hardly understood any of it, but I understood the geometry of the search pattern. So Niles stayed on the CB with Alix on the ship, while I took our bearings and marked the map.

The radio signal was pointing us west and east, so we needed to get a second reading further north, or south. So, we decided to go to Plymouth for the second reading. It was directly south of Campton, so if that's where the transmitter was, we should have gotten a perpendicular vector.

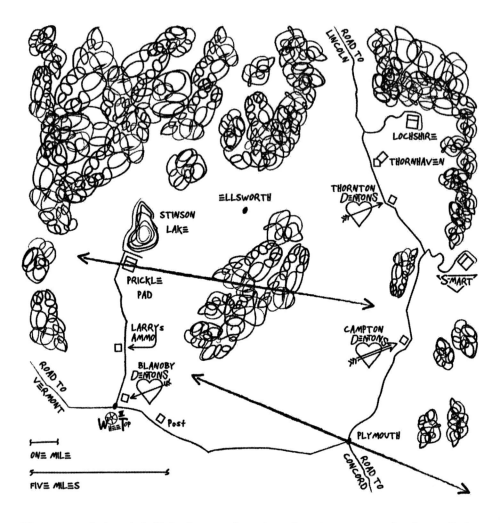

The second signal definitely wasn't pointed at Campton. *That's a relief.* It pointed more northwest, which meant the transmitter was off the map. Probably in Wentworth, or somewhere further along the Primitive trade route.

To confirm whether or not Wentworth was the source of the transmission we drove further south to Dorchester for another reading. It was off the trade route, and more than once we had to push abandoned vehicles off the road, but it was easy for the Ghool Bus. *This thing is a beast!*

The signal in Dorchester didn't point north to Wentworth. It pointed northwest like the others, which meant the transmitter was further out.

Someone in Dorchester took a shot at us from a church steeple, and since we had no reason to start a firefight with territorial survivors we instantly retreated and headed back north.

Next we got back on the trade route and drove north to Warren. We picked up some radio chatter about organic vegetables at a bartertown further north in Haverhill. They called it *Stonecrest*. But the vector in Warren was slightly southwest, instead of northwest like the others, so we headed for Orford.

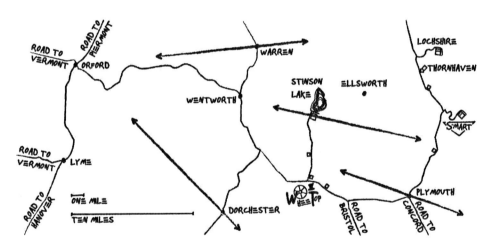

The road from Wentworth to Orford was hardly a road at all. Just two roughly paved lanes winding through dense forest. The occasional abandoned farmhouse, or a covered bridge over a mountain stream. The closest thing to civilization was a baseball diamond someone built in a field near Baker Pond.

Once we were in Orford the signal spun like a compass in a magnetic storm. We were close. And after a few circles around town we tracked the signal down to a campus of buildings called *Rivendell Conservatory*.

It seemed like a suitable place for survivors. There was a perimeter fence, and near the driveway were twenty one recently dug graves. Sure enough, one of them was the grave of Mark Freeman, Jack's father.

Before the collapse, Rivendell had been some kind of school for gifted children. The marquee in front still boasted the victory of their debate team, the *Philosoraptors.*

We circled the campus and narrowed it down to one building.

We tried hailing the ship to let them know we found the place, but we were way out of range for the CB radio. The only thing left to do was go inside and investigate.

> *Our mission is to foster lifelong learners, positive contributors to society and proactive, healthy adults.*

The bubbly friendly letters of the Rivendell Conservatory mission statement greeted us as we entered the facility. I was armed with the Mosquito. Holland had his crossbow.

As a school, Rivendell reminded me a lot of Thornhaven, but it seemed to have the opposite temperament. Everywhere we looked we found messages of student-directed learning, individually tailored curriculums and mentorships to develop real-world skills. Not all the conformity and standardized testing demanded when I was in school.

A thriving community survived here, but now there was almost no trace of them. Every scrap of useful supplies and equipment were stripped from the place. There was not a vehicle in sight. Odder still, we saw no evidence of gunfire, or G attacks. *They must have left voluntarily.* But they left the signal.

From my perspective the transmitter could be anywhere, but Niles had a better instinct about such things. He went straight to the highest point on campus, the bell tower above the library.

Sure enough, inside the housing of the bell was a rack of equipment I barely understood.

"It's not a transmitter, it's a repeater!" exclaimed Niles.

"What?" I asked.

"The signal's not from here. This equipment is receiving a weak signal and retransmitting it at a higher power, so that the broadcast can cover longer distances without degrading. Look." He named all the components as he ran his hand down the rack. "An antenna system, a receiver, a controller and a transmitter. Look here!" He ran to the window. "Solar power, and a satellite dish! This is a hub in a much larger communication network."

I spotted a piece of equipment he missed. "Niles look here. This looks like a Wi-Fi router, but look what's tied to it."

It was a scroll of parchment, tied to the router with a purple ribbon. I pulled the tail of the bow gingerly, almost afraid it was a boobytrap. We both watched eagerly as I unfurled it, revealing an old fashioned script inside.

Twenty Nine: The Pirate Code

In all ages, the prevailing Crown slanders any who refuse to swear allegiance or grovel for licenses. It commissions swarms of officers and privateers to usurp our time, travel, and treasure. The Crown calls it 'piracy' to explore frontiers beyond its influence. So the responsibility falls upon us to define the conduct among pirates.

First, a pirate is the sole authority over their own life, and may not be crimped into service.

Second, duties are created by consent. Claims of obligation without consent are invalid.

Third, no pirate, nor crew, however commissioned, may initiate hostilities against any other.

Fourth, a pirate may, without permission or rank, defend themselves against any hostile party.

Fifth, no captain, nor crew can possess rights exceeding or violating those of an individual pirate.

So, if you agree that the tyranny of the Crown has sailed on sea and land long enough, and wish to shake the shackles of the world, then boldly declare, #APiratesLifeForMe!

"Max, does the BIODAD in the Ghool Bus have web browsing?" asked Niles.

"Yeah, technically, but not without signal. Why?"

"If we can connect to this Wi-Fi network, I want to try something."

We went back down to the bus, and sure enough, the BIODAD was able to connect to a network called "winsome lewsome" but it wanted a password.

"Isn't it obvious?" asserted Niles. "Look at the Pirate Code. *Hashtag a pirates life for me exclamation point no spaces.*"

I typed it in, *#APiratesLifeForMe!*, and sure enough it reported full data signal, except every page I tried to access loaded as, "This site can't be reached. ERR_CONNECTION_REFUSED."

"Great. Full access to a dead internet," I bemoaned.

"Maybe not," injected Niles. I've been thinking about these numbers. Did you notice how often 172 and 192 showed up."

"Yeah, but I didn't know what to make of it," I said.

"Well, that's really common with IP addresses."

"What's an *IP address?*"

"IP stands for *Internet Protocol*," he explained. "It's a numerical address for every device on a network. It's basically a routing number for everything on the internet."

"So, you're saying this transmission, the 128 numbers, could be some kind of directory of active websites?"

"Four numbers per IP address, that's thirty two websites. Probably thirty two different pirate crews," he speculated. "That explains why some of them change from time to time. If a group moves, or networks a new device, they'd have to broadcast the new address. Then when the other groups pick up the updated numbers they repeat it until it proliferates through the network."

"There could be repeater stations like this all over the country," I said.

"And with the satellite dish on the ship we should have no trouble accessing the network," he added. "Open up a browser. I want to try something."

Niles set the Ghool Bus radio to play the numbers and entered first four that sounded like an IP address into the zPad. It brought up the homepage of a merchant ship called *The Black Sale*.

Thirty: Infection Science Hour

Once we got back to the ship, BIODAD used the satellite dish to connect to the Pirate Radio Network. Alix set us up as a radio repeater on the network, and it was pretty much just like having internet like before.

We browsed through a dozen of the addresses in the directory. Some were blogs. Others were radio shows. One was a video channel exploring the skull crushing capacity of various common household items.

The network spanned the country, and included many of the radio hosts Joel Saxen's network before the collapse, so *Info Planet* got it's syndicated audience back.

I was downstairs eating a bowl of Mighty O's, researching weather patterns in BIODAD's records. We didn't have milk, but we had boxes of non dairy creamer, which was almost as good. I was eating when I heard Ellie call from the studio. "Max, come listen to this!"

I drizzled some maple syrup on my bowl and went into the studio. "What is it?"

"I found something." She tapped the knob on the radio receiver lightly with one finger as the signal warbled into focus.

Tap tap tap. "Wwweee . . . ery speci . . . eeooo." The speakers whistled as she dialed passed the frequency and then back. *Tap tap.* "Oooeee . . . irst time we've had a live guest on Infection Science Hour." It was a smooth, sultry voice I recognized from the early days of the outbreak. "And as regular listeners know, I'm Dr. Stephanie Murphy, lead researcher here at Murphy's Lab, and I'm here with the newest addition to our team, right here in the studio."

It was the neurobiologist I saw Joel Saxen interview on *Info Planet* before the internet went down.

"Why don't you tell our listeners about yourself, Bri—"

"Whoa! No real names!" he interrupted. "I'm still in a legally precarious position by sharing what I'm about to tell your listeners."

"You think that's still an issue?" she asked sincerely.

"Well, whatever Feds are left have bigger fish to fry, but they're a pretty vindictive bunch. So for the time being, just call me *Agent Sovryn*."

"Cool!" Ellie leaned in.

"You got it." Dr. Murphy continued. "Agent Sovryn is a former technician from the Centers for Disease Control and handled highly classified records for a team of researchers studying what they termed *Necroambulism*."

"Before we get into it, let me just say, based on the short time I've been here, it looks like you've got an amazing operation here. Your experiments with hypothalamus suppression therapy seem like a real game changer. It's such an honor to be here."

"We'll have to save that for another show. Why don't you tell us what the CDC's been up to?" she asked.

"Oh boy! Well, it was definitely interesting work," he began. "But I actually wasn't directly involved in the research. I was one of a dozen technicians ensuring the security of the CDC's digital records before Necroambulism hit the population. And I certainly wouldn't say it's anything to be proud of. That's why I had to leave."

"What do you mean?" she asked.

"Since this pathogen was discovered the CDC has engaged in ever increasing ethical and human rights violations."

"Oh no!"

"I know!" he continued. "I hate to have to report this, but the public has a right to know. Maybe if they knew sooner they'd have been better prepared before the CDC declared Wildfire in New Hampshire."

"What's does *Wildfire* mean?" Dr. Murphy asked.

"It means that New Hampshire is a *sacrifice zone*. That the outbreak here is so severe that the Federal Government doesn't consider it worth saving. But the first incidents were actually on military bases." he explained.

"I knew it!" yelled Alix as she came into the studio to join us. "Government super soldiers gone wild!"

"Shhhh." I insisted.

She was still dressed in her PJs and rubbing the sleep out of her eyes. "What's going on?

"Ellie found Dr. Murphy on the radio," I answered.

"Dr. Who?"

"Shhhh!" Ellie and I shushed simultaneously.

Agent Sovryn continued, "At first it seemed like random soldiers were snapping and attacking their own. Spontaneous outbreaks were isolated, and put down very quickly. Anything large enough to attract media was spun as PTSD, or terrorism, or whatever. Internally they suspected some kind of biological weapon, but there was no obvious connection between the afflicted soldiers, and with US bases all over the globe it was virtually impossible to determine the country of origin. That's when a secret executive order from President Abedin empowered the CDC to assemble a team of top scientists and military liaisons to investigate the attacks."

"Is that what you found ethically questionable?" Dr. Murphy asked.

"Well, government secrecy is always a moral hazard, but I didn't start questioning my orders until I did some digging and uncovered plans to begin human experimentation," he explained.

"What kind of experiments?" she asked.

"Dr. Blum compiled a list of candidates who fit three criterion. They had to be former military personnel, had to be currently incarcerated, and had to have no living relatives."

"He wanted people with no one to come looking when they went missing," she inferred.

"Well, exactly. He acquired thirty one subjects from prisons all over the country. Most were rapists and murderers, but many were non-violent drug offenders. Dr. Blum needed to determine what triggered the incidents, but he had no idea where to begin. No idea what they were looking for. So he was essentially just torturing living subjects."

"How did you go along with this?" she asked.

Agent Sovryn continued, "Well, it was hard. When I raised my concerns with Dr. Blum he said these men were military personnel who gave their bodies to national security, and wasn't it better to give their bodies to science? He said these men were living wasted lives in prison, and we were giving them an opportunity to contribute to the greater good. I didn't like it, but from my perspective it was all blood work and brain scans. I didn't interact with the subjects."

"Then what happened?"

"Well, everything changed when Jeremy died," he answered.

"Who's Jeremy?" she asked.

"He was just a young kid, serving a life sentence for a minor marijuana charge under some bogus application of a three-strikes law. He was a real anti-establishment type, and the judge gave him the harshest possible sentence to make an example to others. Jeremy decided to go on a hunger strike to force them to release him from the program." Agent Sovryn paused, sounding hesitant. "Well, Dr. Blum decided starvation was worthy of study as a potential trigger, so he let Jeremy starve to death in solitary confinement. That's how they acquired their first active *specimen*. But they still didn't know what the pathogen was, or where it came from."

"We still don't. Not really," she added.

"They still don't know?!" I interrupted.

"Shhh!" Alix and Ellie shushed in unison. "Talk after the show!" insisted Alix.

Agent Sovryn continued, "Once they had a positive infection it became easier to create new specimens. Dr. Blum sent a request up the chain of command to acquire more prisoners. To study their behavior and potential vulnerabilities. The video of Jeremy's transformation was so shocking to the decision makers in the Capital that our department was given unlimited funding and controlling legal authority. When unwitting subjects started showing up believing they were receiving some kind of vaccine, that's when I knew it was time to leave. That was before the outbreak reached the public."

The CDC knew before Dad's email.

"At first I couldn't find anyone in the media who believed me," he continued, "and by the time the crisis was undeniable, the mainstream media was following a gag order from Homeland Security, and only reporting the official narrative."

"I guess it's a good thing you found pirate radio," Dr. Murphy remarked.

"I'm lucky I even survived. When I left Atlanta the CDC was non operational. Most of the staff had fled, or opted out. Police and military were overwhelmed. The city was in ruin, and even survivors were turning on each other for basic supplies. I was in a bad situation," Agent

Sovryn explained.

"How'd you make it out?" she asked.

"I have some basic combat training, so I could handle myself against the alt-life, but–"

"Wait. The what?" Dr. Murphy interrupted.

"The *alt-life*. Sorry, I got sick of colleagues calling them the *undead*. Even the name *Necroambulism* is problematic. It promotes magical thinking. For starters they're not all clinically dead. Sure, bodily death will trigger the transformation, but plenty of subjects became infected and fully transformed while remaining very much alive. I even saw records from fully rabid specimens that still had heart beats and respiratory function. The point is, even if the host body is technically dead, whatever's animating them is an alternate life form, not voodoo."

"I totally agree. Around here we've been calling them *partially deceased*. Please, go on with your story," she prodded.

He continued, "I was rescued by a group that calls themselves the *Pirates Of Savannah*. Before the outbreak they were one cell in a decentralized federation of hackers and crypto-anarchists called *Pirates Without Borders*. They protected whistleblowers, and helped leak government secrets. After the collapse they took over Jekyll Island, just south of Savannah, and they've been working with the *Pirates of Botany Bay* in Maine, and other cells to rebuild a global communication network using pirate radio and the dark web. Really ambitious stuff. They've also been establishing safe harbors and sea lanes, which is how I secured transport to your lab here."

"Well, I'm grateful for the company. Tell me more about the findings of the CDC's research team," Dr. Murphy suggested.

"Well, like I said, I was a technician, so I didn't see the behavior studies first hand, but I did see the reports, and there was a lot of gossip around the water cooler. The rumor was that Dr. Blum had this vision of isolating some of the features of Necroambulism, while suppressing others. He wanted to give the military a serum that would give a soldier the resilience against fatigue and physical injury, but still keep enough cognitive function to follow orders. That was the goal anyway."

"That's terrifying," she added.

Agent Sovryn continued. "At first all the specimens were starved to death like Jeremy, so those specimens were all more or less identical. Some lower brain functions remained, but all the upper brain, the cognitive part, that was gone. They became mindless eating machines. But once they started feeding them they discovered that the initial conditions of the transformation had a huge formative impact on the resulting behaviors."

"Initial conditions like what?" she asked.

"You name it. Cause of death. Brain activity. Even diet."

"Diet? Let's start there. What do you mean diet?"

"The cognitive degradation is slowed when they feed," he explained. "Even the bodily decomposition is slowed when they feed. It's as if the pathogen prefers to consume incoming material instead of the host body. So if a subject was force fed a raw meat diet before infection they're going to be higher functioning over all."

"That's fascinating! How functional can they be? How much can they retain?" she asked.

"In laboratory conditions, there's potentially no limit," he explained. "Dr. Blum thought that with the right dietary supplement a subject could achieve full retention. It's like the pathogen only consumes the host body until the host begins eating. In one case the subject was force fed cow brains and intestines and retained full cognitive function postmortem, although that subject still gradually declined after being starved."

"Full cognition! You mean he retained his memory? His identity?" She was shocked.

"Affirmative. We also discovered that cause of death played a huge role in the speed of the transformation. Subjects that died with high levels of cortisol in their blood transformed more quickly, while tranquil deaths took hours, even days to transform," Agent Sovryn explained.

"For listeners that don't know, cortisol is a hormone produced by the adrenal gland in response to stress or low blood sugar. It also suppresses the immune system, and aids in the metabolism of fat and protein," she elaborated.

"Exactly. They found the same correlation with adrenaline, but cortisol was the leading indicator."

"So, you're saying someone exposed to the infection while under stress will transform more quickly?" she asked.

"Sure, almost immediately," he answered.

"So, that's why an outbreak in a crowded place, like a shopping mall, spreads quickly, but a patient who dies sleeping in a hospital bed may remain asymptomatic for days?"

"Exactly. Stress facilitates the spread. So an officer in a firefight will change instantaneously, but someone who dies of natural causes might stay dead long enough to autopsy, or even bury before they reanimate."

"What about the last factor you mentioned? How does brain activity affect the transformation?" she asked.

"Yeah, this is the spookiest part. Brain scans revealed that the areas of the brain the least used are the first areas the disease consumes, and areas that were stimulated near infection were the best preserved."

"Wow! That could explain the residual behaviors I've observed."

"Like what?" Agent Sovryn asked.

"Like a driver locked in a car that keeps turning the wheel, an author that continues signing books, or a musician that continues to fumble with an instrument."

"Exactly. At the CDC they called that *residual procedural memory*. All the CDC subjects were former soldiers, so they used a salute test."

"What's a salute test?" she asked.

"If an alt-lifer returned a salute, or saluted a flag, researchers knew they were of the higher functioning sort, and selected them out for more rigorous behavioral testing. In custody they would even march in formation."

"That's really amazing! Marching together is so much more impressive a cognitive challenge than individual marching. It's not just bodily-kinesthetic intelligence. It requires audio-rhythmic intelligence to coordinate and synchronize."

"It's bigger than that!" he continued. "It requires ingroup outgroup thinking. It's practically tribal. The streets of Atlanta got so bad if you saw a squad of soldiers you couldn't always tell if they were alive or dead, because they attacked as a unit, like they remembered their training."

"I've seen this in the wild too!" Dr. Murphy exclaimed. "Keene is a college town, and I've definitely seen fraternity members in matching letter jackets hunting in packs."

"Well, they probably did that when they were alive too," Sovryn joked. "But it can be anything. Religious garb, sports teams, even political affiliation can trigger an association. In a big enough crowd, like follows like, and subgroups emerge. In fact, in a feeding frenzy subgroups will even fight other subgroups for food."

"That's incredible!" she exclaimed. "The conventional wisdom suggests they only identify food, but you're saying they distinguish friend from foe."

"Well, only some of them. You have to think of it like a pyramid of brain functions. *The higher the fewer.*"

"You mean the higher the brain function the fewer subjects retain it?" she asked.

"Exactly. The base level instinct to hunt and feed. That's primitive. They all have that. *We* all have that. But tribalism, territorialism, these are higher functions exhibited by only a handful of specimens in the lab. Rudimentary tool use was only about 30%. Primitive vocalization was only maybe 10%."

"That's so high!" she boomed. "I've only seen about one in a hundred try to use tools. I've never seen them try and talk."

"That would be consistent," he responded. "By only using soldiers all the CDC research suffers from a selection bias toward more aggressive subjects," he responded.

"And therefore, higher functioning specimens," she concluded.

"Exactly, but the other thing to consider is that everything I saw at the CDC was in a laboratory setting, and anything kicking around in the wild right now has been starving and deteriorating a lot longer."

"Like most things, it's probably a combination of factors, which accounts for the wide diversity of behaviors," she speculated.

"The important thing to keep in mind is that they are us. They start with an intact human brain, and they're deconstructed from the top down. Some are more intact than others, but everything we've seen is fundamentally human. It's like we're physically fighting against our own beastial impulses."

"Well, Agent Sovryn, it's been a great show. I'm so glad to have you joining me as a permanent co-host, and partner—"

"Lab partner," he clarified.

"That's right. Lab partner. So, tune in tomorrow for more Infection Science Hour when we'll be reviewing the basics of neuroplasticity, and news on a radiation treatment that's shown promise in Amsterdam."

Thirty One: The Road to Primitive

I switched off the radio. "Don't you see? They don't know about the parasite? They don't know about the hidden infection. They still think it's some kind of mad cow disease because of the brain damage."

"So?" asked Ellie.

"So, they need Dad's research on the early outbreak."

"The pack at the bottom of the lake? How do you intend to get that?" asked Ellie.

"First things first. We need a shark diving suit." My mind was racing.

"A what?" she asked.

"It's a mesh shirt, like chainmail. Divers use it to protect against shark bites," I explained.

"What for?"

"They may be ghouls, but they have human teeth," I smirked.

"Ok. Where are you going to get a shark diving suit?" she asked.

I thought. "The aquarium in Portsmouth has a shark tank. They've gotta have scuba gear for their handlers."

"Yeah, but what about the Baron? He sounds like a nutcase!" added Ellie.

"We can handle him," I said as much as speculated.

"Handle him?! We don't know the first thing about him! You think you can just go in there half-cocked and take whatever you want?"

"Then I'll propose a trade," I insisted.

"Trade what? Our scalps?" she protested. "It's not worth the risk. The odds of finding a backpack at the bottom of an underwater graveyard are a million to one."

"I have to try!" I demanded.

"Why?!" she yelled. "Why do you have to try?"

"Because if I don't, Dad died for nothing!" I screamed. "Scott died for nothing. Simon and Staci all died for nothing."

She paused to think. "BIODAD?" she called out.

"Yes, Elliot?" came Dad's digitized voice.

"Access the Ghool Bus navigation system and plot a course to the Seacoast Discovery Center."

"Course plotted," responded the BIODAD. "You may embark when ready."

"Perfect!" she smirked. "Pack up. We're going on a road trip."

I assembled a basic 72-hour bag for each of us, while she prepped the weapons. BIODAD estimated a two hour drive, but that was based on conditions before the collapse. Obstacles made everything take longer. We had to go a little slower on roads that needed to be plowed, and we slowed to a crawl on roads clogged with abandoned cars. With any luck we'd be back before nightfall, but if we got held up we might need to stay the night in Primitive.

We were in the shuttle bay loading the Ghool Bus when Niles came in and started loading his own gear.

"What are you doing?" I asked.

"What? You don't think you're driving over a hundred miles without your navigation officer, do you?" he grinned and fake punched me in the shoulder.

"Holland?" I guessed.

"In the flesh!" he answered.

As gunner, Ellie got first choice of weapons for away teams. It was a balancing act to take enough firepower with us without leaving the ship defenseless, so after Ellie we switched off in order of rank. She took the AR. Alix took her Boomstick. I chose the pistol, leaving the crossbow with Hephae. Holland took the ax, and finally Torrance was assigned the BB gun.

Ellie packed a few last boxes of ammo. "We're ready to go. We shouldn't delay any longer than we have to."

I drove, Ellie sat shotgun, and Holland rode up top. The three of us headed south first, to Blanoby and then east to Plymouth, but as we pulled around the clover on-ramp toward Concord, Ellie screamed, "STOP!" I slowed the bus to a stop before merging.

"What does that look like to you?" She pointed toward a set of deep tracks in a plowed section of road.

"You think it's Dr. Blum?" I asked.

She nodded. "Niles?!" she yelled.

"I think he's answering to *Holland* right now," I whispered.

She grunted in frustration. "Why don't we just refer to them both by their last name?"

"What, call them both *Perry*? It's worth a try." I turned and hollered up to him. "Perry!?"

"Guys, don't call me that." He poked his head through the roof hatch and leaned in. "It's confusing."

Ellie and I exchanged a look.

"By the way," he added, "the new rifle feels like a lot of muscle. What are the odds I can pop off a few rounds on this trip?"

"Maybe," I answered. "Hopefully it won't be necessary."

"No way!" objected Ellie. "The AR is mine. The ax is yours. Keep your hands off it."

"Fine. Whatever," he agreed. "I was just holding it."

"Holland, take a look at those tread marks up ahead. Do those look like Dr. Blum's half-track to you?"

"Totally," he replied. "He's probably out here looking for us."

"Maybe he gave up. Went back to Atlanta." I hoped.

"Fat chance! Keep your eyes peeled up there," ordered Ellie. "We should go after him. End this once and for all."

"It's not like he'd recognize the Ghool Bus. We'd have the element of surprise." suggested Holland, a little too eager for conflict. "Plus we'd save time following his tracks, since he's already cleared the road."

"No. Let's change course," I suggested. "BIODAD can calculate a detour."

"Will it still work?" asked Ellie. "We're out of Wi-Fi range."

"It should," I assumed. "The nav system uses satellite positioning, and the Pirate Radio Network has access to satellites." I flipped on the dash screen and sure enough it triangulated our location right away and brought up a map.

"Check it out. There's an air force base in Manchester. Dr. Blum may be headed there for reinforcements," Ellie speculated.

"BIODAD?" I called out.

"Yes, Max?"

"Plot a new course to the Seacoast Discovery Center that avoids Highway 93," I instructed.

"Calculating," answered BIODAD.

Moments later the nav system popped up with a new route that took smaller roads east, and then cut south toward Portsmouth on the other side of Lake Winnipesaukee. "Looks like It'll add some time to the trip, and it'll be lonelier road," said Ellie.

"A lonely road sounds just my speed right now." I cranked the wheel and sped on.

It was an empty road for a long time. A few times I spotted some animal tracks. They could have been human, but we plowed over them too fast to know for sure. There were no vehicle tracks. Occasionally we passed a small village school house, or a lakeside motel. Lots of campgrounds, but no signs of life. We watched and listened for any survivors, but we were too far off the Primitive trade route for a bartertown. We were in the mountains.

The first real city we passed through was Central Harbor, on the north shore of Lake Winnipesaukee. That's when we started picking up local radio chatter. We listened to their broadcasts all the way through Moultonborough and Tuftonboro before we lost the signal. They mostly talked about islands in the lake region, but they never let slip their name, or location. The signal was strongest as we passed by a mountain resort called the *Castle in the Clouds,* but we never got a definitive answer where they were.

As we came out of the mountains civilization became more dense. We passed a nursing home, a jail, and an animal hospital. All would have been perfectly suitable places to scavenge on another day. We passed a chinese food restaurant, which is practically unheard of in New Hampshire, and we briefly considered stopping just for the novelty, but we were on a mission.

Just before crossing into Maine, BIODAD instructed us to merge onto the Spaulding Turnpike, which followed the New Hampshire side of the border through Rochester, all the way to Portsmouth.

We never picked up any radio broadcasts near Portsmouth, but we started seeing more and more vehicle tracks the closer we got. I didn't see anything as heavy as Dr. Blum's treads, but there was plenty of traffic, until we reached the bridge over Piscataqua River. That's where the tire tracks ended.

Piscataqua River surrounds Portsmouth on three sides, but someone had burned the bridge, probably all the bridges, which meant the only way into the city was from the south.

I was about to plot a course around when Holland spotted a large painted sign near the rubble of the bridge.

"For Tricky's Ferry Yank Chain," read Holland. "What the heck does that mean?"

"Only one way to find out." I pulled the Ghool Bus around and got out to examine the sign. There was a chain next to it that was hanging from a large wooden wagon wheel, suspended above us in the twisted scaffolding of the bridge. From there, a rope was suspended clear across the river, presumably to something similar on the other side, but the river was so thick with fog we couldn't see across.

I pulled the chain, which quarter turned the wheel above us, but when I let go it just bounced back up.

"You didn't pull it hard enough," insisted Ellie as she grabbed the chain and hung her whole body weight on it. The wheel spun a half turn, with the chain attached at the bottom, but when she let go it still just reset to the top.

"Come on guys! The wheel is weighted. It's about momentum," said Niles. "Like the sign says, you really gotta *yank* it." He braced himself and jerked down hard. The top of wheel spun to the bottom and rotated all the way around.

On the upturn it caught the rope, and lifted it up. When it completed a full turn it whipped the rope back down, and rung a loud bell somewhere inside its mechanisms.

The whipping motion sent a wave in the rope that travelled out over the water and into the mist. Moments later we heard another bell ring on the other side.

Holland looked surprised. "I bet that got someone's attention."

The bell signalled a ferryman named Tricky, who pulled his barge along the rope, through the fog, to carry passengers across for a fare of one scalp. *I guess the rumors are true.*

"Come on, Max. Let's just drive around," suggested Ellie.

"No good," responded Tricky. There are checkpoints on every road to Primitive. Your vehicle will not be allowed to pass. Fossil fuel is against the Baron's decree."

"Rumor has it that a scalp is worth a day of food in Primitive. Will you take food as fare instead?" I offered.

"It is an unusual traveler who comes to Primitive with food to spare." Tricky thought for a long while, sizing us up. "But I will honor the exchange."

Without the Ghool Bus it would have been a ten mile walk to the Seacoast Discovery Center once we got across the river. Instead, based on a tip from Tricky, we hitched a ride on a wagon pulled by donkeys.

Near Tricky's Cove was a large brewery called *Stone Ground Ale*. The Baron allowed them to continue operating in Primitive, provided they maintained the roads they used to deliver their products, and obeyed the Baron's environmental vision. As a consequence their delivery wagons were always running, and drivers would often pick up passengers for a fee.

Holland had the foresight to bring his brother's bag of shiny trinkets, which we could easily use for trade. I only hoped Niles wouldn't be upset when he found out. We began seeing tents tucked away in hidden places of the city, especially out of reach places, like the underside of overpasses. Strip malls and restaurants were reclaimed and reopened.

Pilgrims, as immigrants to Primitive came to be known, settled mostly along Woodbury Avenue, which spanned for miles, and ended at *Papa Wheelies*, a bicycle repair co-op. That was our delivery driver's end-of-the-line, but we were still five miles from the seacoast.

The only regular transportation to the coast were the dead collectors. On the advice of our Stone Ground driver we had him drop us off at the South Street Cemetery. Locals held their funerals there with the understanding that dead collectors would carry the bodies to the aquarium to trade. The Baron fed the bodies of the dead to the fish in the aquarium. By chance there was a funeral that afternoon.

The closer we got to the aquarium the fewer tents there were, until there were no signs of life except graffiti. The roads surrounding the aquarium were barricaded with cars stacked four high, and sheets of metal that looked like disassembled police cruisers bolted over the gaps.

The dead collector dropped us off at a booth that probably once housed a ticket attendant, but now it was part of the car wall. A green and black sign read, "State Thy Name and Faction" above an intercom system. It resembled a fast food drive in that forced us to speak into the mouth of a giant ceramic whale. "My name is Max Hartwell. This is Elliot Hartwell and Holland Perry. And we don't have a faction," I said into the mic.

Moments later static came on over the speaker, followed by the voice of a young woman. "Where are you from?"

"Upstate." I answered. "Stinson Lake."

"I've never seen you before. Is this your first time in Primitive?"

"Can you see us?" I leaned my head around the whale, looking for a camera. Then I noticed a woman leaning out of a metal hatch in the wall above the ticket booth. She smiled and waved when I saw her. She was dressed in leather armor and holding a composite bow.

"We're here to see the Baron!" I yelled up.

"You don't have to yell, Sweetie." Her voice came from the whale's mouth as she tapped her headset mockingly. "What Faction did you say you were with?"

"I don't know what that is," I said.

She chuckled under her breath. "That's not really how it works here. The Baron doesn't like outsiders. Someone in good standing has to vouch for you, or you have to be affiliated with a group of some reputation."

"The PorcScouts," I said, thinking the others may have been here before.

"Never heard of them," she said. "Not on my list."

I racked my brain trying to think of anyone who might have a good reputation with the Baron, but all I could think to guess was, "Pirates Without Borders."

"Pirates, eh? And I suppose you're seeking to *parley* with the Baron?"

"Exactly!"

"Well, aye aye, Darling."

The woman walked along a bit of scaffolding that connected her perch to a pole in the booth, and slid down to the ground floor.

"Don't be surprised if he feeds you to the bearsharks," she warned.

"Are bearsharks even a real animal?" I asked.

Holland interrupted before she answered, "Just tell us how we get an audience with him?"

"*It's not that simple.* Around here we got customs. For starters, people here stick together. Everyone here is a member of a faction, like a family that looks out for them, and more importantly takes responsibility if they mess up," she shifted her eyes back and forth, like she was doing us a favor. "Now, pirates are an exception. They're still allowed here, so far, but I'm not supposed to let them in unless they're from a crew with a recognizable banner. So, here's what we're going to do . . ." While she was speaking she removed a lavender scarf she had tucked under her breastplate. Using an arrow tip she split the fabric in three. "We're going to call you the *Pirates of Wednesday.*" She pulled a permanent marker from her hair and marked each length of fabric *POW*. Then giggled, amused with herself. "Now display these as your banner, and I'll add you to the list. Until you find a friendly faction that will vouch for you, I'm afraid I can't let you in with your weapons."

I was trying to size her up when Ellie asked, "Why should we trust you?"

"It's my home, Kiddo. The real question is why should we trust you?" She smiled. "My name's Kimberly. I'm on guard duty till dusk. That's my job. It's really simple. You leave your weapons in a locker just inside, and take a number. When you come back, you give the number to the guard on duty and get your stuff back. They'll open the gate for you when you leave."

214

"What?!" protested Ellie. "No way!"

"It's no big deal." Kimberly insisted. "I don't need to confiscate them. You can put them in the locker yourself, and you'll have the only key."

"So, how do we join some stupid faction?" Ellie asked.

"No," I turned to Ellie, "It'll be fine." I removed the Mosquito from my belt.

"What!?" she screamed at me.

"Elliot, listen." I insisted. "We're not in enemy territory here." I motioned to Kimberly, who nodded. "And we're here with our hands out, hoping to make friends." I set the pistol in Kimberly's hand.

"What about the ax?" asked Holland. "Seems primitive enough."

"Oh no, Hun." Kimberly said. "Bladed weapons are permitted. *Creepers!* We're not savages. I'm just talking about firearms."

"Wait! So, he gets to keep his ax!" pointing at Holland, "but I have to give up my rifle?" Ellie was upset.

"Afraid so, Son." Kimberly answered. "Baron's orders."

Ellie handed the rifle over. "Fine take it."

Kimberly shouldered the rifle and said, "Follow the fence to the left, past the administration building until you reach the turnstiles at the front entrance to the aquarium. Grab a map off the rack there if you want, but you can't miss it. You go straight back all the way to the Shark Tank, but be careful. Baron Steen's bears can be dangerous."

She reached into the wall through a chest high hatch. There was a deep mechanical clunk inside, and moments later a giant heavy metal gate unlatched and swung open. We hadn't noticed it before because it was forged to look like part of the stack of cars.

We started to walk away when she yelled after us. "Hey! If you don't come back, can I have your long gun?"

We didn't answer and went forward as instructed.

Behind the wall was a state park, which was the easternmost point of the harbor, and in fact all of New Hampshire. Inside the park was not only the Discovery Center, but also the remains of five World War Two era anti-ship artillery guns, mounted in coastal fortifications strategically placed along the peninsula's rocky cliffs. One such gun mount was located in the courtyard of the aquarium, and had been maintained as a kind of war memorial. I'm sure they were disarmed after they were decommissioned, but I saw no reason why a clever person couldn't reactivate them. In all likelihood the Baron held the entire harbor hostage under heavy guns.

The memorial cannon was surrounded by more walls, but made from wood, not metal. The park was a maze of new fences, and a team of people were nailing up new boards to expand it all the time. They turned and eyed us suspiciously as we passed.

The wooden fences stretched through the front parking lot, where rows and rows of cars, trucks and vans looked mostly abandoned, or rather repurposed as makeshift living quarters. Car seats were taken out and placed around communal fire pits. Canvas tarps were strung between light posts that lined the parking lot to create cover from rain and snow. They even built outhouses over the sewer drains.

Along the fence people had built wooden cottages, and apple carts where they'd formed a marketplace. They sold fresh food, hardware, even handmade clothes.

The main entrance to the aquarium looked unused since the collapse. Posted schedules still described tours and attractions from September.

We moved in cautiously.

We didn't even need the map, signs all over the aquarium pointed toward the Shark Tank. The gift shop had been ransacked. There was debris all over the place, and the lights in the corridors were all dark, casting the whole aquarium in the blue light of the fish tanks. More than a few exhibits were still full of fish, nibbling on the dismembered bits of corpses that had been thrown in with them.

There was an archway at the end of the main corridor that was made to look like the jaws of a great white. Behind it, a long spiral ramp took us up to the second floor. The room above was a massive circular space, with red sofas all around. It had a high ceiling and all around us sharks of various species circled behind glass walls.

There was pounding on the glass behind us and we all jumped. There was a woman in the Shark Tank, scratching at the glass. Or at least half a woman. Her lower body was removed, and surgically replaced with the tail end of a shark.

"This is a bad idea." Ellie whispered. "This Baron guy is obviously a lunatic. We should get out of here before we end up fish food, or worse."

"Where else are we supposed to get the gear?" I asked rhetorically.

"Oh, I don't know. Any one of a dozen scuba diving shops in every coastal town in the world," she said sarcastically.

"That's a good point. Maybe you're right," I conceded.

A boisterous voice interrupted, "And what is it you hope to acquire from this obvious lunatic?"

Thirty Two: Baron Steen's Bears

We spun around and found ourselves face to face with the Baron, reclining on a sofa with a large black bear and its cub. His hair and beard were black, and untamed, with a variety of beads woven into his curls. He was dressed casually, almost slovenly, in a green woolen tunic, ragged denim jeans, and rubber sandals.

"Do you like her?" He motioned to the creature in the tank. "I named her Nyami."

"He didn't mean it." Holland pushed Ellie and I behind him. "We don't think you're a lunatic. We're just here to trade." He readied his grip on the ax.

The larger bear snorted in our direction, as if asking if we were friend or foe. But the Baron sat up and grabbed its snout, shaking it gently as he made a shushing sound. The bear grunted reluctantly and slumped back down.

"She's part of a series of conjoined predators I'm creating. She was my first." He grinned with pride. "Her tail comes from a species of requiem shark the Swahili people call the *Zambi*. According to legend, they're named after an entire tribe that mysteriously disappeared, perhaps in the jaws of the beast. They also happen to be one of the most aggressive creatures in the ocean, if not the world."

He made four place settings for tea, with sugar and little spoons. "Won't you sit with me, and have a cup? I understand you're here because you need my help."

Holland sat first, reaching for a tin of Turkish delight, and I sat next to him, cautiously. Ellie stood.

"My name is Max. This is Holland, and this is my brother El–"

"SILENCE!" the Baron boomed.

We obeyed.

"Do you think you'd have made it this far if I did not wish it?" He somehow managed to pour tiny cups of tea with calm precision, while simultaneously wracked with vibrating rage.

We all shook our heads.

He finished pouring and motioned for Ellie to sit down. "Then make your request."

"I need shark diving gear," I answered.

"That's an unusual request. I certainly have it in my power to satisfy it, but why should I help three liars like yourselves?"

"Liars?!" we protested.

"Come now, *Elliot*." He said her name with a knowing level of sarcasm, and disdain. "Don't pretend you can fool me with a short haircut and a boys name. Some things are too innate to cover up so easily. So, just dispense with the guile and tell me what the gear is for."

"My Dad was a scientist," I answered. "Doing research on the outbreak before he died. Now we've found another scientist who can continue his work, but his files are at the bottom of a lake."

The Baron looked bored.

"We might be able to cure this thing, or at least figure out a way to coexist. But I have to get to the bottom of the lake and find it, and the lake is full of ghouls."

He scoffed. "Max, this is not something that can be cured with science, because it's not a disease . . . It's nature's revenge. For humanity's decadence. For the destruction of the ecosystem. The poisoning of ocean. Poisoning ourselves!" He stood up, holding his tea cup dramatically, and puffing out his chest. "No. This is no plague. It's Mother Nature's immune system, telling us that humankind has ruled this world like a demented child king long enough! And it's time to move aside and let some other beast that's naturally immune take control."

Ellie became visually uncomfortable when he said *naturally immune*, and he must have noticed because he immediately focused on her.

He smiled. "I already know all about you . . . Elizabeth Paige."

She gasped.

"You see, a man came here looking for you less than a week ago. Dr. Stanley Blum, from Atlanta. Seems he's very eager to find you. Told me all about it. How important you are. He offered me a substantial reward for your return."

"You wouldn't!" I yelled. "I won't let you!" and drew the knife from my belt.

"Don't be stupid!" he yelled. "You're not going to fight a bear with a pocket knife. Now relax! Drink your tea. I have no use for money, and Dr. Blum is a fool to think anyone else does. The old world is dead, and good riddance. Dr. Blum is like all government men. They don't respect the natural order. They don't cherish it. Dr. Blum and his kind represent the most reprehensible of humanity. They use science and reason to justify the rape the natural world. There's no way I'm helping that scoundrel! But that's not why I'm going to help you." He paused.

"Wait, so you're going to help us?" I asked.

He smiled. "I think I have a pretty good instinct about people, and very few people would even consider coexistence with the dead. I'm helping you because the world that's coming is going to need those of us who honor their ancestors. So, go and finish your father's work. Take whatever you need. And in time, if you're sincere, you'll see that I'm right."

Thirty Three: The Claw

We returned to the ship with a chainmail shark diving suit, scuba gear, and enough oxygen for an eight hour dive. The vest also had internal pockets for air, and external pockets for weights to create the optimum buoyancy for each diver. In an emergency I could drop the weights and shoot to the surface using the vest as a floatation device. Unfortunately there was no time for a full training. The Baron showed me briefly how it all worked, but I'd never tested it. I had it mostly figured out by the time we reached home that evening. At least in theory.

"Max! Elliot! Holland!" Hephae came running out of the shuttle bay, looking very excited. "Check this out! I spent all day on it!" We pulled into the shuttle bay, and the moment I got out of the Ghool Bus he grabbed my arm and pulled me toward the workbench where he had Larry's crossbow, a pair of ice skates and what looked like the inner workings of a reclining chair disassembled and spread out.

"Dude!" Holland objected. "I use that crossbow to hunt food. Not to mention it's a rental! What am I supposed to tell Larry?"

"Don't worry. I got it all figured out. I can put it back together whenever. To Larry it'll just look like we gave it a thorough cleaning. But this is awesome! I'm almost done."

He handed me the crossbow body, which included the stock, trigger and foregrip, but the firing mechanism was mounted backwards, so it was pointed back at me. He'd also installed a strap that cinched the stock tight against my forearm.

"I can't aim this thing with it pointed backwards," I objected.

"Don't worry. Watch this!" He snapped together a few pieces of the recliner mechanism he'd been working on, including a giant metal spring, and a gear assembly. He spoke quickly while he worked. "I've been thinking about this underwater adventure you want to go on, and I tried to think of a way to defend yourself."

He fastened the spring contraption where the scope used to be, so it was now facing forward in the assembly. He bolted the two arms of the mechanism to the limbs of the crossbow. It looked like some kind of robotic hand. "I got the idea from this shark toy I had as a kid. You pull the trigger on one end, and the jaw opens and closes on the other. Only this time . . . " He aimed my arm down and stomped on the cocking stirrup he'd attached to the hand, pushing until it locked. "It's spring loaded!" Finally he bolted the blades of the ice skates to the inside of the spring loaded mechanical arms. "I give you . . . *The Claw!*"

"Hephae, this is really cool, but will it take out a G?"

"Try it for yourself." He grinned, shoving a wooden broom handle through a roll of shop towels.

I placed the Claw around the towels, figuring it was about the width of a human neck, and pulled the trigger. The crossbow kicked back so hard I thought it might yank my shoulder out of socket. *That'll take some getting used to.* The spring arms snapped closed like a bear trap and cleaved the towels and the broom handle in two.

Everyone laughed in excitement. Hephae pumped his fist in the air. "Now let's test it underwater."

Thirty Four: Welcome to Creekside

Stinson Lake is no ordinary lake. In fact, it's not really a lake at all. It's a reservoir, with a dam at one end that houses a hydroelectric plant. Still, any body of water becomes a popular destination for summer activities like fishing and water skiing. I don't know if anybody ever went scuba diving in it before.

We had to break up the ice around Dad's fishing boat with the ax to get it free floating again. Then we hoisted it out of the water and shoved it out on the ice. From there it was easy to hack and paddle to the open water in the middle.

The scuba gear was really awkward at first, and hard to move in. I needed help getting it all attached and connected, especially the Claw, which I couldn't buckle with one hand. I took a few deep breaths to make sure the mask was really working before I put my head under the water. Continuing to breathe completely submerged in water was against my every survival instinct. At first I couldn't do it. My lungs simply refused to do what my brain told them to do, until they ached for air and I forced them to go against their primal programming by heaving for air.

It was like breathing through a garden hose, and not being able to get air as fast as I expected caused another kind of panic to set in. I spit out the mouthpiece and went flailing back the surface, choking on all the water I swallowed. Holland and Alix grabbed my arms and pulled me back up.

"I'm ok! I'm ok. I just need to take it slower."

On the next try I closed my eyes and told myself, *You are not underwater. You are having a dream. You're in your bed with plenty of air.* I pushed off the boat into the cold deep and for a few seconds I imagined I was in a flying dream.

I took three long calm breaths before opening my eyes. It was the strangest sensation. When I inhaled my lungs expanded and I began to float upward. Then when I exhaled the bubbles spilled out of my mask and I became heavy again, sinking slowly.

I experimented with slow shallow breaths to keep an average equilibrium, and kicked my fins to push downward until it was cold and dark. I had a halogen light attached to my head so I could see in the depths. In my free hand I had my staff, which I'd attached to a steel hook. I intended to use it to move debris, and hopefully snag the straps of the backpack without getting within arms reach of whatever was down there.

I dove deeper and deeper, until something metallic caught the light through the muddy sediment. I looped the hook underneath it and pulled, flipping a large flat square of metal out of the mud. As it slowly sank back down, and the billows of dirt settled back to the bottom, I could read the writing on the sign, *Welcome to Creekside.*

I looked around and discovered that I was at the foot of a water tower, completely submerged in the reservoir. As my eyes adjusted I could see that there were many buildings around me, as well as traffic lights, and street signs.

Before the dam there was no Stinson Lake. In its place was a small village called *Creekside.* Years ago, when city planners approved designs for the hydroelectric plant they neglected to consider the impact on the residents of Creekside, but by then millions of dollars had been sunk into the project, and it was too late to back out. So, they seized the land with eminent domain, evacuated the residents and moved them to neighboring towns like Blanoby and Ellsworth. But they never bothered demolishing the structures. They just flooded the village and sold the new lakefront property to housing developers. As a result, the village of Creekside was mostly intact, despite decades underwater.

The backpack could have sank anywhere. I swam to the nearest intersection and shined my light on the street sign hanging next to the traffic light. It was covered in years of rust and lake algae, so I wiped it off. I was on Elm Street.

I peered down Elm Street in both directions, trying to decide where to search. The lake water was darker and muddier at the bottom and made the town look cast in thick green fog, but the rooftops reached up into the clear water, and the taller structures caught faint beams of sunlight from above. I swam over the town, scanning below for any kind of clue.

I spotted something large and blue moving along the sidewalk below, but couldn't make out what it was through the fog. I thought it might be some large bottom dwelling lake fish, but when I moved down to get a better look, I spotted a familiar postal worker.

How the heck did it even get here?

It had taken quite a bit of damage. It was waterlogged and decomposing. One arm was torn off at the elbow and one leg was broken and dragging behind the other. Half its face was missing, probably eaten by fish. But I couldn't figure out how the Postman from Lochshire had gotten to the bottom of a lake ten miles away.

I was way above it, and it hadn't even seen me. It moved in slow motion, fumbling to open mailboxes, turn up the rusty red signal flags, and move on. After all this time, the Postman was still trying to deliver mail.

There were dozens of G's wandering around. With all the air out of their lungs and all their putrid gases expelled they sank like stones, and now they just milled about this sunken town, looking a bit like they were walking on some alien world.

It was about the creepiest thing I'd ever seen. They were decomposing, and only held together by strands of sinew. Nibbled by fish, and tangled in weeds. But the most unsettling part was how they carried on as if they were in a regular town. A group of teenagers sitting outside a waterlogged cafe, pretending to sip from broken coffee mugs. A woman dragging a stroller as she window shopped the flooded boutiques. A man in a blue mechanic's jumpsuit slowly pounding on the hood of a car with the nozzle of a gas pump.

I knew they were flowing into the lake from the creek, and I dropped the backpack near the mouth of the creek, so I swam toward the bulk of the G's, thinking that must be the direction they were coming from.

I spotted the remains of the bear that chased Scott out onto the ice. The bones protruded from its putrid meat, with tufts of matted hair floating nearby.

I knew I was close when I saw Scott's fire ax, embedded in the post of an old pier. Nearby a G was sitting in a small boat, holding a fishing pole over the old creek bed. The fishing G was yards away, and at their speed I was in no real danger.

Then I saw the reflective duct tape of the backpack half buried in the mud below the pier.

I swam down and hooked the pack with my staff, but it was caught on something. I planted my feet in the mud and pulled as hard as I could. The mud begin to shift underneath, and I felt it begin to come loose.

The water filled with muck so thick I couldn't see, but once the backpack was free something grabbed me. It was an arm, buried in the mud under the pack.

I dropped the weights tied to my vest and filled the vest with air to give me lift, but the G in the mud was hanging from the pack as I scrambled to get away.

Once we got above the billows of mud I could see it's face. *It was Scott!* Or rather, it was most of Scott. The hand and arm holding the pack were so devoured I could hardly believe he had the strength to hold on. I kicked to dislodge his hold, but he grabbed my ankle with his better arm and pulled closer. Below the ribs was only a billow of black muck, like the ink of a squid, were his putrid entrails oozed out of his gaping abdomen. His legs were completely gone, either left in the mud, or more likely in the bellies of the G's in town.

I struggled to push him off me, but there was so little left of him that he floated with me. He sank his teeth into my chest. The suit protected me, but he pierced the air compartment in the vest, which let loose a blinding flurry of bubbles. By the time it cleared enough to see, we were sinking again.

A pack of G's were attracted by the commotion, and marching off the pier into the mud. We were sinking into their reaching arms.

I kicked and yanked and tumbled until I couldn't tell up from down, but Scott was relentless, biting and gnawing so hard I was sure there'd be huge bruises under the shark diving suit.

I was on the verge of panic, just inches from the G's I was sure would drown me, or break my limbs, even in the suit.

Then I remembered the Claw.

I put my free hand under Scott's chin and pushed his head back by the neck as I shoved the open Claw in his face. He gnawed on the gear mechanism as I pulled the trigger, cleaving his head in half at the jaw. His body went limp and began to sink.

I gasped for air, but my mouth filled with putrid water. Scott had ripped the hose out of the tank as he sank.

I kicked my legs to push up, barely above the grasping fingers of the G's below. My lungs ached as I climbed upward. The Claw was creating too much drag, so I unlatched it and let it go. I abandoned the scuba tank to drop weight.

I strapped the backpack over my shoulders and kicked upward. The belly of the Stranger was silhouetted against the light of the water's surface, but it still seemed like it was getting further away.

Time slowed and my lungs burned for air. I felt weak, and half conscious. My heart was pounding in my throat as I started to panic. Only my adrenaline pushed me to keep swimming.

My vision began going dark, and I reached the breaking point. My throat sucked in one desperate spasmodic breath. It burned like acid as the water flooded my windpipe and lungs. I couldn't move. Couldn't fight. I just floated there for a moment as everything went black. My mind went blank, and the only way I knew I was alive was the pain.

Then everything turned white. There was no pain. And I let go.

Thirty Five: The Stranger

The sky above was blinding. The boat rocked gently on the surface of the lake. The trees swayed back and forth, and somewhere a hawk cried.

"Max, have a look at this. I want to show you something."

I turned around and Dad was sitting facing me, wearing a jackal puppet on one hand and giraffe on the other. "Most kids learn to talk like jackals from their parents. Jackals make demands, and provoke resistance. Giraffes on the other hand . . ." He shifted his attention to his literal other hand, looking amused with himself, "Giraffes ask questions, and make requests."

"Dad!" I put my hand over the puppets and pushed them aside. "I'm too old for puppets. Can we just fish?"

He smiled, even though I could tell it made him sad. "Ok, no more parables." He took off the hand puppets and returned them to his tackle box. "You know, you used to love Jekyll and Hyde."

"Yeah, when I was five. I get it, ok." I rolled my eyes and recited, "Be curious. Be respectful. Don't make assumptions. Always negotiate a compromise."

"Max, it's more than that." He sighed. "You start public school next week. Before your mom passed away she made me promise that I wouldn't enroll you in public school. That I'd always let you direct your own education."

"Dad! I am directing my own education. I want to go to public school. I want to be with normal kids."

"I know." He smiled and put his arm around me. "I'm just worried, because the kids you're going to meet at school were raised very different than you. You're going to be like a giraffe in a den of jackals."

"Don't worry. I'm ready. *Semper Paratus* right?"

"You're right." He laughed. "You're growing up. I know you can handle it. I just want you to understand you're entering into a strange world. People are going to be more aggressive than you're used to. Not just the kids. The adults too."

"Dad, I'm going to be ok."

"I know." He squeezed me and then went back to his tackle box to prep bait.

We fished in silence for a bit before he spoke again. "Listen, I want to talk to you about something unrelated. Well, it's kinda related."

"What?" I asked.

"Something's going on at work. I'm going to be pulling some long hours, and I probably won't be home when you get back from school."

"Well, why don't I come to the lab with you again?"

"No. No. You're going to be in school remember."

I nodded. "Oh yeah."

"Besides, this is pretty dangerous stuff. Some new virus. We're taking every precaution, but we can't have any guests in the lab right now," He said.

"Can't you work from home?" I asked.

"Some. I'll keep all my work files on my zPad and stay home as much as I can. I promise."

We spent the rest of the afternoon fishing, but didn't catch anything.

Thirty Six: Keene Central Square

When I came to, I was coughing up water and vomiting over the side of the boat. My lungs burned. I heaved for air, but could barely catch a breath. Once I was sure I wouldn't asphyxiate I fell back and laid on the floor of the boat. The sky above was blinding.

Two shadows fell over me. It was Niles and Hephae, both with this goofy look on their faces.

"We thought we lost you, Buddy!" Hephae exclaimed.

They'd pulled me out of the lake and administered CPR. I sat up wheezing, relieved to see the backpack in the boat near my feet. Suddenly I remembered the Claw, and looked around.

"Holland! I lost the crossbow . . . I'm so sorry."

Hephae leaned over the side of the boat, scanning the surface of the lake. "There!" He pointed smiling. "In the event of a water landing the Claw can be used as a floatation device!" And sure enough, the Claw had floated to the surface on its own.

I dug into the backpack and confirmed that the plastic bags had protected the zPad and the paper files in the main compartment. But water had flooded the smaller front pocket, destroying my PorcScouts Survival Guide, and more importantly my family photo, which was reduced to soggy pulp that came apart in my hands. Mr. Romero's tomato seeds had begun to germinate in the paper pulp, but they needed to be planted in ground if they were going to survive.

When we got back to the ship I needed time to rest. I spent some time in the aquaponics dome to relax, and planted the seeds in some soil beds I'd prepared. Later that evening I went back to the shuttle bay where Niles was loading the Ghool Bus for another away mission.

"Is Ellie coming with us?" asked Niles.

"Probably. Why wouldn't she?" I asked.

"I don't know. She's been sulking a lot recently. She hasn't left the crow's nest since we got back from Primitive," he explained. "I hope she has food up there, because she hasn't even been taking meals."

"She's processing some pretty traumatic experiences," I said.

"I know. We've all lost people," he said. "And we're all dealing with it in our own way."

"It's not just that. It's about Dr. Blum," I hinted, but didn't think it was my place to reveal any details.

"He sounds pretty awful," Niles said. "Maybe Dr. Blum deserves a little retribution."

"I'm not saying he doesn't deserve it," I admitted reluctantly. "He's done some awful things, and the world would probably be better off without him. But I'm not sure revenge is worth the risk if something goes wrong. And even if she succeeds, and takes him out, I'm not sure it'll actually make her feel better. It doesn't change what happened, and I'm worried it will change her in a way she can't undo."

"She who?" Alix walked in carrying a box of supplies. "Are you two talking about me behind my back?"

"He means *he*," corrected Niles.

"He who?" Alix asked skeptically. "What are you talking about?"

"*Elliot*," answered Niles.

"Why would you call Elliot *she?*" asked Alix.

Crap! The look on Alix's face said she was figuring out something wasn't making sense. I had to distract her. "I meant *you!* I thought maybe you should come with us, instead of Elliot. Since we need your expertise."

She blushed and smiled. "Me?"

"I mean . . . this isn't going to be as easy as it was to find the number station," continued Niles. "Infection Science Hour only broadcasts one hour a day, starting tomorrow morning. That means if we don't find her fast we're going to have to find a place to stay until the next episode."

"Plus Dr. Murphy already knows you," I reminded her. "Or knows *Joel Saxen* at least. It might help us gain her trust if you come with us."

"Ok," she agreed. "I'll go grab my Boomstick!" Alix ran upstairs to pack.

"Why did you do that?!" protested Niles.

"I had to do something," I said. "She was figuring it out."

"I don't want to go on an away mission with her," objected Niles. "It's too hard to be Holland around her."

"What? Why?" I asked.

"I don't know." He paused. "It feels like lying."

"It *is* lying," I insisted. "She thinks you *are* Holland."

"You're not helping!" he protested.

"Why don't you just try being Niles on this mission?" I suggested. "We'll need your technical expertise too."

We knew Dr. Murphy was broadcasting from somewhere in Keene, New Hampshire before the collapse. So, it seemed like the obvious place to start.

"We should go tonight," suggested Alix. "That way our first reading in the morning narrows down most of the city."

We agreed.

The most direct route was only a two hour drive south.

Keene is a little town. Way bigger than Thornton, but still tiny, typical of any little town in New England, with red brick buildings and wrought iron fencing. It's where that movie about the kids getting sucked into a jungle board game was filmed.

Keene Central Square was in the middle of downtown, surrounded by shops and restaurants that all looked looted. The square itself was shaded in trees, with cobblestone walkways and park benches. There was a large white church steeple at one end, and a bandstand in the center. We parked the Ghool Bus near a statue of a soldier at the far end.

The sun had set, and the temperature was dropping.

"Let's camp here for tonight. I'm about ready to eat, what do you say?" I suggested.

"Don't you want to look around?" asked Alix. "I've never been to Keene before. Maybe we'll get lucky and stumble on her lab."

"It's getting dark, and we've got an early morning tomorrow," I countered.

"How about this. Grab your travel mug, and I'll make some hot cocoa to keep us warm." She shook three packets of powdered hot chocolate she had in her own bag. "Let's just take a walk through the square and see what's around."

Niles winced, "I don't know."

"Oh come on!" she insisted. "We can already see this place is deserted. If we run into more G's that we can't handle we'll just run back to the bus. *It'll be fun.* Just a nice friendly walk in the park. Like normal people."

"I'll go if Max goes," Niles counter offered. I could tell it was Niles by the sudden meekness in his voice. Holland didn't sound like that.

"Ok," I agreed. "But we're bringing flashlights."

We all suited up for cold, and grabbed our weapons. I had my staff, and pistol. Alix had her Boomstick. Niles decided the Claw was his weapon of choice, although deep down I think it was Holland that was eager to try it out. He also decided to wear the shark diving suit as an added precaution.

We climbed out of the Ghool Bus with our travel mugs full of steaming cocoa. The air was brisk, but there was no snow. The hot chocolate packs came with little dehydrated marshmallows that were just the right size to clog the mouthpiece of my mug, so I let them disintegrate as the hot liquid gushed around inside.

It was delicious.

We walked the perimeter of the square together, instead of through the middle, checking out all the shops along the way. Cafe seating was scattered around like debris. Windows and glass doors were broken. Everything was desolate.

At one intersection there was an apartment building with huge glass panels on the front.

"Watch out!" Alix whispered forcefully as she ducked behind an abandoned car.

There was a G in the window, slumped down face first against the glass, so that it's feet were spread out behind it. It was wearing a silk blouse, and white jeans, covered in blood. It's hair was completely caked with blood, but I didn't see a wound.

She definitely saw us. her eyes followed us every time we peeked out from behind the car, but she wasn't interested. She was interested enough to track us with her eyes, but not enough to pound on the glass, or try to get to us. It was curious.

"Maybe she didn't trigger because she can't smell us," I suggested.

"No," Alix disagreed. "We definitely look alive." She tapped on the glass and the G moaned softly. "And it can hear us." She waved her hands in front of the woman's eyes, which disoriented it momentarily.

"Look, there's another one." I pointed through the window, where another G in a private security uniform was seated at a desk. "It sees us too. Why isn't it moving?"

"I don't know," Alix admitted. "But they're giving me the creeps."

Niles tried the door, and found it locked. "Yeah. Let's just leave them in there."

We moved on around the square.

"Isn't this beautiful!" Alix exclaimed. "I love all these local businesses. Instead of some big corporate overlord. It's like a real community here."

"Well, except the Bank," Niles whispered, darting his eyes down every side street, and around every corner.

"True. Banks are the worst!" she agreed.

"Alix, try to keep your voice down," I suggested. "It's so quiet around here sound is going to travel for a long—"

"Oh my gawd!" She gasped and ran up the stairs of a large white church at the top of the square. "I remember when I was a little girl, I used to dream about getting married in a church like this . . . Of course, Emma

Goldman said marriage was a tool of exploitation. And don't even get me started about what she said about churches. But isn't it wonderful?"

"Sure, I guess." There was a rustling in the park across the street. I looked, but didn't see anything. I couldn't tell if it was G's, or wind, or what.

"*Church of the Shire: Be your best, and harm no other*," she read the marquee on the front of the building. "That's nice."

"Listen, Alix," whispered Niles. "It's getting late. I think we should head back."

"What's that?" Alix had thrown her head back and was pointing up at the church with her flashlight.

It was another pirate radio transmitter, tucked up in the steeple of the church.

"I think tomorrow is going to be more difficult than we thought."

Thirty Seven: Hide and Seek

I set BIODAD to wake us up before *Infection Science Hour.* We planned to make ourselves a breakfast of canned corned beef hash and powdered eggs, but before we started there was a ruckus in the back of the bus that startled all of us.

"Is there a G in the back?" Alix asked.

"How would it get in?" I asked.

The noise came from under the workbench in the back of the bus. We could hear it scratching and chewing inside a cabinet. Alix aimed her Boomstick at the cabinet door, while I strapped the Claw to my arm, and braced for Niles to pull the cabinet door open.

"Ready?" Niles asked.

We nodded.

Niles yanked the door open and we all tensed, ready to pounce.

"Meow!" Stinky was curled inside, half eating and half playing with the corpse of a mouse.

"Stinky!" I exclaimed. "How'd you get in here? You were supposed to stay on the ship with the others!"

Alix dropped her gun, seeming almost annoyed, and went back to the front of the bus.

Stinky batted the mouse my direction, as if offering it to me. Then darted away and found a spot to sit at the foot of a bunk.

I threw the mouse away.

"TRIGGER WARNING!!"

Dr. Murphy's voice blared from the bus speakers.

"This show may contain content, language and humor that is intended for a mature audience. If that's not you please stop listening now."

"Holland, get up top and hook up the directional antenna! We don't have a lot of time." Alix hopped in the driver seat and started the engine as I turned up the speakers.

"Nothing you hear on Infection Science Hour is intended as medical advice, therapy or really anything but entertainment. Please take everything you hear with a grain of salt."

Niles grabbed three orange sodas and handed them out. "Breakfast of champions." Then he climbed up to the roof and began installing the equipment. With his improved design, once it was plugged in it could be monitored by the BIODAD, and I could control it from the dashboard.

If you're hearing us on the Pirate Radio Network the views expressed here are not necessarily those of the station you're listening on.

"There's only one antenna feed, so we're only going to be able to hear the show when we're pointed right at the receiver," Alix reminded.

"Now that all that's out of the way, let's start the show! This is Infection Science Hour with Dr. Stephanie Murphy, and Agent Sovryn."

The radio blared with the intro music, which sounded like modern Z-Pop played on an 8-bit MIDI player.

"Drive us past the church," I instructed. "I want to check something."

Alix revved the engine, while I adjusted the audio settings.

"Yeah!" Agent Sovryn exclaimed. "Infection . . . . . . Hour! . . . . back . . . . can barely . . . . myself! . . . . Murphy? Are you excited?

Once I zeroed in on the signal I switched to the directional antenna and pointed forward. Alix accidentally threw the bus in reverse, and hit something that crunched under the rear tires.

"Whoops!" exclaimed Alix. "I got this." She shifted back into drive and drove forward over it again.

I took off the headphones. "Yeah but what'd you hit?" I unbuckled and headed to the back of the bus.

There was no rear visibility on the Ghool Bus, except the side mirrors, which meant that a triangular area directly behind the bus was invisible to the driver, but we had installed a speakeasy style viewing slot in the rear door. I opened the slot and looked through.

"It's a G," I called back.

"There's dozens of 'em!" yelled Niles from the roof.

"Want me to flatten 'em?" Alix asked.

"Just try not to. They're all over the place," he warned.

Alix climbed up on the roof of the bus to get a good view. "Max, you're going to want to see this."

I climbed up to have a look. G's were swarming all over Central Square, and wandering around in the street. "We'll be safe in the bus. Can we drive around them?"

"Yeah, but Max . . ." She glanced around the square. "Why aren't they coming after us?"

I hadn't noticed, but she was right. I climbed down a few steps and tapped my foot on the horn.

Honk! Honk! Honk!

Some of the G's glanced our direction, but then went back to wandering whichever way they were going before.

"That's super weird," Alix observed.

"This is freaking me out. Let's go," insisted Niles.

We climbed back down and resumed our stations. I plugged in the headphones and searched for the signal.

>"... *definitely builds trust. It's good* . . . . . . *a partner to keep you accountable.*"

And then Agent Sovryn's voice.

>"*With that in mind, I want to read you a statement from Doctor* . . . ."

Alix hit the gas and moved around the square.

>"*Mill* . . . . . . *sch, an entomologist at the University of* . . . . *normal* . . . . *the* . . . . . *question is always, are these cannibals?*"

"Hey!" I turned to Alix. "Keep it straight! This thing's temperamental."

>"*Implies* . . *intraspecies activity. These* . . . ."

"I'm doing the best I can." She yanked on the wheel. "There's a ton of these freaks."

>"... *that's the difference. They* . . . . . . *and they feed* . . . . . . *warm human flesh. Intelligence?*"

Alix swerved around the ghouls in the street, while I kept the antenna locked on the church steeple.

". . . power, but . . . . . skills remain and . . . . remembered behaviors from normal life . . . . . . are reports . . . . using tools. But even these . . . . the most primitive . . . use . . . "

We curved around the top of the square, passed the marquee of the church, and I turned the antenna directly toward the pirate transmitter.

". . . external . . . . as . . . . and so forth. I . . . . out to . . . . even animals will . . . . . " the . . . . . use of tools in this manner. These creatures are nothing but pure, motorized . . . "

"Hold it right there!" I motioned to her. "Back up to the the church."

". . . instinct. We must not be lulled by the concept that these are . . . family members or . . . "

"Stop right there."

Alix pulled the bus around and stopped perpendicular in the street, pointing right at the church.

". . . . must be destroyed on sight!"

Agent Sovryn finished reading and Dr. Murphy responded.

"Agent Sovryn, I think he's right. Once the identity of our loved ones is gone, I think they're gone."

And then Agent Sovryn's voice.

"Even if that's true . . . . . . a lot to disagree with . . . . . "

I took off the headphones and turned to Alix. "The Infection Science Hour is syndicated on the Pirate Radio Network."

"So?" she asked.

242

"So, we're not tracking one signal. We're getting multiple signals from a bunch of radio repeaters all broadcasting the same content."

"Oh."

"Who knows if she's even in Keene anymore. This might be the only transmitter in town." I unplugged the headphones so the signal played over the internal speakers. "Watch."

I pointed the antenna at the church steeple and picked up the signal.

". . . exploiting non lethal suppression techniques . . . "

I instructed the BIODAD to spin the antenna in a slow circle.

". . . . . and horseradish. Mustard gas causes the lungs to fill with fluid until drowned . . . . "

". . . blocks neurotransmitters and actually causes the nervous system to crash is nerve gas . . . . "

"Blinding lasers, microwave denial systems, sonic cannons and even plasma rifles . . . . "

"See that? Three distinct signals, in addition to the one in the steeple, which is going to interfere with the other signals."

She reached out for the headphones. "You drive. I got this."

I took the wheel and she told me to drive around Central Square over and over. After about the third round all the G's had moved out of the road and onto the sidewalk, just apathetically watching us drive circles around the park. I objected at first, but once I figured out what she was doing I knew it would work.

Alix had BIODAD display a map of Keene on the dashboard so she could start logging radio signals. "BIODAD?"

"Yes, Alix?" came Dad's voice.

"Can you display display signal strength and direction?" asked Alix.

"Affirmative" said BIODAD.

"And can you also ignore transmissions from the radio repeater at the Church of the Shire, to narrow the search?" she asked.

"Affirmative" said BIODAD.

"Do it!" she said.

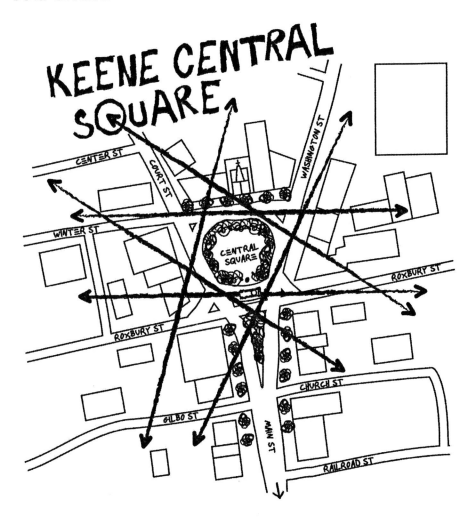

It took the whole hour, but she got multiple readings from each transmitter at multiple points along the loop, and based on the intersections BIODAD was able to determine which transmitters were outside the city, and which one was inside Keene.

Recording the vector of a signal from opposite sides of Central Square produced two lines that eventually intersected. So, the lines indicating transmitters outside of Keene were more or less parallel, and didn't intersect on the local map. But, two of the vectors pointed southwest, and intersected less than a mile away.

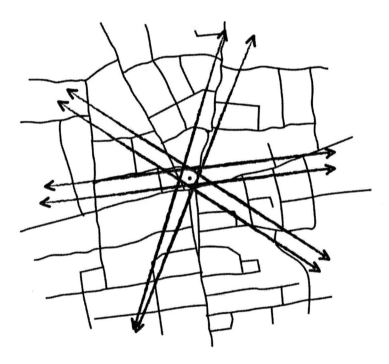

245

Thirty Eight: Doctor Murphy

We decided not to wait for the next episode of Infection Science Hour, and to do a physical search of Keene State College. We took Main Street south to a roundabout on the corner of Winchester and Marley Street. We followed signs for the Putnam Science Center, figuring that's where her lab probably was. We drove onto campus and stopped in a parking lot nestled between the Science Center and a thermal power plant.

We suited up and exited the bus.

"Where do you want to start?" Alix asked.

"If the campus is abandoned she'd probably do her research in the science building, but it doesn't look very secure," I commented.

"At least we know where she's getting power." Niles pointed to the chimney of the thermal power plant, which was billowing exhaust into the air.

"Before the collapse her show was internet based, and now it's broadcast on terrestrial radio, so we just need to find the radio transmitter," Alix said.

Niles walked over to an abandoned car parked near the Ghool Bus. "Here's a clue." He pointed out a black and blue bumper sticker which read, "WKNH 91.3FM Keene State College Radio"

We followed the campus directories to the Media Arts Center, which we approached on foot, but as we walked through campus we began to notice a growing number of G's like the apathetic G's downtown. They were sitting on benches, and fumbling with pay phones. One of them threw a frisbee at another, which hit it in the face and knocked it down. A group of them were sitting around a G clumsily strumming a broken guitar. There were dozens of them around campus, and they all completely ignored us. They'd give us a sideways glance as we walked between them, but there was no hunger. No aggression.

"What's wrong with these G's?" asked Niles.

"I don't know," said Alix. "I've never seen anything like this."

It reminded me of the patrons at Wheel Top, but we weren't wearing any kind of camouflage.

We reached the Media Arts Center, but the doors were locked. Niles and Alix picked up a steel bike rack to use as a battering ram, and were bracing to break the glass front of the building.

"Guys, wait!" I said.

"What?" Alix asked.

"We can't break in," I answered.

"What, why not?" Niles seemed surprised. "We break into buildings all the time."

"Yeah, but this might be an occupied building. Dr. Murphy might be using it," I explained. "If we break it open we could be exposing her to an invasion."

"I don't think these G's are invading anything," Niles joked.

"Hey Max, look at that." Alix's hands were full carrying the bike rack, but she pointed with her chin.

I turned and saw a G looking right at us, and taking steps our direction. As it got closer I saw that it was wearing a red letter jacket with a gold sigma on it. It had an irate look on it's face, and it was picking up speed.

"It's coming right for us!" Niles yelled.

The G in the sigma jacket tackled Niles and Alix, pinning them beneath the bike rack. Alix screamed.

I drew my Mosquito and was about to fire when the doors of the Media Arts Center burst open, and two figures in bright yellow hazmat suits ran out. The first person grabbed the G, lifted it off of Niles and Alix, and threw it face down on the ground. The second person was armed with a large drill.

They both climbed on top of the G, held it down as it struggled to turn back on them. The one with the drill placed it against the base of the its skull and slowly penetrated the brain until the G began shaking, and finally relaxed.

The first person stood up and pulled off his mask, raising his fists in the air triumphantly. "Whoo!" He was tall and bald, in black rimmed glasses

248

and a goatee. "You kids ok? Good thing we were on patrol. What are you doing here?"

"Are you Agent Sovryn?" I asked, pulling the bike rack off of Alix and Niles.

"Are you Max Hartwell?" The second person holstered the drill and pulled off her mask, revealing a grinning young woman with dark curls and turquoise glasses. *It's Dr. Murphy!*

Thirty Nine: Murphy's Lab

"How do you know my name?" I asked.

"How do you know my name?" Dr. Murphy asked, her voice as smooth and inviting as I remembered.

"I'm Joel Saxen!" screamed Alix, barely able to contain herself. "You were on *Info Planet*. That's my show!"

Dr. Murphy chuckled. "Funny, you don't look like Joel Saxen."

Agent Sovryn just looked confused. "Whoa!" He jumped back as the G on the ground started to wiggle back to life.

"What the what!?" I exclaimed, aiming my pistol again.

"Don't worry! This is our new friend . . ." Dr. Murphy rifled through its pockets, removed a wallet, and checked his student ID. "Sherman . . ." She squinted over the top of her turquoise reading glasses. "Howard."

"Whoa! Never trust a man with two first names," interrupted Agent Sovryn.

"What? Why not?" Niles objected.

"It's just a joke, Kid."

Dr. Murphy stuck Sherman's ID in a laminated pouch on a lanyard, and put it around his neck. She zipped his wallet into a sandwich bag before slipping it back into his pocket. "He's going to be matriculating here in the spring."

Agnet Sovryn helped Sherman to his feet, who was now perfectly docile and cooperative. Sovryn snapped a mug shot of his face and ID with his wristwatch, and spoke into it like a voice recorder. "Male patient, admitted at . . ." He checked his watch. "11:10 AM." Brian spun him around to look him over. "Excellent condition. Another Sig-man."

"What's a *Sig-man*?" Alix asked.

"Members of a local fraternity," answered Dr. Murphy. "The Sigmas. We've been observing them as a case study on the impact of previous affiliation."

Sovryn snapped his fingers to get Sherman's attention, and then twinkled his fingers. Sherman examined him, and then imitated his twinkling fingers. "Good mirroring," said Sovryn. He grabbed Sherman by the face and held his eyes open. "Definitely showing signs of dehydration. Let's schedule him for serum injections before the end of the week."

"Agreed," confirmed Dr. Murphy. "Make it Thursday. I want to give him a few days to acclimate."

Sherman got distracted by the G's throwing the frisbee in the quad and stumbled after them. I noticed they were all wearing similar red letter jackets, embroidered with the same gold sigma.

"What did you do to him?" I asked.

Dr. Murphy turned to me and smiled, brushing a dark curl out of her face as she caught her breath. "Let's go inside, and I'll tell you all about it. But first, you are Max Hartwell, right?"

I nodded. "And this is Holland Perry."

Niles waved.

"And you're Joel Saxen?" Dr. Murphy asked skeptically, pointing to Alix.

"It's a long story." Alix laughed. "Joel Saxen basically doesn't exist. He's a hologram and a voice modulator." Alix bounced and giggled. "Dr. Murphy, I am like your biggest fan!"

"Please, just call me Stephanie," she said. "And this is my lab partner, Brian."

"I've been following you online since PorcTherapy!" Alix continued to geek out.

"*Pork*, like pig?" I asked?

"No, *Porc* like porcupine," corrected Alix.

"Wait, what?" I'd never heard of anything with a name like PorcScouts.

Stephanie must have seen the confusion on my face. "Why don't we go inside and have some tea?" she paused, "But first, you should meet DJ."

We walked across campus to the second floor of the Putnam Science Center, now known as Murphy's Lab. On the way she explained that the drill treatment was for hunger. They called it a *field surgery*.

The strangest thing was all the G's around campus. It practically looked like school was in session. Drinking from water fountains, or waiting in line outside bathrooms.

"How'd you keep them from freezing?" I asked.

"Friction and wind cover," she answered. "A few degrees makes a big difference. I used to patrol the campus and make sure the frosty ones came inside, but once I started leaving doors open they figured it out on their own. Plus in large herds they rotate, like penguins."

On the first floor of Murphy's Lab, two G's were dressed in blue coveralls. One was painting a red wall black. The other was spreading black paint on the ground with a mopping.

On the second floor all the G's were dressed in lab coats. The doors were all marked with rainbow colored placards. While walking down the hall Stephanie removed the orange drill from her belt, and handed it to a G in a lab-coat who dutifully carried it to the room with the orange placard.

We entered a chemistry lab, where a G in a lab coat was prominently emblazoned with a sticker that read, "Hello: My name is *Derill*."

"Watch this!" Brian tittered like a school girl as he approached Derill and said boldly, "*Earl Grey, hot!*"

Derill shambled over to an elaborate tea set, built out of a bunsen burner, an Erlenmeyer flask, and some extra bubblers connected with tubes. After a moment's hesitation Derill began to prepare a pot of tea.

Stephanie invited us to have a seat while they changed out of their hazmat suits in a storage closet. By the time they came back, Derill was serving the tea. Stephanie was in a blue dress and Brian was dressed in black slacks, a black shirt, and a black tie.

"Her name is Derill Jamila Lords," Stephanie explained. "But we've been calling her *DJ*."

"I've never heard of a girl named Derill," said Alix.

"You've never heard of Daryl Hannah?" retorted Brian.

Stephanie continued, "She's a patient of mine. Stage four brain cancer. Her general practitioner identified the strangest symptom. Derill had stopped experiencing hunger. By the time she realized there was a problem she was already emaciated. They would have caught it sooner, but she was still eating out of habit, just never enough. Poor thing was slowly starving herself to death. She finally went to her doctor after she fainted from malnourishment. They thought she had a tapeworm or something, but sent her to me when scans revealed the tumor."

I sipped the tea, which absolutely was not Earl Grey. "What flavor is this?"

Brian sat up and sipped the tea. "Dammit! It's oatstraw and ginger." He stood up and held the cup out to Derill. "I said *Earl Grey, hot*!"

"Don't yell at her!" ordered Stephanie.

"I didn't yell, but it's not right," he countered.

"Well then, don't raise your voice at her."

"You're right," he admitted. "I'll make the tea." He got up and went to the counter.

"Oatstraw and ginger is perfect." Stephanie patted Derill on the head. "Thank you DJ. It's delicious," she whispered.

"I wish you wouldn't do that," said Brian. "It confuses her. She'll never learn that way."

Stephanie sipped her tea. "Anyway, DJ was inoperable. The cancer was sloughing cells into her spinal fluid. We found clusters all over her body. All we could really do was make her comfortable. But after she succumbed to the cancer she wasn't like the other PDS sufferers."

"PDS?" asked Niles.

"*Partially Deceased Syndrome*," Stephanie answered. "That's what I started calling it. Because DJ's living condition persisted, and she never felt the drive to eat." She turned her head and raised her voice so Brian could hear, "But she still triggers when she's angry, which is why we don't yell at her!"

"I know. I'm sorry." Brian returned with a new pot.

"Now she's my highest functioning patient, probably because she was put on dietary supplements before she died." Stephanie continued, "Her cancer originated in her hypothalamus, which regulates hunger. That got me wondering if I could replicate her condition. It turns out that we can eliminate their hunger with targeted brain damage."

"Targeted brain damage? Don't be so modest!" Brian interrupted. "It's like drilling a hole through a watermelon seed that's still inside the watermelon. This woman is a genius!"

"Enough about me," she blushed. "Max, what are you doing here?"

"I'm looking for you!" I answered.

She looked puzzled, so I opened my pack and spilled the research out on the table. "I'm Rich Hartwell's son, and this is the only hard copy of the research he was doing before he died. I've also got digital copies of the research my science teacher was doing. I heard your show, so I brought it here hoping you were equipped to continue their work. Find a cure for this thing. Some kind of vaccine, or something."

She sifted through the pages. "Wow! Max, this is amazing." She grabbed the zPad and browsed the digital files. "Do you mind if I make copies?"

I nodded. "Go ahead."

"Awesome. I'll sign you onto the Wi-Fi network and start the transfer." She tapped away on the zPad.

"Download all our research onto his machine too," Brian suggested. "Distributed redundancy, I always say."

"Good idea." Stephanie agreed and dragged the files over. "I'll look these over tonight, so we can discuss it on the show tomorrow."

"That'd be great!" I replied. "So, how do you know me?" I asked.

"I knew your mother," she answered.

"What? How?"

"We were researchers together." She paused, withholding something.

"You're talking about Mom's book, *Psychoclass A*?" I guessed.

"That's right." she said. "Before you were born, your mom and I were studying what we termed *psychoclasses*. Trying to get to the root of human aggression. We knew that there was a strong correlation between abusive and dominating personality types and certain physical formations in the brain. And we knew that adverse childhood experiences had a transformative effect on those areas of the brain. In other words, childhood trauma caused a kind of scar tissue in the brain that permanently altered the way someone thought. I'm talking learned hardware, not software. And we hypothesized that xenophobia, racial supremacy, bigotry, maybe even collectivism itself could all be rooted in this disturbingly common brain damage. Specifically decreased activity in the prefrontal cortex, and increased activity in the amygdala, triggered by child abuse and neglect. We discovered a nearly perfect correlation between adult aggressiveness, cerebral scar tissue, and traumatic childhood experiences, which we classified in five escalating categories. Psychoclass A, B, C, D and E."

"What does that have to do with me?" I asked.

"Well, to us Psychoclass A and E were only theoretical. Psychoclass A described a human brain with absolutely no scar tissue at all, which would require a childhood completely without the minutest degree of abuse, neglect, or any traumatic experiences during the brain's formative years. That's what we wanted to study, but after surveying hundreds of potential subjects . . ." she stopped, pausing to sip her tea.

She sat back in her seat and eyed everyone in the room one at a time. "I need everyone to let me and Max speak alone."

Alix and Niles eyed each other awkwardly.

"Why don't I show you two the studio?" Brian suggested.

"That'd be awesome!" Niles beamed, as they all got up to leave. "You have a synthesizer right?" asked Alix as they disappeared down the hall.

Stephanie leaned forward and spoke with a grave seriousness, but she still sounded like a camp counselor. "Max, we need to discuss this alone because it concerns matters of your medical history, and I feel you've got a natural right to your medical privacy. Before you were born your parents and I involved you in a renegade psychological experiment." She put her hand against her forehead. "When I say it like that it sounds so unethical," she smiled.

"What kind of experiment?" I was dumbfounded.

"The psychoclass data formed a kind of bell curve, with about 80% of the population occupying Psychoclass C in the middle, and 10% groupings on either side. Psychoclass D was exceptionally aggressive, prone to sociopathic professions, like public office. Psychoclass B was the opposite, exceptionally empathetic, like your parents. But to flesh out our theory we had to study Psychoclass A too, and it was only theoretical. Transition from one psychoclass to another seemed impossible. After hours of psychotherapy and regular doses of empathogens we saw marked changes in behavior, and mental processes, but not in the scar tissue, which seems irreversible. In other words, the software can change but the hardware was pretty permanent. So, since we couldn't find subjects, and we couldn't make them . . . we decided to try and raise them."

I was speechless.

"So, for the first five years of your life I worked with your parents to ensure your healthy psychological, and neurological growth. I observed your play, did regular brain scans, planned your nutrition. But we followed a kind of *Prime Directive*, that we wouldn't interfere with your natural development. We decided punitive discipline ran too high a risk of triggering minor scarring. Multiple studies show that brain trauma in young children raised in violent homes resembles that of soldiers in war. So it was important to allow you to direct your own mental development. We were just facilitators."

257

"So, what happened?" I asked.

"When your mom died unexpectedly your dad decided to pull you from the program, and focus on parenting full time. We thought the loss of a parent at a young age probably constituted enough emotional trauma to disqualify you from the research, but we had twelve other participants."

"You mean Ellie?" I guessed.

"Ellie? You mean Elizabeth Paige?"

I nodded.

"How do you know about her?" she asked excitedly.

"It's a long story. She's from Boston," I began.

"I know."

"Ellie and her mom came looking for my dad because she was bitten early on, but it turns out Ellie's immune."

"Wait! Ellie is immune to PDS!?" she asked. "Where is she?"

"She's back home. At Dad's cabin on Stinson Lake," I answered.

"You've got to bring her in. I have so many questions! This is huge! I'll bet all the participants in the Psychoclass A experiments are immune!"

"Well, wait a minute. If Ellie's immune because of the experiment, wouldn't that mean I'm immune?" I asked.

"Maybe . . . You didn't complete the program, but I'd say probably. We'd need to do an MRI scan to identify your psychoclass."

"What's an MRI?" I asked.

"*Magnetic resonance imaging.* It's an imaging process that uses magnetic fields to create a 3D model of your brain, or really any organ. I can identify your psychoclass based on physical structures in the brain."

"And you have a MRI machine here on campus?"

"Yes! I read about these radiation treatments in Amsterdam, so Brian and I retrieved a bunch of equipment from my old oncology lab."

"Well let's do it!" I jumped up.

"Ok! Ooh! But wait. I don't have the electricity, and it's getting late. I want to spend some time looking over your research. Why don't you and your friends grab a room in the dorms. I'll have Brian load the furnace, and we'll do the show in the morning. By then we should have enough power to run the scan, and we'll have the results by lunch. Sound good?"

"Sure, yes. Absolutely!"

Forty: Psychoclasses of the Dead

The next morning I tried to hail Ellie and the others with the handheld CB radio, but we were out of range. There was no reason for them to worry. We'd prepared for a three day trip, and we were ahead of schedule. Besides, odds were they would hear the show, which was a stronger signal, and then they'd know we found Murphy's Lab.

After breakfast we all met in the studio before the show for a sound test. Each of us had a microphone and a headset to hear the live feed, which Brian adjusted on the soundboard to equalize the volume. Niles preferred to assist Brian with the soundboard, instead of being on the show. Alix took the mic to do her own sound test.

"Live from the Info Planet! Waging his crusade on ignorance!"

The voice in headset wasn't Alix, it was Joel Saxen.

Alix and Brian laughed and exchanged a fist bump. "It worked!" Alix beamed. "Isn't it awesome! Brian helped me install the voice modulator last night while you guys were talking. I figured I should go on the air as Joel Saxen."

"That's a great idea!" Stephanie agreed. "I'm sure my listeners will be glad to hear he's alive and back on the air," she smiled. "Oh. That reminds me! We need to connect to the Pirate Radio Network. Brian, do you have the latest pirate code?"

"Affirmative!" Brian spun his office chair around and began pressing keys on the laptop.

"How do you know about the pirate code?" I asked.

"They broadcast it over the radio repeaters. It's the IP address of the Pirate Radio Network portal," answered Brian. "It's how we connect to the dark net."

"I know," I responded. "But how did you find out about it?"

"Twenty seconds!" warned Niles.

"Pirates Without Borders and the Pirate Radio Network existed before the outbreak," explained Brian. "It was just underground before."

"That reminds me! Max, we're going to discuss psychoclasses on the show, but the Psychoclass A experiments are off limits. Don't mention it on the air." Stephanie put on her headphones.

"Ok," I said hurriedly. "But why?"

"Confidentiality of the other participants. If word got out they might be immune they'd be in danger." She gestured at me to put on my headphones.

"Ten seconds!" warned Niles.

I put them on and could hear the intro music beginning.

>"TRIGGER WARNING!!"

Stephanie's voice came from a recording as she frantically got her show notes in order.

>"This show may contain content, language and humor that is intended for a mature audience. If that's not you please stop listening now."

Alix kicked her feet excitedly and adjusted her mic.

>"Nothing you hear on Infection Science Hour is intended as medical advice, therapy or really anything but entertainment. Please take everything you hear with a grain of salt."

Brian spun around in his chair.

"If you're hearing us on the Pirate Radio Network the views expressed here are not necessarily those of the station you're listening on. Now that all that's out of the way, let's start the show!"

Stephanie scooted forward and spoke into the mic, "Good morning and welcome to another *Infection Science Hour.* I'm Dr. Stephanie Murphy. With me as always, Agent Sovryn."

"Hailing frequencies open, Captain!" said Brian.

Stephanie continued, "Today we're doing a special extended edition of *Infection Science Hour* to welcome two special guests we have in the studio. Why don't you introduce yourselves?"

"That's right Dr. Murphy. I am the one. The only. The Patriot of the apocalypse. Joel Saxen!" Joel's voice filtered through the sound system and fed into our headsets with a split second delay. Niles pushed some buttons on the sound board so a roar of applause swelled behind Joel's voice, and then simmered back down. "And I'm here with a good buddy of mine, Max Hartwell."

My heart sank. *She said my name!* Suddenly everyone was looking at me, and I froze.

Brian covered his mic with his hand and whispered across the table. "Introduce yourself."

I leaned forward. "Hey guys . . . Long time listener. First time . . . talker." I began to sweat.

"Max, we're very excited to have you on the show to compare notes." Stephanie pulled out copies of Dad's research. "From the looks of it you're a budding young scientist yourself," she began. "You've brought us some research that really challenges some of my previous theories. Why don't you tell us about it?"

"Well . . . " I began. "My dad was a virologist before he was infected, and he was studying the outbreak. So, after he died I made copies of all his research, and I've been looking for a scientist who can use it ever since."

"Thank you for your service!" added Brian.

"Right . . . Well, he thought it was a virus, and he was wrong about that, but he was right about there being a hidden infection. The active infection is transmitted through bodily fluids, like saliva, and that's obvious. But there's also hidden infection we all carry, and that's airborne."

I paused, but everyone just kept staring at me, so I went on. "Eventually I made it to Thornhaven. That's what they call Thornton Middle School now. And my science teacher was doing her own research. She discovered microscopic egg sacs in the lungs and throat of living subjects, which allows the parasite to spread like the flu."

"That explains why everyone changes, even if they haven't been bitten," she explained. "But that's not the most groundbreaking thing about your dad's research. All this time we've been looking at infected brains, trying to figure out why the spongiform brain damage is different from one host to another. Trying to figure out why some patients retain more cognitive functions than others. We thought we were looking at different strains, or maybe it was just random. But your dad connected his research to psychological research I was going more than fifteen years ago!"

"Cut to the chase here, Doc. Tell the People what we're up against." interrupted Joel.

"Ok, Joel. Today we're going to be discussing the diversity we've seen in the abilities of PDS sufferers. It's been a subject of great speculation. Do they run or walk? Moan or talk? Are they mutating or are there multiple subspecies? There have been many theories, but thanks to Dr. Hartwell's contributions I think we can conclude that the disparity is not in the disease, but in the hosts. We know the prion consumes what it can't use, and hijacks whatever it needs to get the body up and moving again."

"Dr. Murphy, hang on," I interrupted. "You're calling it a prion. But I've got microscopic images confirming it's a parasite."

"Well, you're half right," she agreed. "It's probably a good idea to do a little review. I've been calling it a prion since the early days, because that's the only microbe we know of that causes the spongiform brain damage we've seen. But your science teacher was correct when she identified the parasite as a relative of toxoplasmosis. The common strain of toxoplasmosis even has similar psychological effects on cats and mice, but if you look at her images of the adult parasite you can see it has two nuclei, while common toxoplasmosis has only one. What I think we're dealing with is a symbiotic relationship between the toxoplasmosis parasite, and a prion nestled inside it, which explains the second nucleus. It's similar to the relationship between mosquitoes and malaria, where the malaria matures in the mosquito's gut and makes the mosquito's bite contagious. Toxoplasmosis is usually fairly benign to humans, but by using the prion in its digestion the combination is devastating."

"And what the heck is a prion anyway?" Joel interrupted.

"Good question, Joel," she continued. "It's a *protein infection*. Like Mad Cow, or Scrapie. Incidentally, that's why some people call PDS sufferers *Scrapes*. A prion is a deformed protein that attacks healthy proteins and transforms them to its mutated shape. This triggers a chain reaction through the brain that spreads in a crystalline pattern. But in this case, the location of the damage is not spontaneous."

"Are you saying this protein virus inside the parasite directs which parts of the brain to damage?" I asked.

"It's probably the other way around," she answered. "A prion is a lower order of life than a virus. It's more like a crystal, and not technically alive at all. I don't think there is a mastermind exactly. I think we're seeing an emergent complexity resulting from the symbiosis of two otherwise simple pathogens, resulting in behaviors we've never seen before."

Joel interjected, "If you ask me Doc, the mastermind is the shadow government. The Deep State. Obviously the secret chiefs have decided to initiate their depopulation agenda and they engineered this brain bug to do the dirty work."

Brian laughed. "Joel, as a former CDC employee myself I can tell you you're way overestimating the competency of these people. The CDC didn't invent the pathogen. They don't know where it came from either."

"I'm onto you, Feds!" screamed Joel. "Don't think I don't know that you're part of the conspiracy of lowered expectations!"

Stephanie laughed. "Alright guys. Conflict is good for radio, but let's limit our baseless accusations to a minimum. We're getting off topic. Here's what I'm getting at. During the latency period the parasitic larva congregate in the lungs and circulatory system, but as they mature they invade the brain to complete their reproductive cycle. And they build their colony right between the amygdala, which regulates aggression, and the hypothalamus, which regulates hunger. The colony essentially triggers insatiable hunger and aggression to motivate the host."

"What do you mean colony, Doc? Like they got some kind of queen bee?" asked Joel.

"On the contrary," Stephanie explained. "Each parasite appears completely independent, and under the right conditions capable of beginning a whole new colony. But here's where it gets interesting. In humans, the amygdala, and hypothalamus experience windows of imprint vulnerability during early childhood. So, for example, a child who experiences food insecurity suffers a much greater trauma than an adult, but as an adult that child will still have a distorted relationship to food, because of the physical damage childhood trauma does to the hypothalamus. That could lead to a variety of eating disorders. Similarly, if you trigger a young child's fight-or-flight mechanism during their early imprint vulnerability it leaves a physical mark, like a scar, on their limbic system, and changes how their brain assesses danger as adults. Fast forward to the PDS epidemic, and hosts who experienced different

265

childhood imprints have different brain structures, which provides different assets for the pathogen to exploit."

"And that's where Dad's research on psychoclasses comes in?" I asked. "A psychoclass is a group of people with similar childhood imprints, which means they have similar brain structures as adults, which means they retain similar abilities as ghouls."

"Oh! We don't use the *G word* around here," corrected Stephanie. "But that's exactly right, Max. That's why we've been seeing more complex behaviors in hosts from more violent backgrounds, like police and military. The bulk of the population is in the middle of the bell curve, what we call Psychoclass C. They have only moderate amounts of scar tissue. In these cases the infected host is slow, and primarily motivated by hunger, not rage. But a minority of the population, who experienced unusually traumatic childhoods, have a greater degree of scar tissue. Those we'd identify as Psychoclass D have increased aggressive tendencies as adults, and retain higher cognitive functions as PDS sufferers."

"I went through our records here, and the scans correlate perfectly," Brian volunteered. "Brain scans you'd classify as Psychoclass D come from hosts we observed transforming faster, running, using tools and in one case imitating speech, although only a few words."

"Exactly!" Stephanie agreed. "And, since they are more motivated by rage than hunger, our hypothalamus suppression procedure is less effective in those patients. But even stranger, in Psychoclass D hosts Dr. Hartwell observed increased symptoms even during the latency period, including insomnia, paranoia and self destructive recklessness."

"Hold it right there, Doc. You're talking about living breathing homegrown human?" Joel asked.

"That's right. In the authoritarian and sociopathic psychoclasses, the parasite begins to hijack the limbic system while they're still alive! It triggers paranoia, depression, and even dementia. Really anything to increase risky behaviors, which increases the likelihood of the host getting themselves killed, and continuing the reproductive cycle of the parasite."

"Now wait a minute! You're basically saying that if the global elites get infected they turn into some kind of super cannibals?!"

"The opposite deviation also exists," Brian nudged. "Psychoclass B hosts are more empathetic, and more averse to aggression than average. So, their limbic system is more resistant to the parasite's control. Transformation in these cases is slower. In the wild they are more lethargic than the others. If they hunt they tend to follow more ambitious leaders, but here's the kick, they also respond better to rehabilitation."

After Brian finished Stephanie continued, "Psychoclasses A and E are mostly theoretical. The model suggests they encompass less than one in a thousand people. Living Psychoclass E people would be incapable of natural empathy. Hyper aggressive alive or dead, and much higher functioning post mortem. Potentially even intelligent."

"Intelligent!" I gasped.

"Yes!" she insisted, "Theoretically a sufficiently aggressive host could retain their human intellect if the parasite deemed it useful to hunting, and they fed enough. Psychoclass A is the opposite. Without any scar tissue between the amygdala and the hypothalamus there would be nowhere for the mature parasites to nest. The unique architecture of their brain may make it unsuitable for them. So, a Psychoclass A host would remain a carrier, but could be essentially immune."

"You're saying that immunity is nurture, not nature. It's not genetic," I summarized.

"Exactly, we call traits like this *epigenetic*. It's similar to addiction. There might be a genetic predisposition, but it's an adaptive response triggered by the environment."

"Does that mean everyone is born potentially immune?" I asked.

267

"Great question!" she answered. "I mean, listeners shouldn't try this at home, and we're going to be investigating this in the coming weeks, but yes. Moving forward, we're living in a world where these larva will probably lay dormant in us forever, but every newborn is potentially immune to the adult parasite, if they can survive the early years of imprint vulnerability without experiencing trauma."

"Now, wait a minute!" protested Brian. "If Psychoclass A was less than point one percent of the population before the outbreak, how in the world are parents supposed to shelter children from trauma now? Food is scarce. People are turning on one another. Danger lurks around every corner. It doesn't sound like an ideal scenario to raise kids."

Stephanie seemed perplexed. "I'm not saying it'll be easy. I certainly have no interest in raising children in this environment."

"Me, either," inserted Brian.

"But the stakes have never been higher," Stephanie continued. "Everyone wants scientists like us to come up with an injection, or a pill. They want us to give them a quick fix for all the problems of the world. But that's not how science works. We have to work with the facts we observe. I'm not saying I know all the answers, but I hope we are contributing to the discussion. And maybe not today, but someday communities of survivors around the world are going to start building a life for themselves again. And when they do, it's critical that they have this information."

Brian looked surprised. "That sounds very optimistic. I mean you're basically talking about raising a new kind of human. A much more peaceful and empathetic human. And you're talking about doing it in the worst war zone imaginable."

"I don't think we have a choice," Stephanie continued. "We're dealing with a disease that exponentially increases human aggression, and uses it against us. Long term, I don't think we can afford to be enemies anymore. And in these conditions, that means we can't afford to abuse our children anymore."

"You're not just talking about Psychoclass A individuals," I volunteered. "You're talking about raising Generation A."

"I like that." Stephanie beamed. "That's exactly right."

Forty One: Magnetic Resonance Imaging

After the show, Stephanie brought me to the basement of Murphy's Lab where she and Brian brought a wide variety of medical equipment they'd salvaged, including the MRI machine.

There was a dressing room where she had me change into a hospital gown to ensure there was nothing metal on me, like zippers or buttons. They would be affected by the magnetic field.

The MRI machine was a large narrow tube that looked a bit like a giant clothes dryer, but open at both ends. I laid down on a table that slid along a track into the tube, and Stephanie monitored the process from another room, although there was an intercom inside the tube, and a panic button. Apparently some people get claustrophobic.

The scan took thirty minutes, and I had to stay perfectly still or I'd blur the image. Stephanie said not to fall asleep, because I might nod my head. So, I kept my eyes open.

The machine made a lot of rumbling clunking noises, which made it impossible not to imagine being surrounded by G's in some kind of metal death trap. I tried to put it out of my mind.

A few minutes into the cycle a rhythmic buzzing began that sounded pretty much exactly like a fire alarm of some kind, and my mind filled with images of panic and mayhem.

I closed my eyes and tried to just zone out, ignore the clamour and get lost in my own head.

I tried to think about Dad. About the way it was before everything fell apart. I tried to remember the little things, like hiking in the mountains with the PorcScouts to get a good view of an eclipse, or making banana split milkshakes on a Sunday morning. How Dad said microscopes and telescopes were really the same thing, it's just a matter of perspective.

I kept getting distracted, thinking about how things were built. All those tools, and processes, and trade agreements, and shipping routes it took to even make a banana split milkshake possible. The sugar and the cream came from entirely different countries. The blender was probably manufactured on the other side of the planet, but the electricity was generated at the local hydroelectric plant. Dad used to say, "We want bananas, not republics." It was some kind of point about puppet governments, but from now on we'll have to make our own milkshakes. We'll have to start from scratch again, which is an opportunity to build something better this time.

Then I thought about the enemy. Not the G's, but the brain bugs themselves. Dad used to talk about something called *shadow biospheres.* Closed ecosystems of strange life forms that evolved independently inside volcanoes, or deep in the ocean for millennia. I imagined the parasites seeping out of some arctic crack, or crawling off of some meteorite. Wherever they came from, they wasted no time adapting to exploit us.

Although, everyone we'd met was brainstorming ways to exploit them. Dr. Blum wanted his bioweapon. Syrkis used them for electricity. Baron Steen had his freaky super predators. Even Dr. Murphy was basically using them as servants.

What if the parasites learned exploitation from us? After all, their primary adaptation was symbiosis. The prion and the parasites cooperated to become more than either of them was before. They had a mutually beneficial relationship. They probably didn't even really know we existed. They lived in a microscopic world of amino acids and protein molecules.

Maybe it's humanity that has to learn symbiosis from them. We had to learn to coexist, if not with the G's then at least with each other. To stop taking advantage of each other, and find ways to live and interact to the mutual advantage of all.

The disease itself was a relatively simple thing really. The infected didn't have super powers. They weren't magic. They were essentially the same organism as us. Just motivated differently.

No. Civilization collapsed because people made enemies of each other instead of the real threat. Because people were petty, and vindictive, and power hungry. Civilization collapsed because people refused to cooperate. To band together. To share the science. The parasites were not our downfall. We were. They were no threat without our own aggressive tendencies.

Then I thought about Mom's experiment and realized civilization didn't fail because of the dead, they failed because of their own brains. Because of their psychoclass. Because of generation after generation of abuse, and callousness, and prejudice. They thought it was normal, because it was common. They thought it was unavoidable because they lacked imagination. But it always seemed flawed to me. Pointless. Ignorant. Even tragic. I always felt different.

What if this brain scan proved I was different? Different like Ellie? What if we were the first of our kind? And what if this plague had inadvertently paved the way for people like us? *Psychoclass A.* Not just immune to the parasite, but immune to the human instinct to harm others for personal gain?

But epigenetic immunity was only a theory, and I'd noticed theories had a habit of being falsified. First it was a virus, then it was a parasite. Now it's a prion inside a parasite. But that's just a theory too. Tomorrow it might be an alien fungus, or interdimensional radiation. Who knows, maybe Niles would turn out to be right about the nanobots, or Scott was right about the vampires?

I used to think science was how we know things with absolute certainty, but it isn't really. It's just somebody's best guess. Theories are just ideas consistent with what we've observed so far, but we're seeing new things all the time, and people don't see things the same way. Dad used to say, "The Universe consists of non-simultaneously apprehended events." Even if our ideas get better over time, they're never really perfect, and sometimes everything we think we know is thrown into question by one little inconsistent fact.

Ellie was immune. That was a fact. Ellie was part of the Psychoclass A experiments, and so was I. Those were facts. But did that mean I was immune, or was it a coincidence?

Then I wondered for the first time . . . what does a society look like built by people like us?

Forty Two: Life, the Universe, and Everything

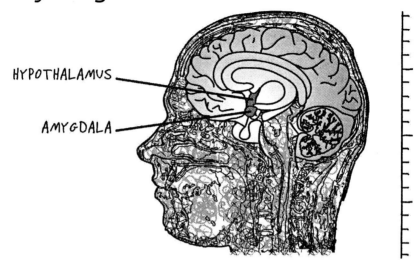

HYPOTHALAMUS

AMYGDALA

Stephanie explained that it would take the computer some time to render the images. After that it should be pretty easy for her to identify my psychoclass. Niles and Alix spent their time with Brian in the radio studio.

Even though Alix still knew him as Holland by name, I could tell that Niles was coming out more and more as he became comfortable. And I don't think Niles could resist geeking out about hacker stuff with Brian.

I went with Stephanie back to the lab upstairs. She was eager to examine the parasite's second nucleus with her new electron microscope, which could see smaller objects in finer detail than anything at Thornhaven.

While Stephanie prepared her report on my brain, I decided to poke around DJ's medical records, which were among the files Brian transferred to my zPad.

Partial death by terminal brain cancer. She stopped breathing first, but after that DJ's transition was practically gentle. Her organs shut down one at a time, but were no longer dependent on one another enough to crash the others. Her heart kept beating for weeks. So, there was debate whether or not to even call it death. It was actually DJ herself who self-identified as *partially deceased.*

The PDS symptoms increased gradually, including sound sensitivity, muscle spasms, and pupil constriction, but insomnia was the most dramatic change that signaled the parasite's take over.

Even though she no longer slept, DJ said she could sense other people sleeping. She said it felt like a magnetic force was pulling her toward them. Stephanie saw no scientific basis for such a sensation, so she attributed it to DJ's growing dementia, but she never actually tested it.

Once DJ's heart stopped, her brain death was rapid. Only what the parasite preserved survived. She lost verbal ability almost immediately, but still mostly understood what other people were saying, and she was surprisingly expressive with her face.

Teaching her was difficult, but possible. It took patience to establish a routine, because DJ didn't learn by instruction, only by habit. But long term, deterioration was in one direction, and it got worse every time she was triggered.

Stephanie and Brian had collaborated on a serum based on DJ's early dietary supplements, and the serum Dr. Blum was developing. Because even if DJ didn't get hungry, the parasite colony did. It was a cocktail of vitamins, hormones, protein and empathogens. She'd been tweaking the recipe since the beginning, keeping all her patients nourished and hydrated with weekly injections.

I was browsing the current composition of the serum when Stephanie interrupted, smiling and holding a manila envelope. "I've got your results!" She removed a set of black and white films and attached them to a light box for viewing. They were a centimeter by centimeter cross section of my brain.

"See here? This is your amygdala and hypothalamus." She pointed to a couple masses of grey matter in the center of my head. "There's no doubt about it. You're Psychoclass A!"

"And that means I'm immune like Ellie?" I asked.

"I think so. Obviously you shouldn't go testing it directly. This is a huge discovery! We've got to move forward carefully. I think the next steps are for me to make contact with the other participants and see if any of them are immune for sure, and you should bring Ellie here so I can do a side by side comparison."

I thought about Ellie's attitude toward scientific inquiry. Given her experience with Dr. Blum and Mrs. Lessard I couldn't imagine her ever consenting to more tests. Lab coats made her skin crawl. And a serious hypothesis could be made that subjecting her to further trauma could compromise the immunity. But before I could explain the situation gunshots rang out somewhere on the campus.

Stephanie's eyes went wide and we ran to the window.

Through the trees in Fiske Quad, I spotted Dr. Blum's half-track blocking the intersection of Main Street and Appian Way.

Two soldiers were firing military rifles, clearing all the G's within range, and triggering the G's in earshot of the gunfire.

"No!" Stephanie screamed as her patients were slaughtered.

One of the soldiers heard her, and took aim. We both ducked as he peppered the building, showering us in shards of glass.

"It's Dr. Blum!" I told her. "He must have heard me on the show and come looking for Ellie."

The gunshots continued in rapid bursts, as the crowd turned and shambled toward them.

"Brian and the others are still in the Media Arts Center. We should get down to the basement and take cover," she suggested.

"Dr. Stephanie Murphy!" Dr. Blum's voice boomed through a megaphone.

I peeked over the windowsill, and saw Dr. Blum strolling toward Murphy's Lab, surrounded by his entourage, still firing wildly.

"You should really be commended for your service!" Dr. Blum continued. "I know we've had our *academic* differences, but leading me to both my escaped specimen, and the traitor Brian Sovryn is above and beyond the call of duty! Cooperate now and I can offer you leniency for your past transgressions."

"We need to get everyone on the Ghool Bus and get the heck out of here!" I said.

"And leave all my research in the hands of that sociopath!" she objected. "No way. There's no telling what he'd do with it. Brian and I are prepared for this. We'll wipe the servers before we let him take this place."

We ran downstairs.

On the first floor the two G's in the coveralls were triggered and clamouring to get out of the building. Stephanie snuck up behind them and pushed a wall mounted handicap door opener to let them out.

The G's ran toward the firefight, triggering others along the way. Dr. Blum's gunmen continued to put down anything that got near them.

Stephanie grabbed DJ and put her hands in mine. "Take her downstairs and wait for me. I'm going to get as many patients out of the line of fire as possible."

"Wait!" I stopped. "I can't hide here. Even if you wipe the servers, if he even suspects that I'm immune like Ellie I'm going to end up a guinea pig on his surgery table!"

Agent Sovryn burst in wearing red paintball armor with a gold sigma painted on the breastplate. He was armed with a fully automatic M16 rifle, and followed by two G's in matching Sig-man jackets. He was exploiting their group affinity for backup. Alix and Niles were close behind them, looking terrified.

"It looks bad out there, but besides the doctor I count only two grunts and a driver," explained Brian. "I know the terrain. If we stick to the plan, I think I can take 'em."

"Plan? What plan?" I asked.

"All you kids go down to the basement and close yourself in. We're going hunting."

"No way!" I held up the manila folder of my test results. "This may as well be a death warrant if he gets ahold of me."

"Good news?" Brian asked Stephanie.

"Tests indicate he's immune," she answered.

"No way!" exclaimed Niles. "That's awesome!"

There was a lull in the gunfire and Brian peaked around the side of the building and came back. "They're on the move again. Whatever we're doing we've got to do it now!"

"Ok!" Niles clapped his hands to get everyone's attention. "Brian, can you lead them south?"

"No problem. I'll take the Sig-men and draw their fire. We'll ambush them down by Brickyard Pond where there's lots of natural cover. But where are you going?"

"The Ghool Bus is parked right behind Murphy's Lap," Niles answered. "If we go now we can get out of here and back on the road before they can even get back to their vehicle. Just buy us as much time as possible?"

"Sounds good to me," said Brian.

Stephanie nodded.

Brian ran out, laying cover fire as he and his squad crossed the Central Quad toward the math building. Stephanie took DJ down to the basement, and the rest of us ran toward the Ghool Bus.

We climbed inside, where Stinky was lounging on the dash. Alix hopped in the driver's seat and started the engine.

"BIODAD," I called out. "Reverse course back home."

Forty Three: The Social Contract

An hour later the gunfire had faded into the distance, and into memory. We were about halfway home with no sign of pursuit when we started picking up something on my handheld CB radio. The voice was heavily distorted. I couldn't make out anything.

"BIODAD?" I called.

"Yes, Max," came Dad's simulated voice.

"Can you do anything to boost the CB receiver?"

"My internal amplifier circuits are equipped with automatic gain control. That could smooth out the audio quality," it answered.

"I got this!" Alix plugged the CB into the BIODAD system. She toggled the dials until the voice came through clearly.

"Max?" It was a gravelly male voice that was familiar, but hard to place. "You left me in the supply closet, Max."

"Who is that?" asked Alix. "How does he know your name?"

"It's Sheriff Nap!" cried Niles. "But I thought he was dead?!"

"Max, is that you?" *It was Ellie!* "Are you nearby? Over."

I pushed the button to transmit. "No! It's not me!" I yelled. "It's the Sheriff. Do you copy! It's Sheriff Nap! Over!"

There was a long pause.

"Max! If this is a joke it isn't funny," Ellie said finally. "Is Alix playing with the voice modulator? Over."

There was quiet again. What could I say? Any message we transmitted would be intercepted by Nap.

Eventually the silence was interrupted by escalating laughter. At first it was just Nap, but before long someone in the background was laughing hysterically. *Is he with a group?* "Quite a pickle we got here, Max," teased the Sheriff. "It seems like I can hear both you brats, and you can both hear me, but your friend can't hear you."

BIODAD had boosted the CB receiver, but we had no way to boost the transmitter. We could pick up Ellie's signal, but she couldn't hear us. *Sheriff Nap must be somewhere in between.*

"Seems like we have a bit of a hostage situation here, Max," said Nap.

"What?!" cried Ellie.

Nap only chuckled menacingly.

"What do you want from me?" I asked.

"What do I want?! I want Thornhaven back. I want control of the leadership council again. I want everything you took from me!"

"I can't do that!" I protested.

"Do you know what happened after you left me at the mercy of Major *Whimpers*? He threw me in the boiler room with the rest of our fallen companions. There was just one difference. I'm still alive!"

"That's impossible!" I said, almost in a panic.

"It was my dead eye that saved me," he laughed. "When I cover my good eye these dead punks think I'm one of them."

My mind raced, trying to remember his face. *Was his eye patch over his good eye in the video?* I imagined him grabbing G's by the head and locking eyes with them until they accepted him.

281

He continued, "I have seen the dead do incredible things when no one is looking. Things you wouldn't believe."

"How are you even still alive!?" cried Ellie.

"Because down in that hot, dank hell I discovered a dangerous servant and a fearful master." Suddenly his voice was cold in a way I'd never heard before. "Death itself! Resist it, and death will devour you, but embrace it, and the dead will serve you! Death and I have forged a social contract. I feed their insatiable appetite, and in exchange they obey me. And today, Max, you and your friends are on the menu."

"You're a monster!" I screamed. "You'll have to find us first."

"Max, I'm the Sheriff of Grafton county." He continued in the same icy tone. "Do you really think I don't know about the cabin? Your Dad registered every weapon in that place."

Forty Four: Sending Out An SOS

Darleen's voice came over the CB. "Alix, if you're there, I'm freaking out here! Do you copy? Over." We could hear gunfire in the background.

Sheriff Nap was silent, but we knew he was listening.

"We're under attack!" yelled Darleen into the radio. "I repeat, G's are attacking the ship! Wherever you are, we need backup fast! Over."

I grabbed the radio. "Darleen? If you can hear me I need a HERD report."

There was no response. They couldn't hear us.

"BIODAD?" I called out. "Can you make a voice recording?" I asked.

"Yes, Max," came the digital voice.

"Good, begin recording. *This is an emergency distress call. We are under attack and requesting immediate assistance from any survivors within the sound of my voice. We are located in a cabin on the south shore of Stinson Lake, north of Blanoby. Please hurry!* End recording."

"What are you doing?" asked Niles.

"Hoping Larry or Syrkis can help," I answered. "BIODAD, repeat the recording on all CB channels."

"Yes, Max."

"Good thinking," said Alix, looking a little frayed with panic as her white knuckles gripped the wheel. "They'll be in range before we are."

We sped north at the Ghool Bus' top speed.

Forty Five: Miles Per Hour

We were headed east on Highway 25 approaching Blanoby. I knew we were almost in range, and was about to try hailing the ship again when Alix slammed on the brakes, throwing me forward against the dash, and coming to a complete stop near the Main Street exit.

"Why did you stop!" I demanded.

She pointed ahead, where Dr. Blum's half-track was waiting in the westbound lane.

"BIODAD," whispered Niles. "What's the maximum speed of the M3 Half-track?"

"In ideal conditions, the M3 Half-track has a recorded top speed of forty five miles per hour," whispered BIODAD.

"We can't go much faster than that," insisted Alix. "Not with the plow, and all the armor on this thing. Not to mention the dome hatch makes us a little topheavy."

The half-track driver revved their engine and flashed their high beams at us, as if daring us to run.

"What choice do we have?" I asked.

"Good point." Alix gripped the wheel and slammed the gas pedal to the floor. The tires shrieked as the bus fishtailed toward Main Street.

Bullets sprayed from their gun ports, ricocheting off our steel plating. We made the turn with the half-track in close pursuit behind us.

"Want me to go top side and return fire?" Niles offered.

"With a shotgun? No point. You don't have the range." I handed him my Mosquito. "See what you can do with this."

"You want me to shoot a .22 pistol at an armored military vehicle?" he protested. "Why don't I just throw marbles at them?"

"I don't know! Aim for the tires," I suggested. "That's the best we got."

Niles took the pistol and ran toward the back of the bus.

Alix jerked the wheel, throwing Niles off his feet. "Hey! Try to keep it on the road!" he yelled.

"You do your job, and let me do mine!" she ordered.

I went back to the CB radio. "This is the Ghool Bus hailing anyone aboard the Porcupette! We are closing on your location with hostiles in pursuit. If you read me, I need a HERD report. Over."

After a moment of static we heard Darleen's voice, "Max? Is that you? What the heck is a HERD report? Over."

"Darleen!" I exclaimed. "What's your status? Is everyone ok?"

"We're totally surrounded by G's! We barricaded the doors and windows, but Elliot has the only firepower. He's up in the crow's nest now, but I don't know how long we can hold them off."

"Put Elliot on," I asked.

"No way," she answered. "I'm in the safe room and I'm not going anywhere!"

"Darleen, the ship has an intercom. There's a panel near the entrance to the safe room," I explained. "Tell Elliot Dr. Blum is on our tail, and we'll need cover fire once we're in range. Then report back to me with what he says. Over."

Alix swerved to avoid obstacles in the road, jostling me around the cab. "We got G's in the street!" she yelled.

Niles took his shots with the pistol, using the sliding peephole as a gun port. "Just plow through 'em!" he yelled. "If we keep swerving like this we're going to flip over!"

Moments later Alix jerked the wheel hard, turning onto Stinson Lake Road, and tipping the bus up on two wheels.

It felt like time stopped.

I thought for sure we were going to roll over, but then the wheels slammed back down. Alix hit the gas, crashing through bodies like soggy piñatas. She cranked the windshield wipers to clear the gore.

"They missed the turn!" Niles reported from the peephole. "That'll buy us some time!"

But not much. In less than a minute they were sprinkling us with gunfire again.

Darleen came back on the CB, "Elliot says he'll do what he can, but a sheriff is hiding in the woods, and if he gets a clear shot he's taking it. Does that make sense to you? Who's the sheriff?"

"Darleen, I need you to get on the computer terminal, turn on the outside cameras and tell me what you see. Over."

"Max, they're everywhere!" I could hear the panic in her voice. "They're in the woods. They're in the street. They're even out on the ice!"

"Darleen, we're coming in fast, and we need to dock in a hurry. I need to know if the shuttle bay door is clear. Over."

"Not even a little bit! The pit traps are full and they're pounding on every door!"

I paused to think. "Holland, save your ammo! We're going to need it."

"What are you thinking?" asked Alix.

"BIODAD, can you open the shuttle bay door from here?" I asked.

"Negative. I will not have that ability until I am within Wi-Fi range," answered BIODAD.

"That's cutting it really close. Do you think you can do it?" I asked Alix.

"What choice do we have?" she answered, pushing the accelerator.

"Ok Darleen. Get everyone to the safe room, and be ready to close the shuttle bay doors the moment we're inside. Here's what we're going to do . . ."

Forty Six: Intruder Alert!

The closer we got to the ship the more G's filled the street. And not just strangers either. I saw some of my old teachers in the crowd, Thornton police officers, the occasional S-Mart employee, and even residents of Lochshire. *Sheriff Nap has been busy!*

They'd breached the perimeter fence and completely surrounded the ship, pounding on the windows and doors.

I heard gunshots as we approached. Ellie was in the crow's nest with her rifle. It was a defensible position, but she didn't have enough ammunition for a herd that size.

Alix yanked the wheel and spun the Ghool Bus a quarter turn. A trail of gore and broken bodies in our wake as the G's piled against the other side. The ship was straight ahead.

"BIODAD, I want you to open the shuttle bay door the moment we're in range," I ordered.

"Understood," it said.

"Hold on to something!" screamed Alix as she revved the engine and charged full speed into the crowd. Dozens of bodies crunched and bounced off the snow plow. Heads crushed under our tires.

The shuttle bay door began to open, and not a moment too soon. Just as we hit the slope of the driveway the half-track rear-ended us at full speed, launching the Ghool Bus up the driveway with such force that we left the ground.

As we sailed through the shuttle bay door the top of the bus hit the ceiling and sheared the dome hatch right off the roof.

We slammed down hard on the shuttle bay floor, skid forward out of control, and crashed right through the back wall on to the deck.

The gunfire began immediately. First Dr. Blum's men firing at us, and then Ellie firing back at them from above.

The path we plowed through the crowd began to fill in as G's stumbled up the driveway, cutting us off from the gunman, who were forced to turn their fire on the crowd.

Niles kicked open the emergency exit on the rear of the bus, pistol at the ready. "Everyone get inside! The door is smashed! This place is going to fill up fast." He fired the Mosquito and caught an incoming G in the face. It was so decayed I couldn't tell if it was a man or a woman.

Niles ran to the door to the lounge, but found it locked. He pounded on the door screaming, "Guys! let us in!"

I grabbed my staff and ran to the back of the bus. Alix followed close behind me with her shotgun. Half a dozen G's were already in the shuttle bay, and more were coming. I joined Niles, pounding on the door, while Alix aimed the Boomstick and opened fire.

Hephae opened the door and we all rushed in. He swung the sledgehammer nearly smashing my face, narrowly hitting a G over my shoulder. It's head, exploding against the door frame.

He slammed the door, as the avalanche of pounding and scratching immediately began on the other side.

"Well, where the heck have you guys been?" asked Hephae.

The glass doors between the lounge and the back deck were shattered, but the plywood reinforcements were holding. Grasping hands pushed through broken glass and started trying to pry back the plywood.

Alix jumped up on the edge of the fire pit and began firing through a knot hole in the plywood. We all piled segments of sofa against doors. It was holding, but still threatening to break as the G's pushed against it.

"We've got to get everyone down to the bunker and seal it!" I yelled.

"I think everyone's in the safe room," said Hephae. "Except Elliot. He's is in the crow's nest and won't come down."

The plywood began to split, and then the first G slipped through, knocking Alix to the ground. She fired the shotgun as she fell, obliterating the G on top of her, but now they were pouring in.

I helped her get to her feet, but she dropped the Boomstick, and it was left behind.

"Run!" screamed Niles as he fired the Mosquito into the mob, crippling more G's than he killed, leaving a trail of bleeding crawlers.

We all ran through the galley toward the front entrance, with the G's close behind.

Alix and Hephae turned the dining table on its side and held it like a wide shield, charging the G's and pushing them back into the galley.

I opened the safe room entrance behind the spiral staircase and started waving people in. Stinky darted between my legs and leapt into Darleen's lap.

"Where's Torrance?" asked Niles.

"Upstairs, I think," answered Darleen. "He took his BB gun and left."

"And you let him go!" Alix screamed.

"Where's Elliot?" I asked.

"Still in the crow's nest I think," she answered.

"Little help!?" yelled Hephae. He and Alix were pushing against the table, but the G's in the galley were overpowering them.

Niles shouldered in between Alix and Hephae and shoved.

"You three hold back the hordes as long as possible. I'm going after Torrance and Elliot," I said.

"Max, help us!" Alix insisted. "I'm your captain, and that's an order!"

G's were already pounding on the front door, the boarded windows, and the door to the shuttle bay in the studio. My mind raced, looking for our next move. "Holland, do you still have the Mosquito?" I asked.

"Yeah, but no ammo," he said.

"Hephae, what about the sledge?" I asked.

"I can't get a clear swing, and if I let go we're dinner," he said.

I had my staff. "I have an idea! We need to push them back to the stove."

"Then what?" asked Niles.

"Just, trust me," I said.

"Ok," said Hephae, "On three."

He counted us down. Then we all screamed and shoved as hard as we could, moving the horde back the few feet we needed. When we passed the stove I pulled the oven open, so the bottom of table was locked against the over door. I threaded the staff between the table legs and shoved one end in the back of the microwave above the stove. Then I wedged the other end of the staff into the cupboard above the sink, so the staff held up the table up for us, and we could relax.

"That won't last long, but hopefully it's enough," I said. "You guys get down to the bunker and reload. Hold them off as long as you can. I'm going upstairs to get the others. If we're not back before the G's get through, I want you to lock yourselves in."

Forty Seven: Her Last Move

I ran upstairs to look for Torrance and Ellie. The gunfire continued as the horde outside went after Dr. Blum's goons.

"Elliot! Torrance!" I yelled up the stairwell. "It's time to go! Everyone's in the safe room."

"If we go down there, we'll die down there!" Ellie yelled back.

I ran up to the crow's nest where Ellie was perched with the AR-15, and Torrance was shooting into the crowd with his Red Ryder BB gun.

"It's not too late!" came Dr. Blum's voice through his megaphone. "We can end this. We can protect all of you! But only if you cooperate with us. Just hand over the girl and all is forgiven."

"Girl?" wondered Torrance. "Which girl is he talking about?"

Ellie and I exchanged a knowing look.

"The G's are getting inside," I warned. "The bunker is our last move!"

"No," she said calmly with her eye buried in the scope. "This is my last move."

She pulled the trigger and landed a shot right in Dr. Blum's chest. Time seemed to stop as blood spat through the front of his lab coat. His jaw fell slack as he dropped the megaphone.

I took a deep breath, and before I exhaled Dr. Blum was twitching and writhing back to life, immediately attacking his own bodyguards.

I grabbed Torrance by the arm. "Come on! "

Forty Eight: Down The Hatch

Ellie, Torrance and I ran down the stairs. Everyone else was already in the bunker and Alix was waiting at the entrance to the safe room, ready to slam it closed once we were inside. But before we reached the first floor the front door shattered as a G broke through boot first.

!t was Private Woz.

He looked more massive than I remembered. Dressed in a crisp new police uniform, but now also in a red motorcycle helmet with the face mask removed.

Officer Cordell stepped in right behind him, in his original fatigues, and carrying a fire ax. But they both stopped in the doorway, as if waiting for a signal to attack.

Moments later Sheriff Nap stepped inside and stood in front of his goons. His dead eye scanning the inside, unable to adjust to the light. The eye patch covering his good eye.

The G's behind them waited for nothing, pushing against the barricade of furniture.

Woz and Cordell looked at Alix under the stairs, then at us, and then back to Alix, choosing the easiest prey. The only thing between us and them was a hasty pile of studio furniture.

"I'm sorry," came Alix's trembling voice, as she slammed the safe room.

Nap's attention snapped to the staircase, and his eye locked with mine. He only smiled, and ordered in a raspy voice, "Get 'em."

Woz made that hysterical laugh which had been his signature while he was alive. It seemed maniacal from a grown man bent on violence, and bone chilling from a dead one.

Cordell raised the ax above his head, dropping it hard on a segment of couch, and splitting it open. He hacked again and again, smashing book shelves and splintering coffee tables until the Sheriff's army poured in.

"Great! These things use axes now?" Ellie cried.

Torrance was the first to scramble back up the stairs. We all ran into the captain's quarters, and slammed the heavy door.

"I'm out of ammo!" said Ellie frantically, changing her grip to use the rifle as a club.

I surveyed the room for big furniture. "Help me move this!" I said, and we pushed a heavy vanity dresser in front of the door.

Woz's boot thuds were so heavy they rattled the floorboards. When he started kicking the door, the vanity mirror shattered.

"What the heck are those things?" asked Torrance.

"It's Private Woz and Officer Cordell," I answered. "G's from my old school."

"Why are they so strong?" he asked.

"They were strong before. I guess Sheriff Nap has been keeping them well fed," I speculated.

The door began to creak and splinter under the heavy footfalls, and Torrance began to cry. Suddenly, the ax head split the wood of the door, and pulled back out.

Officer Cordell peered through the hole, snarling when he saw us. Then he swung again, this time leaving a palm width opening above the knob.

The ax pulled back again and the hole was quickly filled with the mangled face of Sheriff Nap. "I mean, come on. How do you guys expect to beat me?"

I could tell by his grin that he was taking a sick pleasure out of tormenting us, and I realized that he was probably always a predator. The apocalypse just changed the rules. I thought of Stephanie's psychoclass theory, and tried to imagine how brutal his childhood must have been. But what kind of mercy does the merciless really deserve? *If I ever become as malevolent as him, I hope someone will end my misery.*

I grabbed the Red Ryder BB gun from Torrance and trained the sights on his dead eye. "I give you mercy." I pulled the trigger and shot his eye out.

Sheriff Nap hollered in pain and fell backwards. He was forced to use his good eye, which triggered Woz and Cordell, digging their teeth and claws into his body until the hollering stopped.

We were still trapped.

"We need another way out," Ellie insisted. She broke a window with the butt of her rifle thinking we might escape down the outside of the building, but we were surrounded on all sides, with the sea of faces flowing in every battered door.

"Not good!" screamed Ellie. "What now?!"

"Maybe we can get up to the roof," I suggested.

Once Woz and Cordell had their fill of Sheriff Nap they fixed their attention back on us. Cordell swung the ax again and severed the knob. Woz pushed the splintered door against the dresser.

"We need more furniture!" I insisted. "Help me move the bed."

We all pushed together, but it wouldn't budge.

"It won't slide on the carpet," Ellie said. "Help me lift this side and we'll flip it."

We all got on the same end and started lifting the heavy bed frame up on it's side.

"Elliot, look at this!" There was a hatch in the floor under the bed, with a number pad like the one under the stairs. "Remember the ladder in the bunker. This must be another entrance!"

"Well, open it!" Torrance screamed.

Woz shoved the dresser aside, and Cordell came in right behind him, dragging the ax head on the ground behind him.

I punched in the pass code and lifted the hatch. "I got it, now go!"

Ellie and Torrance toppled the upended bed frame onto the two G's, blocking them just long enough to climb down.

I climbed in after them, but when I reached up to slam the hatch, Cordell bit down hard on my knuckles, spraying blood.

I screamed, and in a fit of pain I lost my footing. As I fell, Cordell's teeth tore the flesh off the backs of my fingers, and my hand was crushed in the hatch as it slammed. I tumbled down two stories of steel tube to the bunker below.

Forty Nine: Don't Panic!

The bunker rumbled as the first floor filled with G's, pounding open every door, window and cabinet upstairs.

"Torrance!" screamed Alix, throwing her arms around him. "I thought you were dead!"

"No way," boasted Torrance. "I'm *understructible!*"

"Max, are you ok?!" Ellie climbed down and ran to my side.

I sat up, making sure everyone was in the bunker, then I called out, "BIODAD!"

"Yes, Max."

"Seal the safe room."

A sequence of mechanical locks sealed and secured every exit. The generator kicked on, the lights came up, the life support system activated, and light jazz filled the air.

"At current quantities we have sustainability for three adults, three adolescents, one child, and one cat for one year, four months and eight days," said BIODAD. "Would you like to play a game?"

"Wait . . . BIODAD, are we locked in here?" asked Darleen.

"I will remain sealed until it is safe to exit," answered BIODAD.

"What?!" cried Alix. "BIODAD, unlock the bunker now!"

"No!" screamed Ellie. "If they get in we won't be able to get it closed again!"

"I'm sorry. Your request cannot be processed at this time," said BIODAD. "It is not safe."

"I don't like the sound of that. Max, are we trapped in here?" asked Hephae.

"I honestly don't know," I answered. "But the best plan is to keep quiet and wait. I don't care how many G's are out there. They'd need a wrecking ball to break this thing open," I assured them.

"Max, your hand!" cried Ellie when she saw it. "Good gawd, it's broken . . . bad!"

My body was rattling with adrenaline. I couldn't even feel the pain. But blood was pouring down my forearm, and the bones of at least three fingers were protruding.

"There's a trauma kit in the pantry." I pointed with my good hand and Niles went after it. "But it might not matter."

"What do you mean it *might* not matter?" Darleen asked.

"It's not just a break," I said. "It's a bite."

"What!?" they all screamed.

"Is Max going to turn into a *monster?*" sobbed Torrance.

"No way. We can still amputate!" said Ellie frantically.

"Guys," I said.

"There's got to be a saw, or a machete in here somewhere," said Alix.

"Guys!" I said louder.

"There's no time," warned Hephae. "Hold him down. I'll use the sledge!"

"Ladies and gentlemen, your attention please!" Niles raised his arms like a symphony conductor. "Belay your fears! Lay your head to rest. Max is immune."

"You're immune too?!" Ellie was so relieved she wrapped her arms around me and kissed me.

My stomach toppled. "Dr. Murphy thinks so," I said. "I guess now we'll know for sure?"

"What do you mean, immune *too?*" asked Alix.

"Apparently they're both immune," said Niles nonchalantly. "It's a sibling thing . . . sort of . . . it's a long story."

For a moment I was upset he revealed Ellie's secret, but with Dr. Blum dead, I suppose it didn't matter.

"The cameras!" yelled Darleen. "BIODAD, turn on the outside cameras!"

The computer terminal displayed a split screen of the external video feeds. I selected the feed from the front porch, which was a shot of the front yard. The crowd bottle necked on the porch steps as they pushed inside.

"BIODAD, switch to the internal views," I said.

Every inside feed was filled with shoulder to shoulder G's, trampling over studio equipment and home furnishings as they scavenged for food.

The camera in the captain's quarters showed us a view of the bottom of the stairs, where Woz and Cordell were on their knees, tearing open Sheriff Nap's intestines and eating the contents.

Woz continued laughing hysterically over the cacophony of other G's that joined the buffet.

"What's with the laughing?" asked Alix, covering her ears.

"He was like that when he was alive. Laughter must be hardwired to aggression in his brain," I speculated.

"Well it's creepy!" she complained.

"BIODAD, deactivate videos," I ordered.

Even without the cameras, all the pounding above echoed inside the steel bunker.

"How are we going to get out of here?" asked Hephae.

"I think we've got to wait," I said. "Hopefully Larry comes looking for his late meat delivery, or scalpers come to cash in on the herd. Heck, even wild animals might lead them away eventually. We're ok. As long as we don't panic."

Before long the deafening clamour of walkers, and crawlers, and laughers, and hackers was replaced by the unsettling melody of Syrkis music.

Fifty: Shades of Grey

It turns out Ellie's story wasn't so unique afterall. There were at least thirteen of us, assuming all the participants in the Psychoclass A experiments survived. Their profiles were among the files I'd downloaded from Murphy's Lab. I was surprised to see they were from all over the world. China. Somalia. Saudi Arabia. And if even one in ten thousand people shared our immunity that was hundreds of thousands of people on the planet. The world was smaller than ever now. We'd find them.

In the end, it was Syrkis who came to our rescue. He lured the entire herd back to Wheel Top using a music box, a megaphone, two twinkling rope lights, and an empty cement mixer truck. He said, "There's more than one way to skin a gift horse," by which I gathered he meant we were in his debt.

It was tricky convincing BIODAD it was safe enough outside to let us out. Turns out *safe* is kind of a grey area to holograms programmed to replace a paranoid parent. The problem was that actual risk can have virtually infinite nuance, but his programming was pretty black and white.

Are we ever one hundred percent *safe?* I don't think so, but we had to convince the computer we were.

Niles finally came out to everyone, although he was still Holland to strangers. New people made him nervous, and Holland was the people person. The actual line between Niles and Holland remained kind of a grey area, but even when he was mostly Holland, you could tell he was a little bit Niles whenever he spotted something shiny on the ground.

Alix came out too, in a sense. She and Niles decided to be co-hosts of *Info Planet* using their actual personalities. They both moved out of the cabin, with Torrance, and joined Stephanie and Brian at Keene State College. It was the biggest radio station nearby, and they wanted an audience. Alix passed Joel Saxen off to Torrance, who made excellent use of him as comic relief on the Pirate Radio Network.

Hephae decided he wanted to be sealed in the bunker for as long as BIODAD would let him, and when he told us Darleen said she wanted to be sealed in too. Alix protested, but she couldn't argue it wasn't safe, and they'd still be in radio contact, so she agreed.

After I had some time to mend, Ellie and I went to Wheel Top to see Dr. Blum for ourselves. Syrkis said he passed the electric slide test with flying colors, and he was on his way to being a productive denizen of the Big Wheel.

"I found something I think belongs to you." said Syrkis. "I pulled it off some dead cop, but it says, *Property of Max Hartwell* on it. Want it?"

It was the handheld CB radio Dad gave me. *Now I have the set back together!* I thanked him profusely, and he said, "Just promise me sometimes you'll stop and listen to the music on the wall." I laughed, and agreed.

Ellie and I watched Dr. Blum inside the wheel for a long time. He was dead alright, but how dead was he? How much of him was left? How much did he remember? I'd never know for sure.

Syrkis had harvested all the fuel he needed, and was ready to hit the road to Primitive. Ellie decided to hitch a ride with him, and try her hand at piracy, but before she left we agreed we had unfinished business at Lochshire.

Ellie's mom was easy to find. She'd been frozen in the snow the whole winter, right where we left her. But finding Dad was less obvious.

We searched the parking lot where I left him. He had no legs, so he couldn't have gotten far, but we didn't find him anywhere outside.

I found him on the fourth floor of the east tower, slumped against the door of our apartment. *How did he get here? Why did he come here?*

Someone had obviously raided the apartment. The supplies we'd left were gone. At first I thought it must have been Nap, or someone else from Thornhaven, but then I found porcupine quills in the apartment. The PorcScouts, ever averse to unnecessary conflict, must not have seen fit to give Dad his final death. There certainly wasn't enough of him left to be a threat, but I was still grateful for the chance to give him mercy myself.

I cradled his withered head in my arms, and put the barrel of the Mosquito in his mouth. He was too weak to even gab his broken jaw, but closed his lips around the barrel. He reminded me of a suckling baby, and I pulled the trigger.

Ellie and I dug their graves at the Pine Grove Cemetery in Thornton, next to my mother's plot. We wrapped their bodies in white sheets and deposited them in the rich clay. Then we pushed the dirt back over the holes.

We stood there a long time in silence.

Ellie grabbed my hand and squeezed it, either taking comfort or giving it. "Are you staying at the cabin?" she asked.

"I haven't decided where me and Stinky are going," I answered. "If we stay at the cabin we'll be locked in with Hephae and Darleen . . . but Stinky doesn't like confined spaces."

"Because you can still come with me," she said.

"Maybe." I paused. "I feel like I should go back to Murphy's Lab, and help with the research."

"Max, you have no obligation to anyone you don't choose for yourself."

"I know," I said. "Part of me wants to just load up the Ghool Bus and drive into the sunset."

"You can do that too," she said. "But wherever you go, we're going to stay in touch, ok?"

"Of course," I agreed.

"I'm serious!" she insisted. "I hear pirates in Phoenix are launching their own cube satellites now. You've got no excuse not to talk to me all the time, no matter where you go."

"I'm serious too. There were thirteen kids in the Psychoclass A experiment. They're like our siblings. *Generation A.* We've got to find them, and tell them what we are." I paused. "That reminds me, I have something for you." I pulled the CB radios out of my pack. "I'm going to keep Dad's radio, but I want you to take mine. That way even if we're separated we can communicate, and I can find you." I handed her my radio, and held Dad's in my hand.

She pushed a button on the radio, letting out a piercing shriek of feedback.

I laughed. "I'm going to miss you."

"Ditto," She wiped the tears from her eyes and forced a smile. "I'd be dead without you."

"Ditto," I said.

"Oh! I have a surprise for you too!" She spun around and pointed her backpack at me. "It's in the big pocket, pull it out for me?"

I unzipped her backpack and found a cardboard box about the size of a Mighty O's box. "This thing is heavy!" I struggled to get it out of her pack. "What is it, rocks?"

"Close. It's *a* rock, singular. Here give it to me." She grabbed the box from my hands. "Syrkis knew a guy at the Bizarre Bazaar who got it done. It cost me an arm and a leg . . . *not literally.*"

"What is it?" I asked.

She dropped the box in the mud with a thud. "Ready for the reveal?" she asked rhetorically as she pulled the cardboard away.

It was a headstone. I real one. Cut from granite and carved with our parents names, *Alicia Paige and Rich Hartwell.* And beneath their names there was a single epitaph:

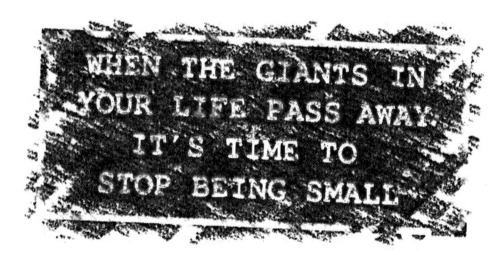

WHEN THE GIANTS IN
YOUR LIFE PASS AWAY,
IT'S TIME TO
STOP BEING SMALL